A
HARVEST
OF
SECRETS

A HARVEST OF SECRETS

A NOVEL

ROLAND MERULLO

LAKE UNION
PUBLISHING

Published by Lake Union Publishing, Seattle

www.apub.com

Amazon, the Amazon logo, and Lake Union Publishing are trademarks of Amazon.com, Inc., or its affiliates.

ISBN-13: 9781542034388
ISBN-10: 1542034388

Cover design by Shasti O'Leary Soudant

Printed in the United States of America

For
Peggy Moss and John Beebe

And when ye reap the harvest of your land, thou shalt not wholly reap the corners of thy field, neither shalt thou gather the gleanings of thy harvest.

And thou shalt not glean thy vineyard, neither shalt thou gather every grape of thy vineyard; thou shalt leave them for the poor and stranger.

Leviticus 19:9–10

One

It was late on a warm and humid Saturday afternoon, midsummer, and Vittoria SanAntonio was walking the paths of the elaborate flower gardens her late mother had planted. From time to time she'd stop and snip the stem of a rose, dahlia, poppy, or bluebell, and slip the delicate treasure into the porcelain vase she carried. Each bright blossom seemed to correspond to one part of the jumble of feelings inside her. Most immediate—a splash of bloodred—was her trepidation about the impending war. Her father and his wealthy friends, the house servants and barn workers, her own acquaintances in Montepulciano—everyone was saying that an Allied assault was imminent, though no one seemed to know exactly when or where the *Americani* would make landfall on Italian soil.

Connected to that—vibrant orange in her mind—were thoughts of her lover, Carlo, called to military service with several of the other vineyard workers. She had no idea where he might be: Greece, Albania, Russia—Mussolini had sent his forces far afield, and she knew it was entirely possible that Carlo was no longer even alive. For a short while after he'd been pulled away to military service, she'd thought she was with child, and in spite of the shame that would have brought her, and the destruction of what was left of her relationship with her father—his daughter made pregnant by a simple worker!—she'd hoped it was true. But no, that was not to be. Not yet at least. Not yet.

Behind the fear of war and the whole-body and whole-spirit ache for Carlo's touch and words stood a background of speckled blue, a longing for her late mother—gone eleven months—that never seemed to ease. Vittoria sensed now, from scraps of recalled conversation, that, beneath her disguise as an obedient wife and central Italian socialite, her mother had been a keeper of secrets. Vittoria was almost sure the secrets were linked to political activity, and that her mother had been about to reveal them to her only daughter. On her sickbed, near the very end, her mother had opened her eyes and said, *Quello che devi sapere, carissima* . . . What you have to know, dearest one . . . and then lapsed into unconsciousness again.

Vittoria heard a burst of laughter fly out through the open barn door. She turned her eyes in that direction and saw Old Paolo, the vineyard foreman, tossing an armful of hay to the mule in its corral. Her brother, Enrico, was there beside his elderly friend, working in happy imitation. In the distance, she thought she heard the rumble of Allied bombers, heading for the factories and rail yards of the North.

She felt a few hard drops of rain splash against her cheeks. The vase was full. Her interior world was still a colorful mess, so different from the neat rows of vines and the manor house's perfect ochre stucco, the image her father liked to present of a famous estate in perfect working order, a famous family without blemish or trouble. The rain began to fall harder. She heard the sound of an automobile gliding into the courtyard—Massimo's car. Her mysterious godfather, come for a weekend visit. She hurried across the patio toward the shelter of home.

Two

Shortly before first light, Old Paolo left his bedroom on the second floor of the main barn, retrieved his shotgun from the smaller of the two first-floor storage closets, and set off on what he hoped would look like his regular Sunday-morning rabbit hunt. He hesitated a moment at the barn's open doorway, said a quiet Ave Maria, and then went past the mule enclosure and across the gravel courtyard, glancing once at the flower gardens and the manor house and the automobile parked near its entrance. Black, beautiful, polished to a high shine, an American *macchina*, Eleonora said it was. FORD, the word on the grill. Although he knew who owned the vehicle and had seen it there often over the years, still, two things surprised him now: that the visitor could find fuel in wartime, and that he seemed not to worry about being stopped by German patrols. The visiting *Signore* must be a man whose money allowed him to live beyond the reach of fear, and living beyond the reach of fear was a great blessing in these times.

Whispering prayers as he went, asking for protection, for courage, Paolo skirted the vegetable plot and climbed past the rows of vines that covered the hillside. Eighty-seven rows there were; he knew the feel of them like he knew the feel of the shotgun resting against his shoulder. Staked, tied, pruned by his own hand, bursting now with their mid-summer greenery, the vines were magnificent creatures, angels of the growing world. By fall, they'd produce tens of thousands of bunches, the juice from their grapes would be turned into thousands of bottles of wine, and the wine would be sold all across Italy—and perhaps, if the war allowed, in other countries as well. Money from those sales would add to the fortune of Umberto SanAntonio, the man who controlled his life and the lives of all the other field-workers and servants on the estate.

The man who controls my life, Paolo thought, as he climbed past the last row of vines and into a copse of chestnut, beech, and pine trees on the property's northern flank. When the war that had been raging across Africa and Europe finally reached this place, as he suspected it soon would, he wondered what would happen to that control. To these vines. To the visitor with the American car. To Umberto, his lovely daughter, Vittoria, and her brother, Enrico. What would happen then to the Vineyard SanAntonio, where he'd worked and lived for all his many years on this earth?

There was no radio in the barn, and neither he nor any of the other field-workers could read well enough to make sense of a newspaper. But the news reached them anyway, passing from one estate to the next, mouth to ear, servant to worker to servant. Paolo knew—everyone knew—that the Allies had been victorious in North Africa and were now on their way to Italy. Their arrival would surely mean that the German and Italian forces would be pushed up the peninsula. Eventually, the fighting would reach this place, north of Rome, east of Pisa, and then suffering would pour over their lives like spring floods over bottomland. Was one supposed to wait for that to happen? Do nothing and wait?

Breathing hard from the climb, sweating, praying, doing battle with his own fear, Old Paolo went quietly along the forest path until he reached a boulder, taller than a man, wider than the delivery truck was long, shaped like a huge table. *L'altare,* everyone called it. The altar. He leaned his shotgun against the stone and left it there, in order to seem as unthreatening as possible, and then, murmuring a last prayer, he took three more steps around the side of the boulder. There, as expected, stood a man he'd never seen before. The man was young, not in uniform, with an enormous beaked nose, dark-brown hair hanging down over his forehead, and an Italian army rifle in his hands. He was pointing the rifle directly at Paolo's face, and Paolo stood still and felt a bit of urine squirt into his pants. "I am sent by the priest," Paolo said. For a long minute the young man held the rifle that way, finger on the trigger, and then he slowly lowered it.

There was something in the young man's eyes—a murderous iciness—that Paolo found alien and terrifying, as if it belonged to another world, a place of hatred. *These are the kinds of people I'm involved with now,* he thought. *May the Lord protect me.*

Three

From her place at the mahogany dining table, Vittoria SanAntonio watched one of the servants carry in a large platter of *reginette*. The long twirls of pasta touched with red sauce were her favorite dish, and as the girl—Eleonora was her name; she'd been with them just over a year—walked past to set the platter near the head of the table, Vittoria could smell the peppers and garlic. *Arrabbiata*, the sauce was called. The feminine adjective for "angry." *Arrabbiata*.

Like the table at which she sat, the formal dining room was ridiculously large, with two serving girls in attendance (one of them did the cooking now that their longtime cook had been called to war). There were curtained windows that reached from the parquet floor to the gilded molding at the ceiling; a sparkling glass chandelier her father said had been in the family for six generations; a tablecloth and napkins of Como silk; eight mahogany chairs with velvet seat cushions; heavy silverware set just so; and a decanter of their own wine—last year's *vino nobile*—on a sideboard near her father's right hand. The flowers she'd picked the afternoon before sat on a marble windowsill like another spirit in the room. Part of her was grateful for the beauty and luxury, especially now, when so many others were suffering. But another part—when she met Eleonora's eyes—felt dressed in finely tailored guilt. As if to intensify those emotions, the room echoed with absence. Her mother's essence seemed to haunt the empty chair. Her beloved younger brother,

Enrico—"damaged," their father always called him, *danneggiato*—had been sent to play in the barn with the workers. Anything to keep him from embarrassing the perfect family in front of a guest.

And there was the other absence, as well, the secret one, the most painful. She lifted her eyes out the window, up along the vine-covered slope, as if she might see Carlo tending the grapes, as if he might straighten his back and turn toward the manor house, hoping to catch a glimpse of her; as if, long after darkness had fallen, she might slip out of the stone manor, hurry along the path to the smaller of the two barns, and meet him there behind the building for an hour of quiet lovemaking and the rare, rare joy—entirely absent from this house— of straightforward conversation.

"They say the Allies will try to land soon. Sicily or Sardinia, they say. Perhaps Apulia. No one knows where."

The voice belonged to Massimo Brindisi, her father's closest friend, and, as far as Vittoria was concerned, the most mysterious and puzzling man on earth. Massimo was her godfather, and for years during his frequent visits, he'd plied her with gifts and stared at her as if she were a painting in a museum. Love, lust, admiration—she couldn't read his eyes, and she wondered, at moments, if he was biding his time, waiting for the right visit during which to ask her father for her hand. The night before, a new layer of confusion had been added to her impression of him. Very late, after Massimo and her father had emptied several bottles of the best recent vintage, someone had tapped on the door of her room, tentatively, as if checking to see if she were awake. When she climbed out of bed and opened it, Massimo stepped inside and swung the door most of the way closed behind him, then put his hands on her shoulders in a way that might have been the gesture of a beloved relative, or might have been something else. "You don't know who I am, you don't know," he murmured. He didn't force her, didn't move his hands, didn't try to kiss her or press against her, but she was half-asleep, and he was clearly drunk, in her room, that late, and—she regretted it now—she'd panicked and started screaming.

"Quiet, quiet, please quiet, Vittoria. It's not what you think!" Massimo said, squeezing her shoulders a bit more tightly. But she screamed and yelled and even scratched at his cheeks and neck until he let go. By then, Eleonora was at the door, and Massimo was making excuses. "A nightmare," he said, the words slurred. He seemed chastened. "My dear godchild was having a nightmare. I came to the rescue. Are you all right, my Vittoria? What was it? The war? The Germans? Of what were you dreaming, sweet girl?"

It was the flimsiest of acts, but what was Eleonora to do, challenge him? The nineteen-year-old serving girl challenging the middle-aged industrialist, a man who practically owned every judge in northern Italy? And what was she, herself, to do, Vittoria thought, further damage the tattered relationship with her father by accusing his best friend, her own godfather, of attempted rape, when she wasn't really sure why he'd come to her room, what his intentions had been? Massimo would act shocked, gravely offended. Her father would stare at her for a few seconds, then shake his head. More female craziness. More disappointment in the daughter he'd raised to take her place in the family dynasty. Vittoria didn't look very much like him, didn't share his political views, and it seemed to her on some days that, beyond the fact that they were sheltered by the same roof, nothing at all linked them.

When Massimo left her room, still muttering his wine-soaked excuses, she closed the door and wrestled an armchair over to block it. She'd skipped breakfast and Mass this morning, claiming a headache. But her father had sent Eleonora to insist she join them for the midday meal, and Vittoria had obediently gone downstairs and taken the chair to his left, facing Massimo across the wide table, smelling his cologne even from this distance, glancing at the thin red scratch mark on the left side of his neck. Had she overreacted? Had Massimo been about to tell her something so important and shocking that he had to be drunk to say it, and had to be out of her father's hearing? Starting to show gray at his temples, but handsome in his own fashion, the man was going on now about the possible invasion, though he had no son in the army of Mussolini, and, she guessed, if Italy fell, he stood to lose only that part of his fortune he hadn't been able to transfer to Swiss banks.

"Between *Il Duce*'s army and the German forces, I don't think the Allies have a chance of taking Italy."

"They took Egypt," Vittoria couldn't keep herself from saying. "They took Libya."

Her father glared at her. Massimo smiled indulgently, mysteriously. "True," he said, lifting his fork as if to begin eating, then looking up at her from beneath his unruly black brows, "but only because the Axis supply chains were stretched thin. I'm sure you understand that, my beautiful Vittoria. Plus, defending one's homeland is the equivalent of defending one's property. It's—"

"Or one's body," she said.

Another indulgent smile. Was he a rapist? Innocent? A loving family friend who'd wanted only a private conversation? "Yes, of course. Exactly. Which is why I feel confident in eventual victory. Totally confident."

"In a *Nazi* victory, you mean."

"Enough, Vittoria," her father said. His cheeks were trembling. *Arrabbiato,* she thought—the masculine adjective—and she lowered her eyes and began to eat.

"She's exactly like her mother," Vittoria heard her father say, as if he were apologizing. "The same politics. A palace radical."

"Yes, and Celeste was also beautiful," Massimo noted. "I still sense her wondrous spirit during every moment I spend in this house."

Vittoria looked up and saw him smiling at her. Such a confusing man! Full of praise for *Il Duce* when he spoke with her father, and yet best friends with her mother, who'd despised Mussolini with every fiber of her being. The two of them would sit together on the patio, conversing quietly and intently over coffee, and when Vittoria approached, they'd look up at her and smile and start talking about the weather, the vines, the price of bread in local markets, in a way that made her feel she'd interrupted something neither she nor her father was supposed to hear.

She tried to concentrate on the delicious meal. The two men went back and forth, piling one agreement upon the next, as if taking turns polishing each other's shoes.

Il Duce's generals will prevail.

Yes, of course they will.

The Americani will never be allowed to make landing on Italian soil.

Never. It isn't possible.

And if they do, they'll lose a million men.

Yes, yes, exactly, and be unable to fight their way this far up the peninsula.

Terrifying as it was to have German soldiers and military vehicles everywhere, shameful as it was to see Mussolini acting the part of Hitler's younger brother—sending troops to foreign lands as if it were he, not the deranged führer, who commanded a fearsome war machine—her father and his friend had made their accommodations. Powerful men themselves, they shared an idolatry of power, seemed to see it as the defining trait of true masculinity. Praise for Mussolini decorated their every conversation—over a game of chess, at a meal, during a walk in the flower gardens. And so far, at least, they'd found ways to placate the Nazis. In her father's case, regular deliveries of fine wine to the SS headquarters in Montepulciano had been enough to convince the Germans to let the grapes be grown and harvested, and the wine sold to those places of business that had managed to remain open during the war. Massimo Brindisi, not a public a supporter of *Il Duce* like her father, had a different kind of leverage: his factories, a bit farther north, were essential to the Axis war effort. The threat of starvation, the violence of Mussolini's Blackshirts and OVRA, and the worry about Nazi retaliation were enough to keep his workers from striking, as they'd done at times leading up to the war years. Profit drove both men, she thought. Profit, luxury, power. Those were their gods, and that was the twisted view of life that had caused her mother to grow ill and die at age forty-nine, Vittoria was certain of it.

She stayed silent through the rest of the meal. First the *reginette*, then tender cutlets of veal in a light tomato sauce with vinegar peppers and polenta; for dessert, a selection of their own cheeses, and glasses of sweet wine from Sicily. Eleonora served them, then stood like a statue in the corner of the room.

Same as me, Vittoria thought. *Listening, and pretending not to.*

"A strange occurrence the other day," Massimo was telling her father, who grunted in response, as if only half-curious, and refilled their wineglasses. "I was driving, just at dusk, through the center of Montepulciano, and I had to take a small detour because of the damage caused by the most recent bombing there. I turned down a road I don't often use, and I happened to go past the house the Germans have occupied. The SS house, everyone calls it. Do you know it?"

"We send them wine," her father said.

"The property is large. It extends from one street to the next, across the entire block. I was driving by the back side, and who do I see coming out the back door?"

"I can't guess, Massimo. Badoglio? The king? *Il Duce?*"

"The priest! Dressed in layman's clothes, as if in disguise."

"The one from the cathedral? Father Giampero?"

Massimo shook his head. "No, no, the local priest, the one in the village. I've crossed paths with him here a few times when he comes to visit you."

"Costantino?"

"That one, yes. The light was weak, but I saw him, I'm sure of it. And he saw me, as well. I drove on. But I kept thinking: What is the village priest doing in the house of the Nazis, dressed like a merchant?"

11

Vittoria noticed that Massimo was studying her father's face closely, as if searching for a reaction to his tale.

"Hearing confessions," her father said, and Vittoria thought, at first, that he might be continuing his merry line of jokes. "They're Catholic, the Germans, many of them." He shrugged and started talking about the war again, and Eleonora stepped in to clear the dessert plates.

Once the table had been cleaned and the men had lit their cigars, Vittoria was able to excuse herself. She made her way down the curving marble staircase and out the front door, and stood there for a long while in the heat of the July afternoon, staring across the rows of vines and the green wooded hills behind them, missing Carlo's company so badly she was on the edge of tears. She caught sight of her brother, Enrico, near the barn, saw him make his happy, heedless wave, then duck into the wide doorway near where the horses and some of the wine barrels were kept, and directly below the place where the workers had their rooms.

After a time, she heard two sets of footsteps on the stairs behind her, then the tiny squeak of the front door's hinges. She turned around to find her father and Massimo joining her in the open air. Smelling of cologne and cigar smoke, her godfather gave her a gentle embrace and a kiss on both cheeks, told her she'd really have to come spend a week at his vacation house on Lake Como while the weather was fine and the swimming comfortable. "That house will be yours one day, you know that, of course," he said, something he'd been saying to her, proudly, confidently, since she was a young girl. Then he sauntered across the gravel, sat behind the wheel of his black car, tooted the horn, and raised a cloud of dust behind him as he left.

"So few automobiles on the roads in these times," her father said as the cloud settled. "But they know who he is. They'll leave him alone."

Vittoria held to a stubborn silence. The air between them felt soiled. Her blood pumped anger. Her father's self-involvement, the impending war, Mussolini's propaganda, Carlo's absence, the false life they lived with their gold-edged plates and silver cutlery and conversations that never seemed to reach beyond business and politics. She was tired of it to the marrow of her bones.

"I want you to go with the next Montepulciano delivery," her father said after a moment.

"As punishment?"

"Nonsense, Vittoria! What's wrong with you? Just ride along in the wagon with Old Paolo, smile at the officers you see. Bring your brother if you want. Make conversation. Charm the SS officers. Let them know what good people we are. I doubt very much that it will, but if the war ever reaches us here, our German friends could turn surly. We need to cultivate good relations, now, in advance. Is that too much to ask of you? Are you so busy with other duties, your drawing and dreaming, your flower collecting?"

She shook her head and kept her eyes out over the vineyard.

"And in the future, try, if you possibly can, to be kinder to my friends when they visit."

"I will, Father," she said, and he left her alone at last.

Four

"Per loro, le nostre vite non significano niente," Pierluigi said. To them, our lives mean nothing.

At first, listening to the trembling voice, Carlo thought his Neapolitan friend was referring to the American and British soldiers in the armada of Allied ships he could see so clearly, hovering there below them on the blue-gray horizon. From the narrow trench that he, Pierluigi, and the others had spent the previous three weeks digging in the hills above one of the Licata beaches, Carlo could imagine those soldiers, waiting in the massive array of destroyers, aircraft carriers, and landing craft. That steel machinery of death. In a minute, an hour, a few hours at most, the Allies would begin their assault on southern Sicily. Uneducated though he was, Carlo had always been curious about the world. From childhood, he'd paid attention—to gossip, rumor, real news, the opinions of wiser people—and lately he'd heard enough to know that the war wasn't going well. Not for the Italians and Germans, in any case. The soldiers on those battleships had crushed the Nazi forces in North Africa, crushed what everyone had believed to be the most fearsome army in the history of modern war. And now the Allies had gathered themselves, licked their wounds and buried their dead, brought in reinforcements of men and matériel, sailed north across the Mediterranean, and set their gunsights on Italy.

But then, Pierluigi, shaking violently and unable to look at him, said, "The rich," and Carlo realized that his friend, in his abject terror, had reverted to a favorite theme. "The rich don't care about us," Pierluigi went on. "They use us. To make their food. To do their labor. To build and clean the palaces where they live. And now, to die for them."

"I'm in love with a rich girl," Carlo said to him. "I think about her every minute."

"You've told me, many times. May God have mercy on you. May you return to your beautiful Vittoria alive and unhurt."

Carlo tried to picture Vittoria's face—the long black hair, fine mouth, beautiful green eyes—but the fear had its grip on him, too. His neck and sides were dripping sweat into the cloth of his uniform. Dry-mouthed, he tried to spit into the ridge of dirt just in front of him but succeeded only in sending a thin spray of saliva onto his shirtfront. *Now,* he thought, *now the war has come home.* The seeds of trouble planted by Mussolini and Hitler had grown like weeds during the past few years, but always in the soil of faraway places. Now the death and misery would belong to Italy, too. He loved his country, loved its food and warmth, the magnificent cities he'd seen on wine deliveries, its people's faith in another world, its music, its laughter. But Pierluigi wasn't wrong: the lower classes were little better than serfs, housed and fed by the landowning families, stranded on the huge estates to work themselves into old age with no hope of escape. You didn't require a rich person's education in order to understand because, in Italy, that style of life stretched back centuries, and the stories had been passed down from generation to generation. Evil landowners, kind landowners, but, as the saying had it, the situation was always the same: *Noi lavoriamo, loro mangiano.* We work, they eat.

It had been that way for centuries, yes, but in recent years a kind of madness had infected his country, a perverted patriotism, the idolatry of a madman. When Carlo made the wine deliveries, he found that the owners of small shops in Pisa and the workers at famous restaurants in

Rome were saying the same thing: *Mussolini will make us great again.* Il Duce *is creating another Roman Empire. A true* man*, he'll never let Italy be disrespected on the world stage!*

Vittoria saw how stupid it all was, and so did Carlo. Now, every Italian was going to pay the price for that insistence on respect, for *Il Duce's* alignment with the German devil. And Pierluigi was right—the poorer you were, the higher the price would be.

Close beside him, Carlo could hear his friend's quick breaths, a kind of ticking clock. He could smell his own rancid sweat. He stared over the dirt mound they'd fashioned, down across a wrinkled sea that was shimmering in the last light of day. The fleet seemed to have crept closer. Beside him, Pierluigi moved on to a new theme. "They'll start with the shelling, Carlo," he said quietly. "And then the paratroopers. And then the ships landing men on the beach. We're in the worst place we can possibly be. Right where the shells will fall."

It was true. He and the rest of the company had their combat knives and pistols, and in their sweaty hands the outdated M91 Carcano rifles the Italian army had been burdened with since the fighting in the Alps in 1915, and the invasion of Ethiopia twenty years later. With some bitterness, soldiers joked that two-thirds of the time when you squeezed the trigger, the M91 actually spat out a bullet. Half the time the bullet flew where it was aimed.

Positioned a dozen kilometers behind them were the German forces with their modern tanks and armored vehicles, their long-barreled artillery, their sadistic commanders and superior arms. The Nazis had stationed the Italians exactly where the ships' guns could shower them with death, and Carlo was sure that, after the opening salvos, they'd order any survivors to charge down the hill toward the beachhead and fight hand to hand against the Allied invaders. A slaughter, it would be. Not a single Italian would survive. But Italian survival wasn't the point. The point was for them to delay and thin out the *Americani* enough so the Nazi tanks would have a chance to push them back into the sea. That was the strategy: Italians up front, Germans behind. And, according to twisted wartime logic, that was only fair: it was the Italian homeland they were fighting for, after all. Occupied by Nazis from bottom to top, yes, but still Mussolini's great and invincible Italian homeland.

Pierluigi was shaking so violently that his helmet rattled against the barrel of his rifle. Carlo reached out and gently pushed his friend's shoulder back a hand's length, and the noise ceased. To their right, the sun dropped over the horizon, but enough light remained so he could see that the ships, even closer now, were certainly within range. The commanders were waiting for full darkness so the assault would be more terrifying, the paratroopers safer. Full darkness. And then the massacre would begin.

Carlo closed his eyes and tried again to picture Vittoria, and her family's vineyard, a thousand kilometers to the north, her beautiful skin and hands, the neat rows of grapevines he and Old Paolo and Gennaro Asolutto had worked for as long as he could remember, each vine staked and tied to a waist-high wire so that the vine ran horizontal to the ground, air would circulate freely around the buds, and the bunches of grapes would hang down for easy harvesting. Prugnolo Gentile was the main varietal, but there were others, too: Canaiolo Nero, Mammolo, Foglia Tonda. From the time he was a ten-year-old, fourteen years ago now, he'd been pruning, mulching, and harvesting those plants, filling the great oaken barrels with the harvest, crushing the grapes, straining out the skin and seeds and bits of stem, monitoring the kegs until, by a mysterious alchemy, ordinary juice was turned into precious wine. For most of those years, too, he'd watched Vittoria SanAntonio grow from his feisty childhood playmate to a beautiful woman. He'd studied her face and body, dreamed of her, eventually summoned the courage to speak a few words in her presence. *Courage*, because it had become obvious to Carlo that Vittoria's father, Umberto, known all across central Italy for his wealth, political connections, and the quality of his wine, had no interest in allowing his grown daughter to maintain anything but the most superficial friendship with a manual worker, a poor orphan, even one as skilled and knowledgeable as his own young vineyard-keeper. When they were very small, a friendship had been tolerable, harmless, another game. Once they grew, it moved into forbidden territory. On a cold winter day, her father had taken him aside in the courtyard, grabbed hold of the front of his work shirt with one hand, and said, *Mia figlia, non toccare. Capito?* My daughter, don't touch. Understood? And what could Carlo have said? What were his options? He nodded obediently, too shaken to speak. Umberto turned his back and walked away.

But, in time, across the vast canyon between Umberto's lovely daughter and the orphaned field-worker, a more mature friendship developed in spite of that warning, something reignited from their earliest years, but decidedly different. A few months before Carlo was conscripted into the army of Benito Mussolini, he and Vittoria started meeting in secret, late at night behind the smaller barn where some of the wine barrels and the delivery truck were kept. Whispered conversation at first, quiet laughter, and then a few magnificent kisses, like promises in the fragrant darkness, like gifts that had sat in a drawer, wrapped and ribboned, for ten years, waiting for the right moment to be opened.

They made love, three times. Three wondrous times, a great risk for each of them, though in different ways. They made love, made promises, nurtured next-to-impossible hopes. And then he was torn away from her, from the quiet beauty of those hills, from the vines he loved. With countless other Italian men, he was sent by the madman to a training camp outside Padova. And then, as if he were bait or fodder, he was shipped to southern Sicily and assigned to the Licata hills to obey the German commanders and await the Allies' first bloody step onto European soil.

Carlo watched now and waited. The stink of fear and the salty fragrance of the sea. His thumping pulse. The peasant resignation to which he'd been bred.

Full darkness fell. He could feel the seconds ticking against the bones of his face. Not yet. Not yet. Not yet.

Except for the rasp of his breathing, Pierluigi had gone silent.

And then, near the line between the dark sky and the darker sea, Carlo spotted a series of small flashes, like the striking of a hundred matches, one after the next. Harmless, even beautiful, if you didn't know what the bursts of light signaled. Two seconds of anticipation, then a hideous screaming above them, and the crashes and explosions began, one after the next after the next. *Boom! Boom! Boo-Boom! Boom! BoomBoomBoom!!* The ground shook, and the air around them filled with dust and smoke and whistling shards of stone and metal. The shelling went on and on, endless. Burning flesh now, screams. He and Pierluigi pushed themselves so hard into the sandy soil it felt as though they were burrowing in, helmet first. The sound was deafening, the air slamming against their arms and faces like bursts of heat from a crackling, windblown fire, pieces of shrapnel screaming past, centimeters above their heads. *Boom! Ba-boom! BoomBoomBoomBoomBoomBoomBoom!* It felt as though they were embedded in a thundercloud, sprays of dirt splashing hard against them like driven hail. Pierluigi was moaning in terror, praying the Ave Maria between his teeth.

Salvo after salvo, an endless hell . . . and then, finally, one last explosion and a long, eerie pause. Minutes of nothingness. "It's over, it's over," Pierluigi muttered.

But it wasn't over.

They could hear horrible shrieks and screams echoing from farther down the trench. They could see the lights of the first landing craft approaching the beach. And then, the captain's voice: *"Avanti, avanti!"* Forward! Forward! For a moment, Carlo's legs refused to work. The captain kept shouting his orders, and at last Carlo stood, Pierluigi beside him. He crawled over the top of the foxhole. Crouching low, he managed to take three quick steps in the direction of the beach before there was another eerie whine, a tremendous crash, and the world went black and silent.

Five

The workers' Mass was held at noon on Sundays, not in the elegant Montepulciano cathedral where the SanAntonios and other wealthy families worshipped, but in the small village church, Santa Serafina in Gracciano, a twenty-minute wagon ride from the vineyard. A few humble storefronts, twenty-five one-story stone houses, and the Church of Santa Serafina—Gracciano was the place where the vineyard staff went to shop, to worship, and on those rare occasions when they enjoyed a free weekday, to celebrate a holiday or religious festival. As foreman, Paolo had Umberto's permission to use the delivery wagon to bring along those field-workers and house servants who wanted to attend Sunday Mass. For unspoken reasons—he swung this way and that with his moods—Enrico had decided not to join them, and so, on this Sunday, Paolo's nine passengers consisted of the old retired foreman, Gennaro Asolutto; a pair of middle-aged women, Marcellina and Constanza, and their five children; and one of the house servants, Eleonora, who'd been with them only a little over a year. He and Asolutto sat on the wagon bench, the others on the straw-covered, railed bed behind.

"Hot today," Paolo said, as the horses left the property and started along the gravel road.

"Hot, hot," Asolutto agreed.

Physically, Paolo thought, there was almost nothing left of the man beside him. Once the strong, quiet keeper of the vines and respected boss of all the field-workers, Gennaro Asolutto had moved into his midseventies and, no longer able to do much work, had descended—thin-armed, weak-backed—into an almost impenetrable silence. He ate, he slept, he relieved himself in the barn toilet or nearby trees, he rode the wagon into the fields now and again to keep the others company and divert himself. Most of the rest of the time he sat out in the courtyard on a flimsy metal chair, watching the birds and squirrels and running rosary beads through his fingers. There were times now, since Mussolini's alliance with Hitler, since the start of the war, when Paolo almost envied him. When he did speak, however, Asolutto seemed to be offering, with a few quiet words, wisdom of a fine vintage, thoughts that had been fermenting in a dark keg for years and had to be tasted the way a succulent glass of wine was tasted, carefully, thoughtfully, with gratitude. "It seems the war is coming to us," Paolo said, quietly enough so that those behind them couldn't hear. "The DellaMonica workers say part of Sicily has already been taken."

For a few minutes he thought Asolutto hadn't heard. The old man kept his eyes forward, head bobbing up and down with the bouncing of the wagon, lips dry and pursed. He was either thinking of an answer or about to fall asleep.

At last he spoke: *"È importante ciò che si dice."* It's important, what is said.

Paolo watched the rumps of the two horses, one black, one brown. He listened to the sound their hooves made on the gravel, a pleasant *clop, clop* that had always soothed him. He smelled the moist earth of the forest they were passing through. And he moved Asolutto's words around and around in his mind, trying to understand what the old man was saying.

"Meaning what, Gennaro?"

Another stretch of silence. "*Il Duce* talks and talks, but words are not air. Words have weight. They're not air."

"Meaning what?"

"Words reach into people's minds. Words draw people toward war." Another long pause, and then Asolutto made a sound that was almost a syllable of laughter, and said, "Some good person should kill the bastard."

Paolo looked over his shoulder to see if any of the three women behind him had heard. *Somebody* should *kill the bastard,* he thought. As if Mussolini were close by. As if they were going to listen to him give a sermon at the church. Or, as if, earlier that morning, the beak-nosed man standing behind the big stone had instructed him to kill Mussolini instead of someone else.

"You know war," Paolo said.

Asolutto grunted.

Paolo hesitated. "I never asked. Did you kill anyone in the first war?"

The older man was quiet for so long that Paolo was sure he'd taken offense. "*Sì,*" Asolutto said at last. "And when you kill another person, you kill a part of yourself. Your soul bears a stain afterward. Forever."

Gennaro Asolutto retreated into his silence. The gravel road merged with the cobblestone streets on the village outskirts, and after a short, bumpy ride and two more turns, Paolo pulled the wagon up in front of the church, beside other, smaller wagons, and tied the horses to an iron ring buried in the curb there. He helped Asolutto down, helped brush the straw from the children's Sunday clothes, and they all made the sign of the cross and filed inside.

The church's walls were made of odd-shaped stones the size of melons and potatoes and loaves of bread, and broken, high up on either side, with six stained-glass windows that admitted a weak light. The nave was filled with a dozen rows of dark pews, mostly empty, and one bank of flickering votive candles in tall, blood-colored glasses. The church's only treasure was a marble sculpture of Mary, pure white, that stood to the left of the altar as they faced it. Where the beautiful sculpture had come from, Paolo had no idea, but Mary was lifted slightly off the ground, and below her, reaching up their arms and hands and trying to take hold of the Blessed Mother, were two men, two women, and two children. From their faces, hands, and clothing, Paolo sensed they were working people, peasants, *contadini*, and, like the music of the horses' hooves, the sculpture had always afforded him a peculiar comfort.

No large framed paintings of saints and angels on the walls, no golden candlesticks, no gold-trimmed marble altar rail—Santa Serafina was nothing like the churches he'd seen on deliveries to Florence, Naples, and Rome. But, modest though it was, the building had always felt to Paolo like an anteroom of heaven. The former priest there, Father Xavier, had left under mysterious circumstances, disappeared one day without warning or explanation. He'd been replaced by a younger priest, Father Costantino, a secretive man, brilliant but unpredictable, a puzzle. And now, in Paolo's life at least, the new arrival had grown to be much more than a priest, a man who gave orders, who risked lives, who knew things about the war, about politics, about life, that floated far over Paolo's head. Usually, the weekly service was Paolo's time of rest and peace after a hard week of labor. Today, no. Today, after the early-morning conversation behind the altar rock, he felt battered by the whispering demons of doubt. The stones of the walls were accusing him. Even Asolutto's words had seemed aimed at him: Was it ever right to kill another human being? Did anything ever justify that? Did words always lead, eventually, to murder and sin, and so was it wiser to remain silent?

But, at this point, could he possibly refuse the assignment?

The Gospel reading that day had to do with workers who arrived to their jobs at different hours, some on time, some not, some on the first day of the workweek, some later. According to the scripture, Jesus wanted them all to be paid the same amount, and Paolo squirmed as he listened. The idea made no sense to him; the words had weight, yes, a weight he didn't like. Father Costantino spoke them with great conviction in his deep, calm voice, and a few minutes later, during his sermon, tried to explain them this way: "There is the logic of earth and the logic of heaven. What seems unfair to us, with our earthly understanding—war, injustice, suffering—is all part of Christ's plan, a plan that will make perfect sense once we're safe and at peace in the next world. Look at what was done to the Son of God! Doesn't that seem unfair? And yet, that was also part of God's plan. We must accept His word, as we accept the word of the Holy Father, without questioning."

Paolo tried with all his heart to accept God's idea of fairness, but he'd seen too many workers in his years, good ones and lazy ones. If they were all treated the same, paid the same, spoken to the same way, there would be a revolt among the others. How could Jesus not know that?

During the second half of the Mass—the Consecration and Communion—he wrestled with the idea, praying silently, reminding himself to be humble, to trust. But the doubts persisted, and around them swirled a cloud of confusion that had enveloped him since sunrise. The Gospel was one thing: important, but abstract. Words from two thousand years ago. The early-morning conversation behind the boulder, so real and recent, weighed on him more heavily. He could see and hear the icy-eyed, beak-nosed young man telling him what the next assignment would be and how it would be carried out. It didn't feel to Paolo like a Christian deed, and, looking at the crucifix above the altar, he couldn't reconcile it with his faith.

After the Mass, while the others went out into the sunlight and chatted with friends from nearby estates, Paolo knelt in prayer for a few minutes, and then, when the confusion wouldn't release its grip, he went and found Father Costantino in the small back room.

"You have the shadow of trouble on your face, Old Paolo," the priest said. He seemed, almost, to be joking, even mocking. He was seated against one wall on an unpainted, backless bench and was taking off the gold-edged stole, folding it, setting it aside. The priest had come to them only a year ago, just at the time of the *Signora's* illness, and no one could understand why a man of such spiritual achievement, a Milanese intellectual, would be assigned to a workers' church in a poor village.

24

Was it some kind of papal punishment? Like all the others, Paolo had been captivated from the first week by the man's charisma and intelligence, his humor, his commentary on the Gospels and his firmness in the confessional. And then, this captivation—it was almost worship—had carried them into other conversations, and the conversations had taken a surprising turn, and led to the priest recruiting Paolo for what he called "God's work. Fighting against the Nazi demons." Small errands, they'd been, until today: carrying a note to a certain person when he made his deliveries; reporting back to the priest on the amount of hunger and unrest in the big cities; counting the number of vehicles on the road to Pisa or Florence or Rome; describing to him the train routes nearby.

Now, it seemed, now he was being led into another realm, a darker room in that secret house. He stood uneasily in the doorway, facing the priest, unable to speak. He thought of beginning with questions about the Gospel reading, but changed his mind—that would be dishonest—and so he simply stood there, mute, studying the priest's face—the dark stubble, the dark eyes, the dark aura that seemed to encircle him. From what Paolo understood, there was a whole network of resistance fighters, and it was Father Costantino who gave orders to the beak-nosed young man, but perhaps it was the other way around. In any case, he was sure the priest must know about the assignment. "It seems a sin, Father, what I have been asked to do," Paolo said after a moment.

Father Costantino studied him, then reached down to untie his polished black shoes. "It *is* a sin," he said, and with those words Paolo felt as if he'd been pushed back hard against the wall. He started to say something more, but Father Costantino raised a hand, smiled, looked up. For a moment, one terrible second, the smile seemed almost evil. "But," the priest went on, "your sin will cause there to be less suffering for the good people of this world. And because of that, the Lord of peace and love shall forgive you. One day He may ask you to do something difficult, as a penance, but He shall certainly forgive you, as He will forgive us all."

Six

By Tuesday morning, as she was due to set off on the wine delivery to the house the SS had requisitioned near the center of Montepulciano, Vittoria had heard about the Allied landing on Sicily. Everyone had heard about it. Radio London was reporting that the *Americani*, as everyone called the Allies, had already taken three-quarters of the island. Radio Italia disagreed, saying that fierce fighting was continuing on the southern beaches—Licata and Gela—with Germans and Italians, brothers in the Great Axis Cause, putting up heroic resistance in defense of the Motherland.

Vittoria knew which report to believe. And she suspected that even the uneducated servants and field staff knew, also. Among the men of the barn, only the old and infirm had been left behind, but in their faces and voices, and especially in the faces and voices of the women, she could sense an impossible expectation, as if the arrival of the Allies would mean not only the disappearance of the Nazis, not only the end of the war and the dismantling of the reign of *Il Duce*, but, for them, some imaginary paradise, a longed-for liberation. It made her think about the claims her communist-sympathizing friends had made before the war, and about the oblique comments her mother had sometimes made, as if there were actual hope for enormous change, for a new social order. That was fine, but how, she wondered, did the workers think they'd make a living in that new paradise? Take over the vineyard? Live in the manor house? Upend a whole system that had been in place for centuries? Like her mother, she felt she'd be happy to see that, or, at least, to see the workers treated like human beings instead of farm animals. But it wasn't simple. Where would she go then? To the nunnery? To Massimo's house on the shores of Lake Como? And how would all of them live?

Loaded with twelve cases of wine and led by the family's two beautiful horses, Antonina and Ottavio, the wagon moved slowly away from the barn and pulled to a stop near where Vittoria stood waiting at the main door of the manor house. Old Paolo the foreman, unanointed king of the workers, sat with the reins held loosely in his lap. Her brother, Enrico, came sprinting out of the flower gardens and leaped into the back, smiling up at her with his mouth hanging open, eyes like stars of innocence. Vittoria took her place on the bench seat.

Paolo whistled through his teeth, tapped the horses' backs with the reins, and they started off.

"Have you heard anything from Carlo?" was the first thing Vittoria said to him, though in as casual a tone as she could manage. *As if he doesn't know,* she thought. *As if he isn't like a father to Carlo. As if it didn't seem to make him happy to see us that one time, walking together.*

"Niente," the white-headed old man replied. Nothing. "I would tell you, *Signorina*, if I heard."

"He's in the war!" Enrico shouted from behind them. As if being in the war were life's greatest adventure. "He'll be home safe! Soon! He's my friend!"

"Yes, my brother. Of course he will."

Paolo grunted and tapped the horses' backs with the reins.

"Did they bother you, the Germans, the last time you did this?" Vittoria asked him.

The old man turned to her for a moment, and in his eyes she saw what she'd always seen there: a tenderness that softened the rough, workman's face. Paolo had always seemed to like her, and always seemed unable to express that in words. Now, midsummer, his skin was brown as breadcrust, creased with wrinkles and scarred from old injuries, frightening in a certain way, if you didn't know him. "They're bosses," he said simply, turning back to the road.

"Like all bosses," she tried.

No response, until the silence grew uncomfortable, and then Paolo added, "They like your wine."

Our wine, she thought. *It's your wine, too. Without you and Carlo and Giuseppe and Gianluca, there would be no wine.* But she didn't say it.

For the rest of the hour they rode in silence, with rounded green hills like sleeping creatures to either side, the horses working hard on the uphill stretches, and a long plume of dust lifting into the air behind, then slowly flattening and settling, like a shaken bedsheet. Enrico was singing quietly, comforting himself as he did when he was nervous. It was a first trip for him, too, and Vittoria supposed he'd been hearing tales of Nazi cruelty when he sat with the workers over their simple meals and helped the man they called "Old Paolo" with the currying of the horses.

Despite the wild tufts of white hair to either side of a bald patch, and despite his deliberate movements and wrinkled face, Paolo wasn't really that old, probably a year or two younger than her father, in fact. The connection she felt with him—subtle, persistent, never acknowledged—must have stemmed from her mother's affection for him and the other workers. She and her mother would be strolling through the flower gardens they both loved, or sitting out on the stone patio on a summer evening sipping lemonade and wine. They'd see Paolo returning from the fields, or repairing a wagon axle in the courtyard, or carrying one of the other servants' little children—he had none of his own—on his shoulders after a hard day of labor, and her mother would say something quietly. *Look at him, how he works.* Or, *Such kindness.* It seemed a one-sided admiration. Vittoria noticed that Paolo never looked in her mother's direction, as if in silent protest of the fact that he toiled all day, while she basked in her luxuries.

Among Vittoria's long list of regrets was the fact that she'd never thought to have a deep discussion with her mother about politics. A remark here and there—*We have too much, Vittoria, too much!*—and the radical Montepulciano soirees her mother loved and her father grumbled about, those were her only clues. It seemed to her that every family had its unspoken rules. In her family, her father imposed them: which subjects could be discussed, which publications and books could be brought into the house, which people one should speak to, or avoid.

Why had she always been so obedient?!

As they approached the crest of the last hill, Vittoria saw the buildings of the city appear, first the towers of two churches with their gray slate roofs, then four- and five-story homes coated with brown- and cream-colored stucco, and then, as they crested the rise and the horses' hooves began knocking loudly on cobblestones, the smaller houses and shops on the outskirts. In the *centro*, the streets were narrow, steep in places, and she noticed that one whole block lay in ruins, stones and wooden beams scattered about, making the street resemble a room littered with a child's broken toys. A smashed table with one good leg, a sofa torn in half, a bicycle wheel, the remains of a ruined radio console. Broken roof tiles. Water pipes bent like strands of straw. "What happened here?" she asked, then remembered Massimo Brindisi saying something about it at Sunday's meal. The debris. The village priest coming out the back door dressed as a merchant.

"The bombs," Paolo said. "The Allies. Mostly they try for the factories farther north—Torino, Milano, Genova. Sometimes they miss. Or they see a few army trucks parked together and think it's a secret headquarters. Or they want to frighten them in other places."

"Which 'them'?"

"The Germans. The Fascists."

Just as he finished pronouncing those words, almost spitting them, soaking them in disdain—*tedeschi, fascisti*—Paolo turned the cart off the main street, made a short detour to avoid the rubble, and pulled the horses to a stop in front of an elegant stone house, four narrow stories with wrought iron balconies, fruit trees, a small lawn with empty metal chairs set in a half circle, and behind, a yard that extended, front to back, across the whole block. A wrought iron gate guarded the entrance to the property. Beyond it she noticed a bespectacled Nazi officer standing on the house's top step with his booted feet spread and his chin slightly lifted.

"You stay, *Signorina*," Paolo said to her, using, as always, the formal *Lei* instead of the familiar *tu*. "Enrico and I will unload. Help me, Rico."

Her brother and Old Paolo carried the first two cases through the gate, clasping the wooden boxes to their chests, bottles clinking. Up the walk and right past the officer they went, disappearing through the front door. The Nazi stepped aside but didn't so much as glance at them. He was staring at Vittoria, and she sat still, feeling his eyes on her, praying silently, already cursing her father for making her take the trip. When the sixth and last load of cases was being carried in, the officer trotted down the steps, strode along the walk, through the gate, and came up close against her side of the wagon.

"*Che bello donna,*" he said in his mutilated Italian. The sunlight reflected off his thick lenses at such an angle that she couldn't see his eyes. "My name is Tobias," he said, and Vittoria thought, *As if I care.* He reached out a hand and rested it on top of her right thigh. She slid sideways, but he held on, massaging the muscles through the cloth of her dress.

"My brother will kill you," she said, but, twisted by fear, the words came out in a squeak.

"Really?"

"Really." She jerked her leg sideways, away from him. "With a pitchfork," she said. *Con un forcone.*

The officer was grinning. He squinted at her—he didn't know the word—then turned the corners of his lips down as if admiring her courage, or mocking it. "Every time now you come? With the wine?"

She shook her head side to side.

"I visit you then. In your house. Where the famous wine is made. SanAntonio Vineyard. We know it."

Paolo and Enrico were coming down the walk, approaching the left side of the wagon. The German, standing on the opposite side, took a step back, and she could see his eyes now. He winked at her and turned away. Paolo and Enrico climbed into their places, and, as they were starting off again, Vittoria felt the contents of her stomach rising into the back of her mouth. She leaned over the side and vomited onto the stones.

"You're sick, Vita!" Enrico exclaimed. "Mama was sick! Now you!"

She reached behind her and put a hand on his head, then pulled him close against the back of the bench for a moment and circled his neck with one arm.

"Let them die," Old Paolo said between his teeth, too quietly for Enrico to hear. The fury in his voice surprised her. "Let every one of them die. Let them burn in hell."

Seven

When Carlo regained consciousness—with no idea how much time had passed, hours, days, a week—he was staring up at the face of a woman. Coal-black hair; kind, dark eyes; a lovely smile—for the time it took his thoughts to reassemble out of the fog of unconsciousness, he thought it must be Vittoria.

But no. Too young. A girl, not a woman. Or someone between girlhood and womanhood. The girl was smiling down at him, one of her front teeth chipped at an angle. Not Vittoria. A wave of pain rose up and over him, shaking him from skeleton to skin. He closed his eyes against it, let it pass. Something wasn't right. The strange girl, the pain. He could feel a piece of cloth across the left side of his face, and the pain there was like nails being hammered into broken bones. His left shoulder hurt, too; at first, he couldn't seem to move more than his fingers and toes on that side.

"You're awake at last," the girl said.

A Sicilian accent. Not Vittoria.

Carlo blinked, stared at her.

"Are you in pain?" she asked. *Sente male?*

Her voice was a line of lavender sky beneath steely dark clouds.

Carlo tried to nod but managed only a twitch of his neck muscles. He closed his eyes and felt something against his lips. A sponge. The girl squeezed it, and a few drops of liquid squirted into his mouth. Wine, it tasted like. Bitter wartime wine. And then another squeeze, different sponge, tepid water.

Very slowly, minute by pain-wracked minute, he began to form an understanding. Above him, he could see rough-hewn roof rafters. He could smell hay, hear the bubbly clucking of chickens. But it seemed the world had been cut in half; only one eye was working, the other covered by coarse cloth. The girl moved her face so that it was directly above him, strands of her hair falling across his bare chest. He closed his eyes again and remembered climbing out of the foxhole with Pierluigi, forcing himself forward into the terror. *Avanti! Avanti!* Then a crashing sound, then nothing.

He tried to speak and couldn't. The girl pressed the sponge against his lips. "Wine for the pain," she said quietly in her velvety voice. *Vino per il dolore.*

Carlo swallowed, lost consciousness again for a few minutes, adrift below the ocean in a dream world with the black clouds visible through a wavering prism of water, high above. He surfaced, took a breath, blinked. There was the girl again, steady as sunlight, and here came another wave. "It's many days you haven't been awake," she said. And then, blushing: "My mother and I washed you."

The accent, the beautiful smile. Working his lips and dry tongue, Carlo found at last that he could produce a word. *"Grazie."*

The smile stretched. "If you sit up, you could eat," she said. "You must be very hungry. The Germans are gone. The *Americani*, too. We have a little food. Tomatoes. Grapes. No bread, but some milk from the goat."

She put a hand behind his neck and lifted gently, and though the pain was like nothing he'd ever felt, throbbing in the bones of his face, in his teeth and neck, he flexed his stomach muscles and, with her help, managed to sit up. Holding him with one hand, she dragged something up behind his back with the other. A bale of hay. He could feel it scratching against his skin, and then she leaned his upper body farther forward and lay a piece of cloth or a towel between the hay and his skin and rested him back on it again.

"I am called Ariana." She waved an arm with her hand flapping at the end as if shooing away a fly. "My family lives here. This is our barn. I found you on the hill after the war went past us. Blood all over you. My father carried you here on his back. Your friend beside you was . . ." She paused. "Gone to paradise. We made a grave for him. You've lost one eye, but you're awake now. You're alive."

Carlo felt an enormous weight descend upon him. He managed one word—"*Grazie*"—but pronouncing it seemed to require every last drop of his willpower. Pierluigi gone. His left eye gone. For a moment, a few awful seconds, he wished the blast had taken him, too. He stared at the girl's beautiful face, and it was as if she existed in another dimension, a vision, a spirit. Not real.

"Your name?"

"Conte," he managed, and then, after another few seconds: "Carlo . . . Conte."

He watched her stand and walk away, and he ran his eye back and forth across what he could see of the barn. One thought upon the next, like a stone foundation being laid, the world began to reassemble itself. A barn. A poor place it was, crooked stone walls and a wooden roof. Bales of hay. A few rusty tools in one corner. Hens pecking in the dust of the doorway against a background of too-bright Sicilian sun. His chest was bare, his feet bare. Instead of his army pants, a pair of worker's trousers covered his legs, rough brown cloth in the peasant style. He was very hungry.

Back through the doorway came the girl—how beautiful she was, sixteen or seventeen—with a man and a woman behind her; the parents, he guessed. Unlike their daughter, they were short, squat people, with coarse hands and blunt noses. The mother had fine, dark eyes, the father a high forehead. The girl—Ariana—was holding a ceramic bowl. Her mother was carrying something, too, making the sign of the cross with her free hand. Her father stayed back a few paces, hands clasped in front of him, face set in an unreadable mask, neither kind nor unkind, neither calm nor worried. Carlo tried to imagine the man carrying a stranger's broken body from the battlefield to his own home, blood streaking down his clothes. He thought of them digging a grave and burying Pierluigi.

Ariana knelt beside him, plucked one grape from the bowl, placed it at the edge of his lips and squeezed so that the pulp popped into his mouth and the skin remained in her fingers. She tossed it aside, fed him three more. Her mother stepped forward with a ceramic cup of what turned out to be warm goat's milk.

He could not remember tasting anything sweeter.

Eight

In August, with the grapes ripening but not ready to be harvested, the main job was the bringing in of the wheat from the SanAntonios' southeastern field. Even as a young man, Paolo had found the work exhausting—the scything and bundling, the hoisting of sheaves into the wagon, hour upon hour in the brutal heat. Now, as foreman, he could have merely supervised, but he'd never been comfortable watching others sweat, and, with the stronger, younger ones at war, every peasant on the property—man, woman, and child—needed to share the labor. Lifting bundles with the women and children, scything, then resting, then scything again; drinking well water from the clay pitchers in short breaks; leaving the others every few hours so he could go into the trees and empty his bladder—it all made him feel he'd been given the right nickname: Old Paolo.

When the day was at last finished, and the others were accompanying the wagon back to the barn, Paolo walked with them only as far as the grassy fallow field between the wheat and the grapes and lay on his back there, gazing up at the clouds. His hands, knees, and shoulders ached, and he knew that when he awoke the next morning, it would take him an hour or more to stop feeling like a piece of machinery that needed oil.

The loss of hair, of muscle, the struggle required now to hoist a case of wine he could have tossed into the air in his youth, the sense that parts of himself—cheeks, belly—were being drawn toward the earth as if yearning already for the grave—he felt, at times, worn down by the decades of labor. Still, there were benefits. The passions of youth had loosened their grip. It took him longer to get angry, and the anger quickly faded, a summer shower now instead of a true *tempesta*. He wanted to tell himself, *Yes, and you no longer make the foolish decisions you made in the past,* but on certain days the decision to get involved with Father Costantino in the secret work, morally right as he believed it to be, felt like a risk he would have been wiser not to take. Then again, in one of their private conversations, Eleonora had told him that people all over Italy were involved in the resistance and, as the priest had said in their first probing conversation, *What are your options, Paolo? Wait for the Nazis to line all of you up in the courtyard and shoot you?*

Lying there with the tall grass like a soft bed beneath him, searching his thoughts for a bit of comfort, he cast his mind back to the times— how many, five, eight? He used to know exactly—when he'd made love here with the one woman who'd ever truly seemed to touch his soul.

He was drifting along in the past, remembering, half dreaming, when he heard voices. Real people, not memories. A couple, he thought it must be at first, come here late in the day, as he had once done, to make love. But then the speakers moved closer, the quiet conversation grew clearer, and Paolo froze where he lay. He didn't understand the words, but he knew what language it was. Two men; no, three. Speaking quietly in German, as if worried they'd be overheard, or as if plotting something. Paolo drew in and let out a series of shallow breaths. He could feel the pulse pounding in his neck and temples. The men came closer still, the voices slightly louder. He waited, only partly hidden by the tall grass around him, expecting at any moment to be seen. At the very least, he'd be questioned. If the Nazis had caught and tortured the Nameless One with the beak nose, and if that man had given a description of the old field-worker on the SanAntonio estate, then he'd be tortured, too, forced to give up names, taken out in the courtyard and shot in front of all the others.

A few seconds that passed at the pace of years, and the speakers—three soldiers, he guessed—moved on, voices fading. Paolo lay there for a long while, watching the day lose its battle with night, feeling the worst of the fear leak out of his arms and legs. In time, he turned, slowly stood up, and made his way back to his evening meal.

The main barn—stone foundation, water-stained gray stucco walls, tile roof—housed the horses, some of the kegs and bottles, and all the field-workers, and was long and narrow, two stories tall with a triangular attic storage area above. The first floor was broken up into a series of rooms: a huge locked storage closet beside a smaller unlocked one; then two sets of stables; then two large, high-ceilinged rooms where some of the kegs were kept (others were kept in a separate outbuilding), and a smaller room at the southwest end where the workers gathered for their meals. A toilet and sink were squeezed together behind a wooden door there. Upstairs there were bedrooms and a simple kitchen; above them, an attic with a window for loading hay at one end. Cold in winter, stifling hot in summer, no privacy, the kitchen awkwardly placed, but the building had housed the SanAntonio workers for generations and was now the source of few complaints and no improvements.

As soon as Paolo walked in through the wide main entrance—its doors were kept propped open in summer—he sensed that something wasn't right. At that hour, the women would normally be talking and working noisily in the kitchen above, the men would be sharpening tools, washing hands at the rust-stained sink; the children would be feeding the horses or hiding from each other behind bales of hay or the thick oaken posts that supported the second floor. But all was quiet. He stood still and listened.

Nothing. Even the horses were silent. And then he thought he heard a raised voice from the last room to his left, and he wondered if the meal had already been served and an argument had broken out.

He walked tiredly through the stables and past the kegs, and when he reached the room at the end of the building, he came upon the shocking sight of Marcellina, one of the barn's two middle-aged mothers, holding a pitchfork at waist height with the sharp tines pointing away from her. Barely a meter beyond the metal points stood three young men in German military uniforms. They were armed—pistols at their hips—as Paolo noted immediately, but it was Marcellina holding them captive, not the other way around. The rest of the workers watched, eyes fixed on the soldiers, their heads leaning slightly forward, as if they were ready to attack the three Germans, or run from them.

"Che succede qua?" Paolo asked in his foreman's voice. What is happening here? Every face in the room turned toward him.

"We were bringing the food down"—Marcellina gestured with the pitchfork toward steaming dishes on a low table—"and they came inside and started talking to us. No one can understand them. They have guns."

"I see that they have guns. But I also see that they haven't taken them out and shot you. Put down the *forcone*."

Marcellina reluctantly lowered the pitchfork. Paolo went up close to the men and peered into their faces, one after the next. They smelled like dirt. Not one of them reached for a weapon. *"Avete fame?"* he asked, bringing one cupped hand to his mouth. Hungry?

Three eager nods.

"Feed them," Paolo ordered.

"They're Germans. Nazis," someone behind him said. Marcellina again.

"I see that. Feed them. Share the food."

Paolo gestured for the soldiers to arrange themselves on the bales beside the table. He remained standing and took the pitchfork from Marcellina, watching, making sure none of the men reached for their holstered weapons. They looked very young, not yet twenty. Their uniforms were dirty and unkempt, as if they'd slept in them for days. When

Marcellina put a single plate in front of them—white beans, dried beef, slices of tomato and peppers from the garden—the men scooped the food into their mouths with bare hands as if they were starving.

"Wine," Paolo ordered. Three cups were brought out, the unlabeled bottle passed. He suddenly remembered a moment at the door of the manor house kitchen, a surprise there. "Gaetano, go and fetch Eleonora, but secretly. Don't let the *Signore* see you. If she's busy, just signal her to come when she can. Run. Hurry."

The boy dashed out of the building. Hungry though he was, Paolo stood with the pitchfork in one hand and watched. Deserters, he supposed. A first. He'd never heard of German soldiers deserting, and couldn't imagine how they'd be able to avoid capture, trapped in the Italian countryside as they were, with German army patrols on every road between the vineyard and Montepulciano, and between Montepulciano and their homeland.

Less than two minutes later, Gaetano came through the door, out of breath, Eleonora on his heels, wiping her hands on her apron. She met Paolo's eyes, scanned the group, fixed her gaze on the uniformed trio, and said, without hesitation, a phrase in German that brought weary smiles to their faces and one word from each of them. She turned to Paolo. "How did you know I could speak to them?"

He shrugged, held the answer in his mouth, asked her what she'd said. The mule had started braying crazily in its outdoor corral.

"I asked them if they liked our food," Eleonora said. Everyone was watching her. She exchanged another few sentences with the soldiers, then turned to Paolo again.

"They've run away. They don't want to fight anymore. They don't want to kill Italians. They're asking if we can hide them for a few days and give them some other clothes."

Marcellina laughed sarcastically. "So if they're caught here, we'll all be killed. And they speak no Italian. How are they going to escape? How will they eat?"

The questions spun in the air like hornets. Paolo studied the soldiers' faces. They were light-skinned, light-eyed, and they watched him intently, as if he were an executioner and they the condemned. He glanced sideways at Gennaro Asolutto, the foreman who'd preceded him, and who sat now, quiet as ever, in a corner. Asolutto was the true expert on growing grapes and making wine and had lived among them for decades. Among them, yes, but half of Asolutto had always seemed to stand apart. He'd wielded his authority in the quietest of voices, never raising a hand to any of them, never cheating them of their share of the food or the small sums they were paid at the end of every season, going days without speaking to them at all. When a decision had to be made, he stood quietly in their midst and pronounced a sentence or two, and there was never any thought of challenging him. Their world was a world of hierarchy, of bosses above bosses, all the way to Rome, and, from there, all the way to heaven. When Asolutto grew old, and Paolo took his place in the hierarchy, he'd tried to behave in the same way. But whatever decisions Asolutto had been charged with making—when to harvest, how to ferment, how to settle the arguments that sprang up from time to time among the workers—none of those decisions had ever put lives in danger. Paolo stared at the old man now, wondering what he would have done. Asolutto nodded at him, milky old eyes steady, gnarled hands in his lap, and the nod seemed to contain a message. One of the soldiers coughed and turned his face away, as if he were about to start weeping, and Paolo made up his mind.

"They'll sleep in the attic," he said. "Only a few nights. None of us can say a single word about them to anyone outside this building. We'll find clothes for them and burn their uniforms."

"And they'll keep their guns?" Marcellina asked.

Paolo just looked at her.

"And so now all our lives are in danger. If they're found here, we'll all be killed."

"That's true," Paolo said to her. "But if our men were in the same situation, we would want people to help them."

"Our men aren't murderers."

"The attic," Paolo said. He set the pitchfork aside and walked out of the barn without touching the food. For a long time, he stood alone in the courtyard, looking at the stars. Father Costantino and the man with the beaked nose had put his life in danger, burdened him with the heaviest weight, but he'd agreed to that from the start. Now he'd passed that weight to every worker on the property, and none of them had asked for it. They were all involved now, linked by a frail bond of trust. Another sin, he supposed. He heard noises coming out of the manor house windows, a woman's sobs, it sounded like. He listened for a moment, wondering if it was the house servant Cinzia, or Vittoria, then went back into the barn to tend to the horses and eat what remained of the food.

Nine

After many restless nights following the trauma of the delivery to Montepulciano, Vittoria decided she had to speak with her father, alone, something that had always required a summoning of courage. Since the death of her mother, it had become even more difficult to have a rational conversation: her father's political sympathies—perhaps held in check by her mother, whose politics were totally different—had burst into the light like noxious weeds. He'd hung a photo of Mussolini in the manor house entrance; his comments on current events had turned into bitter rants. Always a gruff man, lacking in tenderness, he seemed, as a widower, to have given free rein to the harshest side of himself, as if he were somehow repaying fate for the hand it had dealt him. *The Italian people are too stupid to appreciate what* Il Duce *has done for them!* was a typical remark.

It was late, an hour after their mostly silent dinner, and Vittoria found him sitting in the third-floor library, his favorite room, in a chair upholstered in tobacco-colored leather. She sat opposite him on the leather sofa and told him what had happened in the city.

"Well, you're a beautiful woman," was her father's response.

"Papa! He's grabbing me! Next thing he'll be dragging me into their house and raping me!"

Her father sighed impatiently, closed the book over one finger, and looked at her across the top of his reading spectacles. "What would you have me do, Vittoria?"

"Stop trading me for protection from them!"

"Stop shouting, please. The servants will hear. And what you're saying is absurd. I'm not *trading* you."

"The servants know how evil those men are!" she said in a slightly quieter voice. "Paolo sees it. Enrico sees it."

"Enrico doesn't understand what he sees. And Old Paolo is simple-minded, a man I should have sent away many years ago. I keep him on as an act of charity."

"I won't go there anymore. I refuse to go."

"You refuse to go," her father said, spluttering now, his face suddenly pinching up into a mask of barely contained fury. "Which means the officer will then come here, to this house, and find you anyway and no doubt torment us. Send his men to ruin the grapes, shoot holes in the kegs!"

"And the grapes and kegs are more important than me, than my body?!"

"It is our grapes and kegs that allow your body to be clothed, sheltered, and fed!"

"You can't stop them?"

"Of course I can't stop them! Nobody can stop them!" Her father looked away, drew and released a long breath, gathering himself, Vittoria thought, holding back a more serious eruption. He turned back to her and said, in a somewhat softer tone, "If you want to leave, for your safety, I can send you to Massimo. He has a beautiful second home above Lake Como and has always intended to leave it to you when he dies, as he's promised you for years now. Your mother and I took you there three or four times when you were a girl, don't you remember?"

Vittoria did remember, but she shook her head violently—no—one heavy tear flung to the side.

"You'll be perfectly welcome there. You'll be comfortable, and—"

"I don't want to. Never. No. It will never happen."

"This is precisely the problem," her father said. "And has always been the problem, from the time you were a small child. Your wants are very narrow. This, not that. That, not this. Only this food for breakfast. Only these clothes for school. Only this hairstyle, no matter how impractical. You want the world to conform itself to your wishes. That never happens. One would think the premature loss of your mother would have shown you that." He slipped a playing card into the book and set it on the table beside him, straightening it so that it sat perfectly parallel to the edge. "And in case you haven't noticed, Massimo would marry you in an instant."

"Never!"

"More narrow wishes. He's a bit older, true, but he'd give you the life you've grown accustomed to, and more. When the war is over, you could travel the world. Have whatever you wanted."

"I already have whatever I want, and what I want is to be able to choose the man I love, as you chose Mother."

"And whom would you choose? What kind of man? Someone who can support you in all your thousands of narrow wants?"

Vittoria came within a second of telling him she'd already chosen, but she held the remark in her mouth and said, "I'd choose for love, as you did."

"As I did, yes, but from among my own kind. Our own . . . stratum of society."

"I don't want to talk about this now, Father," she said. "Your politics, your friends. Sometimes I think you're more German than Italian."

Her father's lips stretched into a tight grin. Frightening, she thought; beneath the dignified mask he was a frightening man. "And sometimes," he said coldly, "I think you're more peasant than noble. Your mother had an exaggerated sympathy for the workers. You seem to have inherited that."

She shook her head, long hair swinging, and stood up. "That's not the issue now, Father. I've made my last trip to the city in that wagon, to that house. If I go again, I'll take a pistol and shoot the German through the middle of his hideous face!"

She whirled around and was out and through the door before her father could speak again. Half blinded by tears, she ran down the curving marble stairway, tripped on the bottom step, fell forward, and let out a cry that echoed in the foyer. For several minutes she lay there, sobbing, arms spread out above her head as if in surrender. She sobbed small puddles on the tile, sobbed and wept and pounded the marble with one fist and eventually fell silent. There was no sound in the house beyond the ticking of the grandfather clock, another item her father claimed had been passed down for generations. *What difference does it make?* she thought. The grandfather clock and chandelier and silver cutlery and emerald-studded gold rings. *What difference does any of it make?*

After a time, she got up and sat back on her heels, staring at the framed photo of Mussolini on the far wall. Their *Duce* seemed to her at that moment to stand as a symbol for everything that was wrong in the world. The divisiveness, the violence, the mistreatment of women, the pitiful urge so many Italians seemed to have to idolize someone.

She wiped the tile dry with the bottom of her skirt, stood, and walked out into the starry night. Once she turned thirteen her father had ordered her to stay away from the barn—she'd loved the place with its rich smells and textures, enjoyed joking with the workers, and had been Carlo's childhood playmate for as long as she could remember. Her mother, a lover of horses, had insisted that she learn to ride, and Paolo had even taught her to drive the wagon, sitting beside her at first, and then letting her sit alone on the bench with the slick reins in her hand. When her father forbade all that, there had been a terrible fight between her parents, shouting in the upstairs study, a slammed door, days of icy silence afterward. Her father's remark, *more peasant than noble*, reminded her of that argument, which had caused a fissure to appear between different stages of her life, and, day by day, an entire cold ocean to form between her and Carlo. After that, years passed with them hardly speaking, as if they'd been made into enemies overnight, forced to look at each other not as friends and fellow humans but as members of different classes and nothing more. The princess and the servant.

The guilt of that, the frustration, had caused her to become physically ill, stomach upset, periodic headaches that chained her to her bed. Her friends—mostly girls from other estate-owning families that gathered for picnics on summer Saturdays, or after Mass at the cathedral—began to seem superficial and false, waiting only for a husband of means, an adulthood of luxury. Carlo avoided her, spending time with the older men, working the vines or the wheat, caring for the horses, never even turning his eyes toward the manor house. She imagined him meeting secretly with servants from nearby properties, girls of his own class, and finally, unable to bear it, she confided in her mother. They had made a retreat at the nunnery in San Vigliano and, halfway home, were walking their tired horses along an uphill stretch of road. "We're both human beings, Mother. We've been friends our whole lives. Now, suddenly, I'm forbidden from speaking to Carlo. Father must have said something to him, as he did to me."

Her mother kept her eyes forward, seemed suddenly uncomfortable. "In this country," she said at last, in a voice lined with pain, "there are walls between the classes. Those walls have been there for centuries, Vittoria." She paused, made brief eye contact, looked forward again. "But sometimes you can find a door in them, and step through it. Perhaps later, in a few years, in some better future, you and Carlo will be able to resume your friendship."

Her mother hadn't said anything more on the subject, and hadn't lived to see that better future, to know about that friendship. Standing with her back to the manor house, still trembling with anger, Vittoria thought back over that conversation, and the silent years that had followed it, and wondered why she and her mother had allowed her father—with his shouts and threats and table pounding—to rule over them like some kind of domestic *duce*. Much later, she had, in fact, discovered a doorway in that ancient wall, and found the courage to step through it, and, in that risky territory, she and Carlo had made something more than a friendship. Much more. But they had never been brave enough to talk about the lost years, not yet at least. She felt too guilty, and, no doubt, his hurt was too deep.

Now, in the warm starlight, she walked across the courtyard to the barn, as if she might find him there and apologize for old insults. Inside the large, open doorway she stood and let her eyes adjust. The air smelled of hay and horseflesh and, faintly from another room, old wine. There were tools of all shapes and sizes lined up neatly against one wall, and, through another door, the horses. She felt wrapped in a warm blanket of memories.

In the shadows she could see Old Paolo grooming Antonina, the black mare Enrico loved, running the brush in practiced motions along her withers. Ottavio neighed, seeing her, and Paolo looked up. "Foreign territory for you, *Signorina*," he said, and it was hard to tell from the tone whether he was merely stating a fact or making a comment about her luxurious life and long absence.

"Let me do that," she said, reaching out a hand. "It's been so long since I touched them."

"No, *Signorina*. If the *Signore* saw that I'd allowed you to groom a horse again, within one hour I would be on the road with my belongings in a sack, walking toward the land of hunger."

She stood by silently and watched him work. "We argued, just now."

Paolo grunted, didn't make eye contact. "Not my business, *Signorina*," he said, but she saw, or thought she saw, something new running across the sharp planes of his face. Fear, worry, anger—she couldn't read it, but she felt again a deep affection for the man, a tenderness from her younger years. He hadn't shaved in several days, and the white whiskers put her in mind of the few times she'd seen snow and ice coating the grasses between the vines. Something—a thought, an idea, an emotion—had just scurried along beneath that frosty lace, she was sure of it. The rest of the barn was bathed in a deep silence, the other workers up in their beds, she guessed. But something wasn't right; she could feel it in the air, sense it in Paolo's voice. Why wasn't he with them as he normally would be?

"I told him I wouldn't go on the deliveries again. No more Nazi fingers on my leg. No more leering SS officers."

Paolo grunted, patted the horse's flank, then faced Vittoria with his strong arms hanging straight down and the sides of his mouth turning down and the outsides of his eyes, too. *"Signorina,"* he said, and then he paused, one hand squeezed into a fist, the other clutching the brush.

She waited.

"Signorina, I have been breaking my mind, thinking about this. It is why I am not asleep. I have something to ask you. And for this something, I could lose my life. My work and my life. And I could endanger yours, also. If you wish me to remain silent, I will."

"Ask," she said. And then, since it had sounded too much like a command, and she was suddenly embarrassed in front of him, she added, "Please ask. I'll make sure nothing happens to you."

He nodded, glanced at the doorway, then over his right shoulder, into the other rooms. He shuffled a half step closer. "First," he said quietly, "I am sorry I can do nothing about the Nazi officer. I saw what he did when you came with us on the delivery. I could do nothing then. It makes me feel—"

"I didn't expect you to do anything, Paolo."

"Second . . ." He paused and looked at her for almost half a minute. "Second, ah . . ."

"Speak freely, please, Paolo."

"Ah," he said. He placed the brush on a shelf behind him and turned back to her. "Since the Germans, you know . . . since you aren't liking the Germans much, there are . . . people. We know people. *I* know them. Who . . . who are fighting them. Partisans, they're called. *Partigiani*. Fighting the Germans . . . in secret. In the hills and . . . and here, near us. Sabotage, passing arms, passing secrets, studying movements of troops and giving that information to certain bosses . . . Hiding deserters. Even, sometimes . . . killing. I have heard that there are many such people in Italy now, all over Italy." He stopped and watched her. "I myself now have something to do with them, and by telling you this I am handing you my life."

"You can trust me, Paolo."

He blinked, seemed unsure. "These people want to know if they could use this barn to sleep in when the cold nights come, and have a little food or water in the meantime, when they're passing by."

"My father would turn them in."

"Yes. If he knows."

"I won't tell him, is that what you're asking? Of course I won't. I can have Eleonora bring food out, if she knows."

"She is the lover of one of them. She's involved."

"Eleonora?!"

He nodded.

"Then why are you telling me?"

"Because," he said, and reached out to rest one hand on the head of the horse, as if to comfort, not Antonina, but himself. It seemed to her that he was biting down on what he really wanted to say, and she had an urge to step closer, take him by the shoulders, and tell him she needed to hear the truth, no secrets, no obsequiousness. "Because you are in a . . . position," he said. "A position . . . to help."

"How? With money? My father controls the money, not—"

"Two ways. First, you have the key to the storage room here," he gestured toward one end of the building, "where your father keeps his

50

hunting rifles and ammunition, some spare clothing. You have it, or you can get it and pass it to me. I could ask Eleonora to do it, but that would be making her into a thief, and so I won't. The weapons will be borrowed and returned."

"My father doesn't use them anymore. Carlo used them. Carlo and Giuseppe and—"

"Yes, I know."

Paolo turned his eyes away, then back. More hesitation. "There's something else I have to ask of you. The man with the car, the guest—"

"Massimo Brindisi?"

Paolo nodded. "There is a need for him to visit here again."

"For what reason?"

"I have been told that there is a need. Maybe your father could invite him? You could suggest it to him, but it would have to be done . . . with grace. Do you understand what I mean?"

She nodded, watching him. "There's something else, Paolo, isn't there?"

He glanced to the side as if in pain, then swung his rough face back so that he was looking directly at her. Something passed between them. She felt the skin on her arms lift and ripple, as if a cold breeze had skipped across it. "Speak, please."

Old Paolo was pressing his lips tightly together, holding the words in his mouth. "There are two more things, *Signorina*. One, and then another. Two more."

"Tell me."

"Eleonora told me what happened . . . in the night. With . . . the, the friend of your father in your room. This Brindisi. Don't be angry at her for telling me. She cares about you. I'm sorry, I would stop him if—"

"Paolo, speak freely with me."

He nodded. "Yes. And, the other—I . . . There are German soldiers in the attic here," he said suddenly. He lifted an arm above his head.

"Boys. Very young. Deserters. I decided to let them stay here. Not long. I think . . . I . . . maybe . . . if . . ."

"And you trust them?"

"*Sì, Signorina.* I have a feeling from God that I should. They have pistols. They didn't raise them against us, so I haven't taken them away."

"When did they come?"

"Tonight. Earlier."

"And you fed them?"

"They were starving."

"And it's they who want the clothes, not the partisans?"

Paolo nodded, watching her intently.

"I'll send the keys. And food. They'll leave soon?"

"Soon, yes. Very soon, *Signorina.* I'll try to send them to Father Costantino, in the village. He—"

"Works with the partisans, yes?"

"Uh . . . yes, *Signorina.* And now you know everything."

Vittoria watched him and felt—how strange it was—on the edge of tears. At last, it seemed to her, one part of the wall between them had crumbled. At last, the truth was being spoken to her on this property. At last, she was something more than a princess in waiting.

Ten

On the morning after the German deserters appeared, the morning after his difficult conversation with the *Signorina*, Paolo awoke just at sunrise, his joints aching, and his mind caught in a sticky web of fear. His sleep had been broken into short stretches tormented by terrifying visions: Nazi jeeps racing into the courtyard, Allied bombs falling on the manor house and setting it afire. Lying awake in the darkness between dreams, he felt as though he were looking into the actual future.

He shook himself fully awake, stood up slowly on aching knees, and climbed the wooden ladder to the attic. There, tucked against the far wall, he found the three Germans sitting in a half circle. A bit of sunlight angled into the attic through openings around the edges of the small door they used for loading hay. Vittoria must have given Eleonora the key the night before, soon after they spoke, and Eleonora must have used it, because the soldiers were dressed in workers' clothes that fit them poorly—the jackets, trousers, and shirts of the young men of the barn, who'd gone to war—and the Germans' discarded uniforms lay folded in a neat pile on the plank floor beside them. Their boots were so badly worn and caked in mud that Paolo hoped they might be unidentifiable as German army boots. Maybe, as long as they didn't speak, the men might pass for Italian workers. But, assuming they avoided capture here, and assuming he would soon send them away, where could they go? Toward what destination? Back to their mothers and girlfriends at home, where they'd be seen as traitors and cowards? To some imaginary place on the Continent that was untouched by war? He didn't know if it was true, but he'd heard that Switzerland had remained neutral, so perhaps if the men could find their way to the Swiss border, and managed to sneak across, they could avoid starvation and survive. But Paolo guessed the Swiss border was five hundred kilometers away, and it would be fenced and guarded, he was sure. He felt a breeze of pity blow through his thoughts—a strange thing, because, until that moment, he'd always associated German soldiers with the purest evil. The Nazi occupation—growing by the week—had brought stories of rape and massacre, of inhuman torture of the innocent, and the Nazi soldiers he'd come across on his deliveries had strutted about like all-powerful demons, cold, superior, vicious. Now, for the first time—maybe because they were out of uniform, hungry, and terrified—he saw the three young men as human beings. Caught, like everyone else, in the bloody teeth of war.

The deserters were looking up at him eagerly, their faces marked by a degree of hunger that was a close cousin to starvation. Paolo could think of nothing to do but make a reassuring gesture—cupped hand to mouth—signaling that they'd be fed, and then take the uniforms into his arms and carry them away. The men could eat and sleep in the attic, but had to go downstairs to use the toilet, so there was always a chance Umberto SanAntonio, who made rare visits to the barn, would see them. Or that someone else—the *Signore*'s rich friend, a delivery-man, a visiting wine merchant—would happen by and look through the doorway at just the wrong moment. In one of his tormented hours of half sleep, Paolo had imagined the SS officers from Montepulciano demanding to search the premises. It seemed to him that every waking minute he could actually *feel* the presence of the three men, as if, instead of blood, his heart was pumping the risk of death into his arms and legs. And not just risk for himself: all their lives were at stake now, everyone on the property. He'd promised Vittoria and the others that the deserters would leave very soon, but what, exactly, he was going to do with them, he wasn't sure. Simply chasing them back out into the world seemed cruel, a breach of Italian peasant morality, another sin.

The gray-green cloth, the strange insignia, the smell of sweat and dirt—it seemed to him, as he shoved the uniforms into a canvas sack two floors below the men, that the material was soaked in the putrid vapor of death.

Just as he was tying the sack closed, Marcellina appeared in the doorway. An unattractive woman, with an unattractive husband, off in Russia now, she believed, a good daughter and two rambunctious boys who avoided work whenever they could, she was always loud and bursting with complaint. In their small society of peasants and house servants, the foreman stood one step higher than the others on the lad-der—a step below the village priest and local tradesmen, two or three or five steps below members of the landowning families. Without anyone ever talking about it, they all understood their places, but from her low place on the ladder, Marcellina was continually throwing stones and mud into the shallow pond of their little society, spreading circles of discontent among the others.

Wide, strong, bristling, she stood in the doorway, backlit by the first morning light. When she spoke, the words came out in a low hiss. "You're putting all of us in peril, Old Paolo. And for what? For three Germans!"

Paolo didn't answer, watched her move closer. He could feel the anger and impatience radiating from her body like actual heat. But— another chapter in this strange day—the cool air of pity he'd felt in the attic seemed still to be surrounding him. Instead of the Queen of Complaint, *La Regina dei lamenti*, as people called her behind her back, he saw, in Marcellina's bloodshot eyes and pinched face, a woman also caught in the teeth of war. No husband, misbehaving children, endless work, a life without a scrap of pleasure.

"You've gone insane," she hissed. "They're killing our people. My husband. Carlo, Matteo, Giuseppe—they're killing all of them. They're raping our women . . . and you give them food! And you protect them! What has happened to you?!"

By this point, Marcellina had approached to arm's length. Paolo could see the spittle at the corners of her mouth, and tremors of anger shaking her shoulders and heavy breasts. She started to say something else, but Paolo reached out and wrapped his arms around her and pulled her against his chest. For a second she stood still, cold and stiff as iron, surprised, resisting, and then she burst into the most terrible weeping. Sobs, tears, uncontrollable shaking. Paolo held her and held her and let her cry, and at last she wrapped her arms around his waist and sagged against him, and they stood there like that until she quieted. "Feed them," Paolo said to her. "One more night they'll stay, and then, I promise, they'll be gone. Christ would want this of us."

He felt her nod against his shoulder, once, and then she turned away, wiping her face with the bottom of her dress, and climbed the stairs toward the kitchen.

Paolo carried the sack into the stable area and dropped it in a corner. While he used the toilet, washed, and ate a bit of bread and the tomato that had been left for him on the table, the bundle sat there, crumpled in the straw, a living creature breathing fear into the world.

Germans in the attic, Marcellina driven to the edge of insanity, Vittoria almost assaulted in her own bedroom, the SS officer, the terrible assignment from The One with No Name—carrying the weight of all of that and exhausted from the difficult night, Paolo brought the sack with him to the far field, holding it casually over his shoulder with one hand as if it contained nothing more dangerous than the shavings of a carpentry project. As if they guessed what it actually held, none of the other workers asked about it. For the rest of the morning and into the afternoon he worked the wheat, his mind spinning. When the day was finished and the others were returning to the barn, he thought of starting a fire to burn the sack, but that would have required too much effort. Instead, he brought it to the edge of the ravine and attempted to throw it to the bottom. But his arms hurt, he was exhausted, the sack looped out weakly from his hands and, halfway to the bottom, was caught by its strings in a gooseberry bush. The deadly bundle hung there, out of reach, swaying side to side in the wind, the tip of one pant leg sticking out. Perfectly visible.

Eleven

Vittoria knew that her father considered himself the epitome of an organized man. He often boasted about it, claiming it was the trait that had made him so successful in business (when, in fact, he'd inherited the vineyard three generations after it had already made its name). Part of his obsession with a neat and orderly operation manifested itself in his labeling of things other people would have left unlabeled. Though they surely could have functioned without doing so, and though most of them couldn't read, he insisted that the workers hang their tools on hooks beneath labels—HOE, RAKE, SCYTHE, and so on—and that the shelves in the kitchen had small labels saying GLASSES, KNIVES, BOWLS. Disorder and spontaneity were intolerable to him, and Vittoria knew—from comments, facial expressions, and the sound of frequent spats—that the fierce regularity of his daily schedule had been next to unbearable for her mother.

On one wall of his upstairs study, her father kept keys, two dozen of them, to the doors of various closets and rooms in the manor house and elsewhere on the property. As a child, she'd thought the rusted pieces of metal belonged to just another display of things that had been handed down from earlier generations, like the framed sepia photos on the living room sideboards, or the elegant quilts that were brought to the beds in wintertime. But these, too, were labeled. After her conversation with Paolo, she went immediately, in a kind of waking dream, to her father's study, took a particular key from its nail, and handed it to Eleonora. Fifteen minutes later, Eleonora brought it back—both exchanges wordless—and soon it was hanging in its usual place.

The next morning, from the minute Vittoria opened her eyes, all she could think about was what Old Paolo had told her. German deserters hiding in the barn! *Partigiani* fighting the Nazis in the hills! Their sweet Eleonora involved in the secret battle! She'd never heard anything about partisans, but the truth was, since the Germans had started pouring more men and matériel into the country, with the exception of weekly visits to the cathedral in Montepulciano for Mass, she'd had almost no contact with anyone outside the house, and the word had never been mentioned in the conversations her father had with Massimo, the village priest, and the estate's few other visitors. *Partigiani!* Old Paolo, Eleonora, and that same priest among them! Those thoughts crossed her mind again and again like a troupe of dancers crossing back and forth on a stage. Twirling, somersaulting, disappearing behind the curtain, reappearing. *Partigiani!*

What, she wondered, would Carlo think of them? They were, in fact, fighting on the opposite side. But Carlo had been the most reluctant of soldiers, completely open to her educated criticisms of Mussolini and Italian fascism, perfectly willing to agree with what Vittoria told him of her mother's radical opinions. He'd be a partisan himself, if he could manage it. She was sure of that.

She sat with her father at the breakfast table, caught in a swirl of emotions. Worry, guilt, confusion. Germans in the barn. War on Italian soil. Partisans in the hills—men and women both, Old Paolo had said—fighting the Nazi war machine. Her small act—the passing of one key—made her feel as though she were taking off the clothes and jewelry she'd lived in all her life, the silks and satins, the sapphire earrings and diamond bracelets, and walking out into the world unprotected by the SanAntonio wealth and privilege. The world was wrapping its cold arms around her. The real world. A place of risk and death. A place where honor and courage mattered more than money.

But, if the deserters were captured, wouldn't they turn in Paolo and the others to save their own lives? Change their minds, fight with their countrymen again, murder Italians in the streets? For a moment, her doubts extended even to Paolo and Eleonora. Were they people she could trust, or ones who'd betray her and her father to save themselves if the Germans discovered what they'd been doing?

To complicate matters, there was a piece of news—a confirmation of weeks of rumors—that seemed strong enough to shake the grapes from the vines, to shatter the red-tile roof and send cracks running through the stone manor house walls: Benito Mussolini had disappeared! Now even his own radio was saying so—his Fascist Council had surprised him with a vote of no confidence, and he'd been deposed for bringing the war to Italian soil. Reports claimed that the king and General Badoglio had taken Mussolini prisoner, left Rome, and were ruling the country from a secret location.

That news fed the strange new excitement in her, made her wonder if Italy might surrender now that its murderous leader had disappeared, if Carlo might soon come home.

At dinner she waited for the right moment—her father seemed absolutely distraught at the disappearance of *Il Duce*—and then, honoring Paolo's request, said, "Father, I've been thinking about what you said, and while I don't ever see myself marrying Massimo, I do agree that I was rude on his last visit. I only wanted to say that to you. I hope he'll visit us again."

Her father had his wineglass halfway to his lips. He held it there for a moment, then set it down without drinking and looked at her more closely. "Could you possibly be learning how to become a woman?" he said.

Instead of reacting to the remark as she would have in the past, Vittoria only tilted her head and raised her eyebrows. Amid all the other emotions, she felt a twist of thrill inside her, something shocking and different and exciting: the ability to disguise her true feelings, the ability to put on an act, to fib. She had no idea where this new talent had come from.

Twelve

For the first few days, Carlo stayed in the barn, leaving only to use the outhouse and, once, to clean himself at an outdoor spigot while Ariana's father chased away the children who wanted a peek. The face and shoulder were a constant source of pain, but day by day, gradual as the deepening of a season, the pain receded. His body began to heal.

It seemed he'd been blown far up into the air by the Allied shell and had landed in the embrace of the kindest family on earth. Bruno and Miracola were the names of Ariana's parents, and, as he healed, Carlo became aware of a flock of black-haired children, boys and girls from ages four to fourteen, some of whom seemed to be part of the family, and others—neighbors, he guessed—who wandered in and out of the barn, and across the arid land, curious to catch a glimpse of the wounded soldier. He'd always loved being around children—he and Vittoria had talked about and looked forward to raising a large brood—and he welcomed their company now, let them stare at his face, even touch a finger gently to his scarred cheek. He told them how he'd been hurt—they listened with mouths open and dark eyes fixed on him—and he let them follow him every morning when he went to pray at Pierluigi's grave.

The sight of that grave, which was just a berm of raised dirt marked by a cross fashioned from two branches of a fig tree lashed together, seemed to say everything that needed to be said about this war, and about war in general. The life of a good man had been erased from the earth far too soon. His parents back home in Naples—Pierluigi had been their only child—would be devastated. And for what? Because *Il Duce's* lust for power had driven him to emulate Adolf Hitler, another maniac? Because Italians wanted to return to the supposed glory of Rome and boast of their greatness in the world? Repulsed by the politics, bitter at the waste, Carlo would kneel there in the dirt, with the sun casting the day's first golden light upon the Sicilian hills, and he'd feel an urge to apologize to his late friend. Apologize for leading him out of the ditch on the hill above the Licata beach; apologize for surviving; apologize on behalf of the world's rich and powerful, who never ended up in battle themselves, but seemed all too willing to send others off to die.

The daily climb to Pierluigi's grave was part of his exercise regimen, part of his rehabilitation, mental and physical. It took Carlo two more weeks to recover his strength, and almost that long to come to terms with the fact that, for the rest of his life, he'd live with one eye, a scarred face, and dampened hearing in his left ear. Only after he'd asked her four times did Ariana agree to bring him a small handheld mirror. Carlo didn't have the courage to lift away the bandage and look at what lay beneath it. But even with the white cloth in place, he could see how misshapen his face had become, the skin of his left cheek disfigured by a shiny scar. He looked like a killer now, someone you wouldn't want to meet on a dark road at night. No wonder the children were fascinated and horrified! He wondered if Vittoria would even want to look at him again, never mind kiss him, make love with him, marry him and bear his children. At times he felt it was all a fantasy in any case, all a fantasy. The princess and the peasant. But he clung to it even so, to their mutual promise, to the memories of being with her, to the sense that, out of all the many places on this earth, the two of them had been set down on that same fertile piece of land, ten kilometers east of Montepulciano.

Though there were many mouths to feed, and though food was still in short supply, Miracola made him three small meals a day—a boiled egg from one of their hens, a cup of milk from their goats with a handful of walnuts from their own trees, a ripe apricot or apple or a bunch of grapes. There was no bread—not yet—and very little pasta, but every few days that passed seemed to bring a slight improvement to the life of the Sicilian countryside. The family cultivated a vegetable plot—zucchini, peppers, tomatoes—and Bruno's fisherman friends would bring over an octopus, or a sea bream, and sometimes Miracola would place on the table a dish of steamed clams sprinkled with olive oil.

Soon, the family was inviting him into the house for meals, though Carlo kept the barn as his sleeping place. Night after night he was tormented by vivid dreams, as if the halving of his sight during the day had doubled his nighttime visions. Time and again in sleep he kissed and held Vittoria, made the familiar jokes with Enrico, felt himself working the vines, saw himself on Umberto SanAntonio's property, beside Old Paolo, walking that lovely, undulating piece of land with its straight rows of grapes, and groves of olive and fruit and nut trees, the woods, the wheat and hay fields, the deep ravine on the far side where he'd once watched a pack of wolves tearing a wild piglet to pieces; the stone-and-stucco, tile-roofed main barn where some of the wine kegs were stored and the horses kept, and the tiny bedroom above—cold in winter, hot in summer—where he'd lived from the long-ago days when his mother was still alive.

Waking up to the reality of the morning was a torment.

Once he was able to, he ventured up the steeper hillside to where Bruno and Miracola owned a small plot planted in wine grapes. Zibibbo grapes they were—they gave a wine similar to Marsala, or could be made into grappa—and so poorly maintained it pained him to walk along the rows and study them. He began to make the trip up there as a ritual, every morning after his visit to Pierluigi's grave, as if convincing himself he would get back to the vines at home, as if the sight of the bunches might hasten his healing.

One hot Sicilian morning he came upon Bruno between the rows, digging near the roots so the soil would catch more of the brief, infrequent afternoon rains. Carlo wondered if Bruno knew how to properly prune the plants, to encourage them to send their roots down deep for water, through layers of dirt and clay and all the various minerals there. *That's what gives wine its richness,* Gennaro Asolutto had told him. *The plant is reaching down to find the secret tastes buried there, the gifts of the earth. You want to push it down, not let it rise up.* The grapes Carlo could see weren't full-fleshed and formed into firm spheres like those at home, but smaller and narrower with speckled skins, the bunches themselves meager and pocked with empty places.

Bruno was a proud man, Carlo sensed that already. So he squatted beside him and talked about other things at first—the progress of the war (word had reached them that the Nazis had been chased from the entire island, that thousands of Italian soldiers had surrendered, and, most surprising of all, "maybe just a rumor," Bruno said sadly, that Benito Mussolini had been deposed by the king and could not be found), the number and ages of his children (eight in all, Ariana the oldest), how many years he'd lived on that land (from the day of his birth, and his father, grandfather, and great-grandfather before him).

"This is my work," Carlo ventured at last, speaking guardedly, gesturing with his chin at the grape vines.

"Vero?" Bruno said. Truly? "Where?"

"Near Montepulciano. I work for a man who makes wine. SanAntonio, have you heard of him?"

Bruno shook his head, embarrassed.

"Northern wine," Carlo hastened to say, dismissively, as if the famous product of Montepulciano might be inferior to its sweet white, or black-red Sicilian second cousins, as if the SanAntonio name wasn't famous across half the peninsula. "I'd like to help if I could," he told Ariana's father. "I won't stay much longer. You and your family have been so kind to me. I'd like to do a little work for you before I leave."

A shadow came over Bruno's square face. The man wouldn't look at Carlo, and for one long minute he worked the soil clumsily with his thick hands. "You don't have to leave," he mumbled at last, still without making eye contact.

Bruno glanced at him, then quickly looked away. After a few seconds of confusion, Carlo understood. *But she's only sixteen,* he wanted to say. *And beautiful. And I'm . . . deformed. And I have someone waiting for me at home.* But another grown man would be helpful around the farm, he knew that. And all over rural Italy it wasn't unusual for girls to marry at sixteen. The idea that Vittoria SanAntonio would give her lifelong love to a workingman, a deformed and half-blind workingman at that, was beginning, with each passing day, to seem more like a fantasy. The idea that her father would allow it, all but preposterous. But in the center of him Carlo could feel—had always felt—a small stone of determination, almost another person, a soul, a spirit. It was the same presence that had given him the strength to live without a father, and the courage to speak to Vittoria again, once their childhood friendship had been buried by her father in the vast space between their lives. That same determination was the part of Carlo that had pushed him to learn the secrets of making wine, the part that had pushed him up and out of the trench with the battle raging around him; maybe even the part that had kept him alive, when another man with the same wounds might have perished.

Frozen in surprise for a few seconds, he at last found his voice and pretended not to understand the offer. "I can show you a few things about the vines, if you like. I can make it so they produce more, so the roots are healthier."

"Show Ariana instead," Bruno said, and then, obviously lying, "she works them, usually." And with that he stood, brushed the dirt from his pants, and walked away.

The next morning, Carlo awoke to see a hard-boiled egg and a cup of weak coffee beside him in the barn, and, next to the food, the pair of clippers Bruno had been using the day before. It was a wordless acknowledgment: Here, you know the work better than I do. Please help us. Please consider staying with us. Carlo had never known his own father (*A passing worker,* his mother had told him. *He left me with the great gift of a son. He blessed my life forever.*) and for a short while, chewing the egg's rich, crumbly yolk, and sipping the coffee, feeling the southern heat change the air of the barn, minute by minute, like water in a pot on a stove, he wondered what it would be like to put down his roots in Sicilian soil. Work he loved in a place where he could make a real difference, a devoted young wife, a father-in-law and mother-in-law instead of the emptiness of the barn in Montepulciano and the cold, grudging, strictly limited respect—a business arrangement—of Vittoria's father. The war had left Sicily now, and probably wouldn't return. The winters were milder, the food as good, the people kind. For a time, he sat there in the barn's warmth, his belly full, the pain in the bones of his face almost gone, and contemplated the life that seemed to have been presented to him without his asking. All he had to do was say yes.

He could feel himself being drawn to that life, but at the same time a stronger force was tugging him north. Vittoria, of course, mainly, and the friendship with Old Paolo and Enrico. But something else, besides, something beyond logic and emotion. A kind of summons he could feel but not name. His fate, perhaps. His purpose and place on earth. He didn't know exactly what it was. But he knew he'd have to make every possible effort to get back to her and to the vineyard. Every effort. If he made it back, and Vittoria had fallen in love with someone else, he'd decide then what to do. But he had an intuition that she'd wait for him, that she felt what he felt: they were part of each other's destiny.

Later that same morning, he took the clippers and climbed up to the vines, tasting a few of the grapes as he walked, wincing at the flavor. It would soon be the end of summer, time for the harvest, not pruning, but here and there he clipped off a wandering vine, something that would suck energy from the fruit. He hadn't been there long before he saw Ariana climbing toward him from the house, her sandals throwing up puffs of dust behind her. On her head she balanced a blue-and-white ceramic pitcher, steadying it with one hand. In the other hand, she held what turned out to be a dried fig. She came and stood beside him, let him drink from the pitcher, handed over the fig.

He twisted it in half and handed the other half back to her.

"My father said you could stay if you wanted to," she said shyly.

Carlo nodded and looked away, the sweetness of the fig in his mouth, the sweet, imaginary life playing in his thoughts again, bumping up hard against the *No* of some interior counselor. Ariana's dark eyes—so much like the eyes of her siblings—were fixed on him, a question. "You're very young and beautiful," he said at last. "I'm . . ." He brushed a hand up near his face.

"I don't mind." She watched him. "The young men here are *brutti.* Crude, awful. The women to them are like animals."

"All of them?"

Ariana shrugged and turned her face away, and he watched a tear wander crookedly down one dusty cheek. He reached out and gently took hold of her wrist, but she wouldn't look at him. "You have someone, I think," she said, tilting her forehead north. "There."

"Yes," he said. "I'm promised to someone, and she to me." The tears were running down both Ariana's cheeks now, a cascade of sorrow. *You've known me for only a few weeks,* he wanted to say. *It's an infatuation.* But there was something so perfectly sincere about her, such a cool, pure well-water of feeling, that he couldn't make himself speak. At last he brushed the tears from her face, took her hand, put the clippers there, and said, "I can show you how to make the grapes better. For your family," but she was sobbing openly now, and the words felt like dust in his mouth.

Thirteen

Late that night, when Paolo had checked the wine barrels in both the main and secondary barns, as he'd done every evening for the past four decades, making sure there were no leaks and that the mice and rats hadn't made a nest or started chewing through the oak, he heard a familiar signal—three well-spaced taps—at the main barn's back wall. He went quietly through the door there, walked a little way, and, when his eyes adjusted, saw Eleonora standing half-hidden behind the trunk of the massive chestnut tree. A glint of starlight caught her bare left forearm and the braid hanging at the left side of her face. As Paolo approached, she moved back into the shadows. "He's coming," she whispered. "Father Costantino. He called the house and let the phone ring once, an hour ago. The signal. Please give him this for my Antonio." She pressed a folded scrap of paper into his palm and whispered, "I brought the Germans in the attic more food."

"Good, good," Paolo said quietly. Eleonora, he now understood, was a true *partigiana*, a fact that, given her sweet, bashful disguise, still seemed almost impossible to grasp. *She* had been the one to suggest he speak with Father Costantino, and that conversation had drawn him into the secret work, but Paolo didn't know whether it had been her own idea, or the priest's. In either case, why had they chosen him? What had made one or both of them believe a simple old field-worker would be willing to risk his life for a cause that seemed, at times, to have no chance at all of success: a few Italians fighting against an entire army!

Then again, he'd always seen Eleonora as a strange and mysterious person, a young woman of many secrets. And so, as a man of many secrets, he'd always gotten along with her. Part of the mystery came from the fact that she hadn't been born on the property like the rest of the household and field staff, but had been brought to the vineyard to care for the *Signora* when the illness was first taking hold of her. Another part was linked to the fact that, unlike the rest of the help, she could read well, knew German, and spoke Italian with a slight accent. Brown braids, brown eyes, freckled skin, a way of walking that made it seem she was floating along, half-connected to the earth, Eleonora seemed so shy, but Paolo sensed a fierce courage beneath that thin surface layer. How and why she'd been brought to the vineyard, how and why the village priest had started to work with her, Paolo didn't know, but he trusted her, admired her. Had he been younger, he might even have been in love with her.

"The three men, they'll be gone soon?" she asked, with the smallest note of fear running beneath the words.

"*Sì.*"

"Good, because everyone's afraid."

"We'd be afraid anyway, wouldn't we? Even without them."

Instead of answering, Eleonora shifted her weight in the darkness and asked, "How did you know I speak German? I've always tried to hide that."

Paolo shrugged again, embarrassed, and then, when she kept her eyes on him, he admitted that he'd overheard her swearing once, in the kitchen, when she thought she was alone. He'd been standing at the back door, waiting for her to leave the stove so he could hand her a basket of eggs. "You were having a kind of fit, swearing—I think—and going on."

"I have a temper," she admitted. "And I was born in Bolzano, which was Austrian before the first war."

"Bolzano. To the north."

"Yes, near the border. Bozen is the German name. My father was Italian. My mother, Austrian, but Jewish."

A long pause. Paolo tried to read her face in the darkness. She shook her head so that the braids swung gently side to side, willow branches in a wind. "My mother. There were camps there. She was taken to one. But, Paolo—"

"Yes, yes, I won't say it to anyone. I give you my word. I'm sorry about your mother . . . You go to Mass, though."

"I do, for protection. But in the church I say Jewish prayers in my mind."

"Ah."

"And I know the Mass because nuns raised me after my father left and my mother was taken. The nuns helped me get away, and sent me here, through Father Costantino."

"I wondered."

"So I have been trusting him. I don't know why he asked me to do these things. He thinks I'm Catholic. He asked me to tell him what I hear in the house, what people are saying there, the *Signore* and *Signorina* especially, and their visitors. He asked me to see if you wanted to, you know . . ."

"Yes, I also trust him," Paolo said, but without as much conviction as he'd intended.

Another pause. "You should go," she said. "He'll be coming. And Paolo, something else."

He waited.

"I heard the *Signore* on the phone the other day. He speaks German, as well. I don't know if Father Costantino knows that."

"You're sure? All these years no one ever heard him say one word in that tongue!"

She nodded. "He was talking quietly, saying, 'They deserved it.' *Sie haben es verdient*. Later, Cinzia told me that when she went to the village to shop, she learned that the Nazis had made people in Castagniello stand in a line in front of the church and then shot all of them. Children, even. Twenty people."

"Why?"

"Because someone had disrespected one of their soldiers."

"You're sure he said that? That they deserved it? And you think that was what he was talking about?"

"I think so." She nodded, and he saw the glint of tears on her cheeks. Paolo put a hand on her forearm, so thin he could have wrapped his fingers all the way around it. He wanted to say something to comfort her, but the only words that came out were, "The *Americani* will chase them away, you'll see."

She nodded, swiped at her face, and floated back toward the manor house in the darkness.

Twenty Italians, Paolo was thinking as he walked. Twenty lives taken, and for what? *One* insulted soldier?! What kind of people were these Nazis? What kind of devils? And the news about the *Signore*! And Eleonora, part-Jewish all this time! Going along in the starlit darkness, he realized that there were the surfaces—the ordinary workings of the vineyard—which he understood very well, and then, beneath those surfaces, there must be another world, one of secrets and mysteries. Spies, hidden abilities and sympathies, layers of trust and suspicion, deceit, complicated plans, painful histories. A man like him, a simple man, should never have involved himself in that world. He should have contented himself with work, with the vines and horses and fields, straightforward things that were understandable, dependable. But it was too late now. Eleonora had asked him to speak with the priest, and he'd done so, and that conversation had led him into a sticky web of treachery. He'd never escape.

71

The path that led to the cistern was faintly lit, but Paolo had gone along it so many times he could have managed with closed eyes. Forty-three steps. Chestnuts in their spiky green shells littering the path. Starlight on the cistern's rounded, stained concrete. He stood beside it for half an hour, waiting, worrying, imagining every terrible possibility, until at last he heard footsteps. A familiar figure emerged from the shadows, dressed in a priest's black trousers and shirt, but without the white collar. And then Paolo realized that there was someone else there, too. A man, it seemed, very tall. The tall figure hung back in the shadows, and Paolo couldn't see his face. No greeting was exchanged. Paolo handed over the note, said, "For Antonio." Father Costantino took it, made a humming sound, and handed him in return a small, surprisingly heavy, paper-wrapped package. He leaned forward, held his mouth close to Paolo's ear, and said, so quietly that the older man had to squeeze his eyes tight and focus intently in order to hear, "This is for the assignment you were told about. You take this and you attach it by the laces to the exhaust pipe of the car. The laces have been coated, so the heat will set it off before the laces burn through. That takes time. It won't happen right away. He'll be far from here when it happens, so no one will be able to trace it to you."

"Like nothing I've ever done."

"I know, I know," the priest whispered. "But no one else could do it as well. Your hands are a gift from the Lord."

Paolo nodded skeptically, waited, smelled tobacco on the priest's breath. How did one find cigarettes during the war? "And if I'm caught?"

"If you're caught, Eleonora will send word. Try to hold out as long as you can without giving my name. And don't mention the one with the beak for a nose."

"The one who told me to do this."

"Yes, never mention him."

"I don't know his name."

"You don't?"

"No, Father."

"Then I can't tell you."

Paolo grunted, waited, felt his heart slamming in its cage of ribs. "Father," he said, "there are deserters in the barn. Three German soldiers. Young, hungry. I decided to let them stay, but we can't keep them."

When Paolo stopped speaking, there was a terrible silence. His guilt, his willingness to risk the lives of all the others, echoed in the black night like the voice of God, condemning him. *Say something, please, Father. Help me now,* he wanted to say, but the words he'd spoken had shone a bright light on what he'd done. Why hadn't he simply fed the soldiers and sent them on their way? What difference would it have made? They'd have to leave eventually. The tall figure behind the priest shifted his weight in the darkness, as if he'd heard, and Paolo flinched. "Father?" he squeaked.

"Va bene," the priest whispered at last. "All right. Listen to me. It was foolish to keep them, but listen. Dress the men in Italian clothes."

"I already have."

"Burn their uniforms."

"I was too tired. I tried to throw—"

"Can any of the women drive the wagon?"

"Yes, all of them."

"Can Vittoria, Umberto's daughter?"

"Since she was a girl. I myself taught her. But someone else should go—"

"No, no. If she's stopped, she can say she's a SanAntonio and they'll leave her alone. If it's someone else, they'll search the wagon. Has she ever been to the nuns in San Vigliano?"

"Yes, with her mother, but long ago."

"Then have her take the wagon and make a delivery to them. A case, two cases, five cases of wine, it doesn't matter. Make sure she goes along the Zanita Road, understand? It's safer."

"The Zanita Road. I understand."

"Find a way to hide the men in the bed of the wagon and send them to the nuns with Umberto's daughter, and I'll figure out what to do from there. The Nazis have left the nuns alone so far. Even if they see the wagon, they won't follow it through the gate."

"No men can go through it."

"Only the sisters' priest and confessor," Father Costantino said. Almost a joke, Paolo thought, judging from the tone. And at such a time. "Hide them there, and I'll find a way to help them."

"A sin, wasn't it, what I did? And what I'm going to do?"

"Yes, yes, you're a terrible man, Paolo. Now go. Go with God."

Father Costantino and his silent companion disappeared into the darkness. Paolo tucked the package carefully against his side, started to whisper a *grazie*, changed his mind, and turned back toward the barn. He was caught already in another swirling current of doubt, hoping the last part of the conversation had been Father Costantino's idea of a joke. A second joke. The priest was young, new to the area, a strange figure in so many ways. Who could tell about his sense of humor? *You're a terrible man, Paolo,* he'd said. What if it was true? And what if Vittoria was caught on the Zanita Road and killed because he'd let the Germans stay in their barn? How would he live with himself if such a thing happened? How was he going to live with himself in any case?

Fourteen

On the morning—a burning, late-August day—when Carlo left the Sicilian family that had nursed him back to life, Bruno crushed his hand in a goodbye grip but couldn't meet his eyes; the young children crowded sadly around as if at a burial, reaching out to touch the one-eyed northerner, clamoring, prancing about, trying to convince him to stay; Miracola handed him a small cardboard box holding matches, and a burlap sack filled with food; and Ariana tenderly removed the bandage over his eye and replaced it with a black patch she'd sewn by hand. Her lips were trembling. Because Carlo asked her to, twice, she walked with him for a quarter of an hour, as far as the dirt road that ran not far beyond the edge of their property.

Caught between dreams, Carlo turned and stood facing her, then leaned forward and touched his lips gently to hers. When he leaned back, she had her fingers to her lips, feeling them lightly, as if they'd been electrified. "You are beautiful," he said. "I will remember you always." He watched her eyes fill with a silvery flood, looked at her face a last time, waited for her to speak, and then, when he couldn't bear the moment any longer, he turned and walked off, listening to her weep and forcing himself not to look back. *Vittoria, Vittoria, Vittoria,* he kept saying to himself, a prayer for courage.

Up through the southeastern quadrant of the island he went, sack over his shoulder, army pistol on one hip, combat knife on the other, walking twelve and fifteen and sometimes twenty kilometers a day in the heat.

Miracola had given him a dented tin cup, which he refilled at road-side spigots and from the frail summer streams that cut through the Sicilian countryside. He slept beneath pine trees, washed himself in a desolate stretch of the Gornalunga River, lived at first on the food the family had given him, and then on pieces of too-ripe fruit he found in the dirt of abandoned orchards. He had six rounds in his pistol, and perhaps it still worked, but, though he searched and searched, he saw nothing living that might be shot and eaten. Not a *capriolo* or a hare, not so much as a single pheasant or quail. The war and the scorching Sicilian summer seemed to have stripped all life from the landscape.

By the time he reached the outskirts of Catania, he was starving and exhausted. He'd been walking for days through mostly empty interior countryside, a landscape little touched by the fighting. But now, on both sides of the road close to the big city, he came upon the scars of war: chassis of burned-out German army vehicles; stone houses broken in half by bombs or tank shells; an American helmet stained with blood; the half-rotted carcass of a mule that had been blown up and left in the scorching sun. Here and there he passed old men scraping the parched earth of garden plots, women hanging clothes on a line, kids playing in the dust. He waved or nodded to them, but even the bravest ones eyed him warily, an armed stranger with a black patch over one eye, dirty, tired, shuffling along, wearing on his broken face an uneven week-old beard.

It seemed to him that he was seeing Italy without its clothing, naked and crude, stripped of niceties. In the North, "Sicily" and "The South" had always been synonyms for poverty and hopelessness. That made sense to him now: everything he could see bore the mark of gen-erations of want. The words of Pierluigi kept coming back to him. *When the war is finished,* his friend had said more than once, *we will change the way we live. You'll see. The poor won't be so poor. The rich won't be so rich. You'll see.* What Carlo saw was that they had each been clinging to a dream intended to get them through to the end of the fighting. Pierluigi was imagining an Italy of fairness and justice, free of want, some heaven of shared labor and shared luxury, as if, once the country was finished with war, the nobles were going to be so grateful to the soldiers that they'd voluntarily portion off pieces of their huge estates and give them away. And it was the same for him: a different dream, but with the same purpose. Where were he and Vittoria going to live? In the manor house? The barn? On their own piece of property at the edge of the vineyard? Did she ever wonder about these things?

But he kept repeating her name, kept walking. *Vittoria.*

As the ninth or tenth night fell—he'd lost count—Carlo realized he could go no farther without asking for help. North of Catania, on the outskirts of a small city—Acireale, a bullet-ridden metal sign said it was—he came upon a house that seemed undamaged and inhabited, and, after mouthing a prayer, he walked up and knocked on the door. A woman answered, stooped, gnarled hands, crooked nose, watery eyes. Half his height, she stood before him either unafraid or so accustomed to being terrorized that fear had lost its power over her. *"Sì?"* she said, as if, before him, scores of men had knocked, or simply broken in, taken what they wanted, and left. A stranger at her door, and yet her "Yes?" held no surprise in it at all.

"Could you give me a little food? I'll work. I'll help, but I—"

The woman reached out, took hold of him by the side of his shirt—a grandmotherly gesture—and pulled him inside. She sat him at a table in an unlit kitchen, fussed at the stove for a while, and lay a bowl of cooked lentils and a spoon in front of him. Then a glass of a pale wine, some kind of rosé. It took Carlo less than three minutes to clean the plate and empty the glass. The woman sat down wearily opposite him.

"Was the fighting here?" he asked.

She nodded.

"The Germans?"

"For a long time. And then the *Americani* for a short time. Gone now. To the mainland, people say. To Calabria. Now Sicily is left to stand up again, like a beaten child. On its own feet."

"I can help you. I can work for a few hours. Do you have grapes?"

"I have a small garden," the woman said. "They left it alone. My son is in Albania, I think. Or Russia. I don't know why."

Because of Il Duce *and his insanity,* Carlo almost said, but he bit down on the words. As was the case with Ariana's parents and Umberto SanAntonio, there were still many Italians who worshipped Mussolini, in spite of the wreckage he'd brought them. It was unwise to insult him in front of a stranger. "I was wounded," he said. "At Licata. Lost my eye."

"Yes," the woman said, without sympathy, as if, from her life, so much more than an eye had been lost. And then, "Have you heard the news?"

"I've been alone for more than a week. Walking. Sleeping in the hills."

"He's gone."

"Who?"

"Il Duce."

"I thought it was a rumor. Gone where?"

The woman lifted and dropped her bony shoulders. "No one knows. His own people, traitors, have sent him away. Kidnapped or killed, no one knows. I pray for him every hour. If *Il Duce* comes back, we'll win the war," she said. "If not, we shall lose it, and starve."

We're starving now, Carlo nearly said. But he kept all expression from his face. What he wanted to say was: *This is the man who has ruled our country for twenty-one years, who befriended Hitler, stripped the Jews of their jobs, sent his Blackshirts to torture anyone who opposed him; the man who brought the Germans here, who sent your son to Albania or Russia to die. And you pray for him?*

"A good man, don't you think so?"

Carlo hesitated a moment, then: "I don't know him."

The woman's face underwent a sudden change, lips tightening, eyes narrowing. She watched him suspiciously, and for a moment Carlo thought she'd chase him out the door or call some local Blackshirt police chief to come drag him away. Mussolini was truly gone, apparently, and the war was gone, too—from this part of Italy, at least—but no one could say what the country would look like when the fighting was finished. Maybe *Il Duce* would reappear and take power again. Maybe the Blackshirts and Fascists would continue to dominate Italian life, painting their slogans on the walls and drumming their philosophy into schoolchildren. Or maybe, as Pierluigi had believed, things would be different.

"You can sleep here." The woman gestured to a sofa in the small stone-walled room next to the kitchen. "I have a bathroom. I have food. You're not a deserter?"

Carlo shook his head, pointed to his eye, but the woman's wariness had been sparked to life and it lingered in the air between them like the smell of burning rubbish.

"They killed a young man in Catania yesterday," she said proudly. "Beat him to death in the square, in front of his mother and sister. The man was a deserter. A traitor to his country."

"I didn't run. I fought, or would have fought. I was wounded on the first day of the invasion. My friend was killed. A family saved me."

The woman kept nodding, but it seemed to Carlo that no amount of truth would sweep her suspicion aside. He wasn't like her son, wasn't fighting, didn't adore *Il Duce*. Nothing else mattered.

She handed him a single sheet, and Carlo removed his boots, lay down on the couch, and rested, turning this way and that, clinging to old memories.

He and his mother had lived in a small room—just a corner of the barn loft walled off with wooden planks. They'd been sweating and mosquito-bitten in summer, shivering in winter. They had a rusty toilet downstairs for their needs, a spigot of cold water for washing, and they'd eaten the worst cuts of meat from the manor house kitchen, day-old bread, fruit and vegetables from their plot and from the fields, in season; pasta, polenta; old potatoes, onions, and turnips in the cold months.

Vittoria's father, lord of the manor, had let them live that way, with a dozen other workers housed in similar circumstances. If they'd been walnut trees instead of human beings, he and his mother would have been cared for more kindly. But, he thought, really, they'd been treated more like animals than trees, like oxen who serviced the fields and were brought to the barn to sleep, and then buried in poorly marked graves when they perished. Pierluigi had been correct: their lives meant nothing. Nothing to Mussolini and his generals. Nothing to the Nazi or Allied soldiers. And nothing even to the lord of the manor, Umberto SanAntonio. True, Vittoria's father had given them work, a place to sleep, enough to eat. But when Carlo's mother fell ill, *Signore* SanAntonio had been notified and was finally convinced, after four terrible days, to send a doctor. "Keep her warm and give her water to drink," the doctor had said on his one hasty visit, and it had been left to Carlo and one of the women field hands to wash her and care for her in her final agony. He, Paolo, Gianluca, and Giuseppe had dug the grave and buried her in a workers' cemetery at the edge of the far orchard.

Carlo was ten and was immediately put to work like a grown man. Gennaro Asolutto, wine master and veteran of the first war, had taken a liking to him, brought him along when the vines needed pruning, let him help with the filtering and keg maintenance, talked to him for hours on end about the fine points of winemaking, the mistakes that could be made—overwatering, careless pruning, leaky kegs, improper amounts of sugar, letting the wine turn to vinegar—the reasons why some years produced a finer vintage than others, the different types of soil, the benefits of morning fog and cool winters, the deadly Tignoletta moths, the beetles that had to be captured and put into jars of gasoline before they chewed through all the grape leaves and devastated the crop. The threat of powdery mildew that had to be treated with sulfate and lime. Those conversations were what Carlo had instead of school. The friendship with Vittoria had persisted, which by itself was a kind of miracle. Her mother would usually allow Vittoria to come to the barn—especially when the *Signore* was away—and she and Carlo would groom the horses together, or walk to the cistern and sit with their backs against it, peeling away the rough chestnut skins, polishing the hard brown shells, talking about what he'd heard people say in the barn, and what she'd heard people say in the manor house, or at the Catholic-run school in Montepulciano where she took her lessons.

And then, as they grew into adolescence, her father had ordered him to stay away from her—and apparently ordered her to stay away from the barn—and there was no choice but to obey him. In true peasant fashion, Carlo had buried his resentment, buried his hopes, and, in time, moved on to harder work and different pleasures: the nighttime visits of young women from nearby properties, as beaten down by work as he was, and as toughened, taking a little comfort for themselves on Saturday nights when there would be no work the next day, expecting nothing in the way of tenderness or commitment, leaving before dawn with strands of straw clinging to their hair and the possibility of pregnancy weighing heavily on their shoulders.

He was twenty when Gennaro Asolutto grew too old to work, and for the first time, Umberto SanAntonio seemed to regard him as something other than a threat to his daughter's purity. There was one face-to-face meeting at the well beside the barn: both Old Paolo and Asolutto had recommended him. Would he take over the wine operations? Would he accept ten lire every two weeks in payment? Did he want to move to a small cottage in the hazelnut grove?

Yes and yes and no. Carlo remained in the barn, supervised the winemaking, rode with Old Paolo in the truck to make deliveries. He discussed the fine points of fermentation with the older foreman, helped create two of the best vintages the Vineyard SanAntonio had ever produced.

But, though his hopes were deeply buried, he'd never stopped thinking about Vittoria, never forgotten the warm thrill of their child-hood friendship. A grown man by then, and she a grown woman, Carlo had started to find ways of crossing paths with her, started to risk saying hello, then making small bits of conversation—about the weather, the grapes, the deliveries, her schooling, her brother, her mother's failing health—though now the conversations were different, with something new, an electric charge, running beneath them. Once, when her father was away, she'd accompanied him and Enrico on a short trip into the city in the wagon, and they'd stopped there for coffee, and she'd reached out and touched his hand as she spoke. Carlo felt that a new kind of connection was being made, a spark of some forbidden attraction shoot-ing across a bridge that spanned the chasm between their lives. More conversations after that. And then the first secret meeting—her idea. A first kiss—his idea. And then more.

Remembering that "more" on the suspicious old woman's sofa, he finally fell into a troubled sleep, that, after a time, was broken by the sound of footsteps. He lay there with his eye open, listening. He'd heard that when the Blackshirts came for someone, they forced their victims to drink castor oil, glass after glass, until their captives erupted in diarrhea so violent and persistent that, humiliated and drained of fluids, they died of dehydration. He couldn't be sure, but he thought he could hear the murmurs of a quiet conversation just outside the back door. Weary, hungry, half-awake, he waited a minute, two minutes, then decided there could be no reason for a conversation like that in the middle of the night. No good reason.

He tossed the sheet aside, and, without even bothering to lace up his boots, slipped out the front door into cool darkness. Stars sparkled like living creatures in the black sky, and a sliver of moon shone among them, a sibling keeping watch. A dog bayed in a nearby yard. Even if he'd imagined the conversation, even if what he'd heard was only the woman mumbling her prayers, listening to the radio, or speaking innocently to a neighbor who couldn't sleep, he wasn't willing to take the risk. Soon enough, she'd realize that he'd fled, and that would make her only more certain that he'd deserted. She'd spread the word, the Blackshirts would be looking for him, a crazed mob of politically connected Fascists who'd avoided service entirely and whose love of their Benito overwhelmed all other considerations, all human compassion, all morality.

He hurried away from the house, leaving the road after a few hundred meters for a dusty path that wound along through bushes, cacti, and stunted trees near the shoreline. By the time the sun rose, he was shivering and hungry, but he'd put five kilometers between himself and the old woman's narrowed eyes.

Up along the coast he went, with the triangular bulk of Etna to his left, snow-topped even in the first part of September, and signs of war wherever he looked. Piers ruined, buildings without roofs, craters in the middle of the road, and charred military vehicles lining the shoulders like the droppings of the animal of war. The path merged with the road again, and a farmer with a horse-drawn wagon stopped and took him as far as Santa Teresa di Riva, telling him that, as they fled, the Germans had come through Taormina, raping and stealing, shooting men they thought should have been fighting for them. Then the Allies, racing through with jeeps and tanks, tall men, some with pale faces. "And some of them black!" he said, as if, dark-skinned himself, those men were the most surprising thing he'd seen in his long life.

"But now the war is over," Carlo suggested.

"Sì, sì," the man said. "For us, for the *siciliani*. But it has gone to Italy, the mainland. You're going there to fight?"

"Yes," Carlo lied. "I'm hoping to find my unit."

"Keep your *pistola* ready then, young man. The war will find you as you go."

Fifteen

Two days after the difficult conversation with her father, Vittoria saw Massimo Brindisi appear in the courtyard again, driving his black Ford automobile and wearing a light-gray summer suit, white silk shirt open at the neck. Brindisi and her father played a game of chess—the pieces made of brown-speckled and white-banded marble—drank glass after glass of wine out on the shaded stone patio, and took a long walk together in the summer twilight. Then she was summoned to a typically late dinner *alfresco*, on that same patio, with a sliver of a moon rising over the hills. Eleonora carried out to them heavy silver tureens of cold vegetable soup, then platters of beef with rosemary and potatoes, an escarole salad, nuts and chocolate cake for dessert. They were accompanying the meal with one of their finest vintages, a 1938 *vino nobile*. One bottle. A second. A third. Vittoria wasn't accustomed to drinking that much, but the wine was so elegant, angels dancing on the tongue, and, she realized, as the meal went on, that she was using it to hold down the volcano of doubts bubbling up inside her.

"We eat almost as well as before the war," Massimo said, flashing his smile at her and laughing his gentle laugh.

"While others starve," she said.

"Who starves?" her father asked. "Not our help. Not anyone on this property!"

"People in the South, from what I hear."

"Hear where?" her father wanted to know.

From Eleonora, she wanted to say. But she shrugged the question away, paused politely, did what she could to bury her anger, and inquired after Massimo's work.

"Ah," he said, a flicker of delighted surprise on his face. "Two of my factories make soap, as you perhaps know, and while ingredients aren't so easy to come by these days—one must make one's payments in the proper places—prices are high, and soap is always needed."

"And the others?"

Massimo's smile widened. All was forgiven, it seemed, at least from his side of the table. "They produce cloth for military uniforms. Leather for boots. Tires for jeeps. We have to watch continually for saboteurs."

"So the war has been a bonus of sorts."

"Of sorts, yes." He fixed his eyes on her and said, with some irony, "I am doing my patriotic duty."

"But many Italians are unhappy about the war," she said.

It was as if she'd thrown a bucket of ice water on the faces of the two men. "Politics are complicated," her father noted after a moment.

"Too complicated for women?"

"Sometimes, yes. In this case, complicated for everyone. We try to do our work, to make our contributions to this world. I with excellent wine, Massimo with other products. We keep whole families alive and fed, each of us, and for that, sometimes, we are demonized."

"By whom?" Vittoria asked sweetly.

"The communists," her father said without hesitation.

"The labor unions and socialists," Massimo added, but it seemed to her suddenly that he, too, was acting. When he veered off into politics, something in his tone of voice sounded strained, half-serious, as if he were holding up a facade for the benefit of her father. The man who'd come to her room, drunk, late at night, had disappeared along with the scratch on his neck. He was sitting there, staring at her, talking about himself so happily on this beautiful evening, but different somehow, and somehow not quite genuine. A mystery in a fine silk shirt. *It's not what you think,* he said on that night. *You don't know who I am.* She watched him while pretending not to. Who was he, then? Loyal Fascist? Greedy businessman? Spy for one side or the other? Secret *partigiano*? And why had Paolo asked that he be invited back for a visit?

"And even," her father said, "sometimes, the very people we feed turn against us."

Vittoria asked for more wine. She sipped, avoided her father's eyes, took small bites of the cake. She was caught by a sudden memory. Her mother at an upstairs window, looking out at the workers in the courtyard. They were bringing the horses inside during a storm of sleet and cold rain. *How they live,* her mother said quietly. *Look at how we make them live.*

Until that moment—she must have been seven or eight—the servants had been her babysitters; in the case of Carlo, her playmate. She thought it exotic and wonderful that he and the others lived in a barn. The men who labored in the fields and worked the vines were creatures from a fable, as happy as anyone else in her child's world. To her father and perhaps to Massimo, as well, the workers still weren't quite human. Her father had next to no interaction with them, as if they spoke another language, or worshipped an alien god.

She had a handful of memories of her father's parents, who'd been alive and living here—it had been their house—for the first years of her life. In a country where people touched constantly—hugging, kissing, lifting children onto their laps—she couldn't remember a single gesture of physical warmth from her paternal *nonno* and *nonna*. Proper, rigid, rule bound, accustomed to their wealth and privilege, they were like statues on high pedestals, unreachable. Her father must have grown up that way, in a desert empty of love, unable even to imagine real affection. She wondered what being married to such a man had been like for her mother.

"I've enjoyed the dinner," she said, folding the napkin and setting it on the table. "I'll leave you, Father, to your complicated manly discussions." She kissed her father's cheek, and reached out a hand to Massimo Brindisi, who held it in both of his for a moment.

"So beautiful," he said. "You should visit me at *Lago di Como*. There are people there I'd like you to meet. I'm leaving for the lake directly from here. Tomorrow morning. Would you join me?"

"Not this time, but thank you for the invitation." She felt slightly unsteady on her feet.

"Are you sure? A two-night visit, perhaps? A small vacation? You could take the girl, Eleonora, if you wish. For company. As a chaperone."

"No, *grazie*."

In her room, Vittoria washed her face and changed into her nightdress, and, less worried about another intrusion, half-heartedly moved the armchair so that it blocked the door. She spent a few minutes writing in her diary, then set the book aside, switched off the light, and prayed, as she always did, for her mother's soul and for protection for Carlo and the other men off at war. She tried to picture Massimo's lake house—her parents had taken her and Enrico there several times, many years ago. She remembered the view down over the blue water, tile-roofed houses dotting green hillsides on the opposite shore, and the pink-tipped mountains behind them at sunset; she remembered fireworks displays on summer nights, and riding the commuter ferry from town to town, her father keeping a tight hold on Enrico as if he might fall overboard and drown, her mother buying a set of ceramic plates in one of the villages they visited, Massimo showing her proudly around the grounds and even swimming in the lake with them one time, on a burning hot day. Tonight, he'd seemed so different, offering to let her take Eleonora "as a chaperone," a strange gesture for a man with evil intentions, if, in fact, he had such intentions. So there must have been some other meaning to his *You don't know who I am* when he burst into her room. There must be complications she couldn't see or imagine. As she'd done hundreds of times, she wished her mother were alive so she could confide in her, ask her what she knew. She wished she could talk about it with Carlo. Lacking a formal education as he did, Carlo nevertheless had an excellent understanding of people, and a quick mind. She thought of getting up and writing him a letter, but where would she send it? Her head was gently spinning, and she was exhausted in a way that often happened after she'd come close to an argument with her father. She rested her head on the pillow, closed her eyes, and was instantly asleep.

Next morning, after a breakfast of coffee and pastries, Massimo said his goodbyes, went out into the courtyard, started his car, and then seemed to change his mind. As if the cost and scarcity of gas meant nothing to him, he left the engine running and returned to the patio, where Vittoria was standing with her father, ready to wave farewell. "Please reconsider," Massimo said to her, and she peered into his eyes as if she might discern the man behind the act. "The weather is fine now, at Como. There's no bombing there. You can swim if you like. I can take you and Eleonora up to Cadenabbia for a meal with a spectacular view of the lake. My friend owns—"

"I'm so grateful," Vittoria said, summoning all her own acting skills. "But now is not the right time for me. Please travel safely."

Massimo hesitated, as if he were trying to read her voice, clutching to a thread of hope. He held her in a light embrace, bathed her in his smile, shook her father's hand again in a kind of gratitude, sat behind the wheel of his black Ford, and drove out of the courtyard.

He'd gone only as far as the gate at the top of the first rise when the American car exploded with one tremendous *boom*, sending tongues of flame into the cool morning and showering the road with shards of metal and glass.

Sixteen

Paolo was working the wheat, sweating through his shirt—they were within five or six days of finishing the harvest—when he heard the explosion. Gennaro Asolutto, Marcellina, Costanza and the children, every one of them reacted the same way: jerking their faces up and sideways toward the sound, and then, after a few seconds, staring at a thin plume of gray-black smoke as it lifted into the sky beyond the crest of the hill.

"The barn!" Marcellina shrieked. "It's the barn! It's the *Americani* bombing our barn!"

But Paolo knew it wasn't the barn, and, though their planes were passing overhead more and more often now, he knew it wasn't the Allies, either. For a moment he wanted to order Marcellina and the others to keep working, but that would have given everything away. And it was too late, in any case: the children had already started sprinting toward the top of the hill so they could see where the smoke was coming from, and their mothers were hurrying after them. He was left there with Gennaro Asolutto—who sat quietly in the wagon, a loop of rosary beads in his gnarled fingers—and with the most horrible feeling he'd ever known. *When you kill another person, you kill a part of yourself,* Gennaro had said. *Your soul bears a stain afterward. Forever.*

Slowly, as if holding a heavy sack of hazelnuts on his spine, Paolo climbed up onto the bench seat, rapped the reins once on Ottavio's hindquarters, and brought the half-loaded wagon as far as the top of the hill. From there, they had a clear view down over the vine-covered slope. Asolutto let out a grunt, as if he'd been punched in the belly. Paolo felt as though he was about to vomit. Beyond the manor house, just past the wrought iron gate at the vineyard's boundary, a few tongues of flame and a billowing column of smoke marked what was left of the beautiful *macchina*. Only its skeleton remained—the tires and interior on fire, pieces of the roof and doors and sparkling bits of glass scattered in the weeds to either side of the road. Father Costantino had said it wouldn't happen until the bomb was thoroughly heated, wouldn't happen until the car was far from the property. Perhaps, Paolo thought, in his haste and fear, on his back in the dirt in the middle of the night, he'd attached the explosive incorrectly. Or perhaps God had wanted him to see what he'd done, so the deed would haunt him forever.

"*Una cosa,*" Asolutto muttered. A thing.

Paolo couldn't turn his eyes away. The children had sprinted down-hill as far as the vegetable plot, then stopped and were standing there, arms at their sides. The women, holding up their long skirts and hur-rying behind, were screaming for them to get no closer. The *Signore* and both house girls, Eleonora and Cinzia, had come outside onto the patio, the *Signore* still as a tree trunk, the girls with their hands to their mouths, weeping. Paolo looked for Vittoria, and for a moment was afraid she'd been in the car, too. But then she stepped onto the patio, staring with the others at the burning wreckage, and he saw her turn and look at the children, then at the mothers, and then lift her eyes up farther, to the top of the hill, searching, he knew, for him. Paolo forced himself not to look away. Before that moment, even with all the sins he'd committed in his life, venial and mortal, he'd never felt so horribly soiled. Now, not only had he killed a man—murdered him—but, and this was so much worse, he'd involved this pure young woman in the murder, made her an accomplice. She'd never see him the same way again, perhaps even feel guilty enough to tell her father who it was that had convinced her to encourage his friend to visit. She, herself, would be tainted for the rest of her life. For a few seconds, before Vittoria whirled around and hurried back into the manor house, Paolo tried to tell himself that the *Signore*'s powerful, fearless friend had been an evil man—why else would the priest have given such an order? And look what the man had tried to do to Vittoria in the night! But it didn't work. A blanket of guilt had been draped over him now: nothing could justify such a sin.

Beside him, Gennaro Asolutto spat into the weeds, started to say something, then pressed his lips tightly together.

Seventeen

Vittoria left the others on the patio and climbed the stairs to her room. The two windows there faced in the opposite direction from the smoking ruin—out over the courtyard, the vegetable garden, and the vines. But, looking through one of them, she could still see the women with their children, and, farther up, Old Paolo and Gennaro Asolutto in the wagon. She was glad her brother had wandered off early that morning, as he liked to do, and was probably exploring the fields and woods that led toward Cortona and the central mountains. He could go like that, alone, for the whole of a day, always finding his way home for the evening meal. Although it was sometimes difficult for him to explain the encounters, Enrico had told her many times that, in the high forests and meadows there, he met with witches and spirits. *They talk to me about God, Vita*, he'd say. *They show me where the walnuts and berries are, so I don't get hungry in my belly.*

She stepped away from the window and lay on her bed, eyes open. Automobiles didn't simply blow up by themselves, she knew that. She understood what she'd done—felt it in the very core of her spirit—and knew what Paolo, or someone he worked with, had done, too. The *partigiani* getting their revenge. She wondered if her father would connect her to the killing, and, while she did feel the dark weight of guilt in her bones, she felt something else, too, in equal measure. Tobias, the disgusting SS officer, was at the center of this "something else." Before her trip to Montepulciano, evil had been an abstraction to her. She'd heard about Mussolini's Blackshirts torturing his opponents, and about the kidnapping and killing of Matteotti, the one member of Parliament who'd stood up to him; the alignment with Hitler; all kinds of Nazi atrocities. And she'd believed those things were real, of course. And yet, she saw now that the life she lived, the fine wine and servants, the leisurely days and luscious meals, had been like a soft fur coat protecting her from the horrors of the war. She knew—the death of her own mother had shown her—that there was suffering and pain in life. But until the Nazi had grabbed her leg as if she were an animal, she'd been protected from that at some level, in some way.

Now the protection was gone. The guarantee of a comfortable tomorrow—of any tomorrow—was gone. She felt the rawness of being alive, the icy reality of evil, true evil. Of sin. Her own and others'.

She felt a fresh wave of remorse, a putrid wash of bitterness tinged with a feeling about Old Paolo that was a mix of puzzlement and anger: she'd clearly helped him to murder her own godfather! She tried to ease the regret by wondering what secret crimes Massimo Brindisi must have committed in order for the partisans to have imposed a death sentence on him. His factories made clothes for Mussolini's army, tires for its jeeps. But, unless Paolo and the partisans were grievously mistaken, there must have been more. Her godfather, her father's closest friend, a man who'd been so kind to her at times, who had loved her mother, must have been deeply involved with the Nazis; otherwise, why would the partisans have decided to kill him?

Eighteen

A fisherman, steering a patched and rusty boat with three worm-baited lines over the side and torn nets hanging from the foremast, agreed to ferry Carlo across the Strait of Messina to the Italian mainland without asking for payment of any kind. They bounced along on a choppy sea, past the hulls of sunken German naval ships and as far as a half-broken pier on the mainland at Reggio Calabria. It seemed to Carlo that, among the many other riches that had been lost—the abundance and enjoyment of food, even for poor people like himself; the elaborate festivals in which every man, woman, and child participated—the war had stripped Italians of the pleasure they took in language. So much lay below the surface now, unspoken, as if the enormity of the suffering caused by decades of fascism, the Allied bombing raids, the German occupation, and now the actual fighting on Italian soil, had rendered words so insufficient that people no longer bothered to use them as they had in the past, freely, creatively, joyfully. Everyone had been made wary—of the Germans, the OVRA, the Blackshirts, the Allied bombing raids, of each other's political views, of the cruel hand of fate. In the past, he and the boat owner might have enjoyed a leisurely conversation, asked about each other's lives, talked about love, work, food. From the least to the most educated, every Italian loved those kinds of impromptu encounters. Now, instead of engaging in a lively conversation, they sailed along in silence. At the pier, with the steep hills near the shoreline hovering over them, he thanked the fisherman with a nod. The man nodded in return, left him, then pointed his boat out to sea again, probing the invisible underwater world for something to sell, or eat.

As the days passed, Carlo pushed himself north through Calabria on tired legs, caught rides on farmers' carts, and, once, in an American military truck, though he and the driver couldn't understand more than a few words the other was saying. To his right, east, as the truck bounced along the rutted roads, the peaks of the Apennines rose like a ragged line of gray-blue sentries, beautiful and still and unfazed by the wars they'd seen, the centuries of occupation. To his left he caught glimpses of a sparkling sea. A day later, walking again, he was able to shoot a rabbit with one of the precious bullets left in his pistol, butcher it and cook it over a fire (started, gratefully, with one of the matches Ariana's mother, Miracola, had thought to give him) in a grove of olive trees somewhere in the long toe of the boot, and it was as glorious as any Easter feast at the Vineyard SanAntonio. He sucked the bones clean of every last morsel of meat.

From time to time he'd spy what he assumed to be Allied planes high overhead, but, though the wounds of war grew more apparent by the day—freshly dug graves with makeshift crosses, abandoned German and American tanks burned black, cisterns with fresh water stains below bullet holes—he had not yet drawn close enough to hear the sounds of conflict.

South of Sambiase, he walked along the edge of a small vineyard, the vines here better kept than Bruno and Miracola's, yet still nothing like the prized and vibrant plants he'd nurtured from before he was old enough to shave. They made him think, for the thousandth time, of home, of Vittoria's face, of all the taken-for-granted joys of peacetime.

In spite of the way he and his mother had been made to live, Carlo felt a bond to the estate, and indebted to its owner. Umberto hadn't thrown him out on the street to starve, as he might have done all those years ago when he was orphaned. And then there was also Vittoria's younger brother, Enrico—body of a fifteen-year-old, mind of a small child. Enrico adored him, Carlo knew that. And he supposed that, even if he arrived back at the vineyard and Vittoria had married the son of some nearby landowner and gone to live on his estate, Carlo would likely remain, keeping Enrico company, pruning grapes and making wine for the rest of his days, like Gennaro Asolutto before him, living above the barn, moving into a lonely old age, teaching some younger worker what he himself had been taught, someone who loved the grapes as he did, who felt the life in them, the gift of them, who understood that wine, consecrated or not, was God's blood.

Not far beyond Sambiase, when Carlo came upon another vineyard, with a stone farmhouse beyond, it reminded him so much of the SanAntonio property that he almost believed he would see Vittoria standing in the doorway.

He knocked, two hours before dusk, and a woman in a stained apron opened the door for him and invited him inside. Violeta, she said her name was, a woman of early middle age, plump even in these difficult times, with black hair touched with the first strands of gray. She asked Carlo where he had come from and where he was going, then prepared a simple meal—peas and olive oil with a few anchovies mixed in, and set it on the table. "My husband is gone," she said to him. Unlike the fisherman, she seemed not to have lost the love of language. "Killed in Russia. My sons, also gone there. Our daughter is married to a Milanese, and I've barely heard from her since not long after the war started. One letter, 'A lot of bombing here, Mother,' she wrote, and then silence. You can cut your beard with my scissors and shave with my husband's razor. And you look like you haven't slept in a bed in a long time. Well, you can have my sons' room. We never use it now. You can stay as long as you like. It's safe here. The trouble is north of us now. We live in the ruins."

Before darkness fell, before he accepted her kind offer and shaved and bathed, Carlo spent an hour in the vineyard, trimming, plucking, bringing back a bowl of purple grapes and explaining to the woman what she might do with the plants when the cold came.

Violeta shrugged, as if caring for the vines mattered little to her, and she wished him a restful night. Not long after he'd gone to sleep, she came into the room, partly clothed, shook him awake with one hand, and asked if she could get into the bed beside him. "Not to do anything," she said. "You said you have a woman waiting for you at home, and I'm old and sad and the urge for lovemaking has been wrung out of me." She was standing there, close beside the bed, in the darkness. Carlo could see her white undergarments and her hands clasping and unclasping in front of her. "I just . . . I'd just like to lie beside someone again for one night. Can you do that?"

He nodded, said a quiet, "Yes," and Violeta climbed into the bed with him, her skin warm against his, a strand of her hair resting on his bare shoulder. She said not one word, just lay on her back at first, and then rolled over and leaned against him, weeping, tapping her forehead again and again against his collarbone as if nodding in prayer. "You've lost an eye," she said, when the spasm of pain had left her, and she was lying still again. "I've lost a husband and perhaps also two sons and a daughter. For what? *Me lo sai spiegare?*" Can you explain it to me?

"I can't."

"But do you wonder? Do you think about it?" Her quiet words floated up and tapped against the stone ceiling.

"Yes. Every time a child looks at me as if I'm a monster. Every time a girl turns her face away. Every time I think about my friend Pierluigi and his family."

"You're walking from Sicily to Montepulciano. For love, you're doing that. Love. The opposite of war."

Violeta began to weep again, quietly. Carlo could feel her body shaking against his, and he wrapped an arm around her and held her against him until the crying stopped. "I know so many good people," she said. "Simple, good people who only want to live and be left alone. Why is the world like this?"

He let the question echo in the dark room. In time, Violeta's breathing changed and he felt her body relax into sleep. He lifted his arm gently away from her but lay awake for another hour. *You have a good mind,* Asolutto the old vinekeeper had said to him more than once. *You're not educated, but curious. A philosopher.* The questions Violeta had asked—simple but unanswerable—swirled through Carlo's thoughts. He wanted to understand why the God who made grapevines and clouds and the turning of day into night would allow His world to descend into the madness of war. Feeling the body beside him, its warmth and breath, he wanted more than anything to be lying beside Vittoria, to be able to discuss with her the great questions, the mysteries, the meaning and purpose of life. There had been nothing sexual in Violeta's request, and he felt nothing sexual now, as if his urges, so long suppressed, could be reawakened only by one woman. He'd tell Vittoria about this strange, sad night, he knew that. And she would understand, he knew that, too.

Violeta left his bed before sunrise, and as first light angled into the room, Carlo lay there, awake again, thinking about the questions she'd asked. The war twisted morality into crooked shapes, made potential killers out of good men like him and Pierluigi, and turned women, crushed by grief, into people who'd grab at any pleasure, any scrap of what passed for companionship in the night. Why, as she said, did it happen?

In the kitchen, in the morning sunlight, Violeta made him coffee from chicory and, without looking at him, set the cup and a plate of grapes and a sliced apple on the table. Carlo told her he'd be leaving and felt that she was ashamed, not of sleeping next to a younger stranger, but of her own loneliness, the small puddle of emotion to which her life had been reduced. Without speaking, she wrapped a half dozen walnuts and two figs in a cloth bandanna, handed Carlo a bunch of grapes, embraced him for a long while, pressing her breasts against him, then released him and watched him go. "In Montalto, ask for Father Ascoltini," she called, and he turned back and looked at her—silhouetted against the doorway—and raised an arm in thanks.

Nineteen

Paolo went through his days by habit, like a machine, a truck that had been started and put into gear for the thousandth time and was rolling blindly along the road. Marcellina told him that, while he was off with the wheat, the *carabinieri* had come to investigate, two policemen in uniform going into the manor house and spending an hour there with Vittoria and her father. A van from the police medical office followed an hour later. What remained of the body was put into a bag and taken away for burial. Two days passed. Eleonora told him that, ever since the *carabinieri* interviews, the *Signore* hadn't gotten out of bed, was eating almost nothing, speaking to no one, staring up at the ceiling and mumbling to himself.

But, guilt feelings or no, fear or no, the work went on. Paolo and the others continued with the harvesting of the wheat, bringing it, wagonload after wagonload, to the second barn, where it would be stored until it could be taken to the mill. Although he suspected it was foolish, he held to the hope that there might be no consequences for the explosion. That it would be considered an accident, an error in the construction of the American automobile, a tragedy.

That fantasy evaporated at the end of the third workday. He returned from the fields to a scene from one of his nightmares: two German military vehicles—a jeep, and a railed, flatbed truck—coming to a stop in the dusty courtyard, men in uniform climbing out, shouting orders in what they thought was the Italian language, herding him and the other workers into the part of the barn where the horses were kept. Enrico, too, was caught up in it—he'd been grooming his beloved Antonina—and Paolo could see that the boy's big shoulders were shaking in fear and that he was trying, without success, to speak. Faces buried in their mothers' dresses, two of the smaller children had started to weep; all the others were pressed back against the wall. Paolo could feel the terror in his own belly and chest. How long would it take for the soldiers to decide to search the attic, find their three comrades, beat them to death, and then line up the families of the barn and shoot every child, woman, and man? As the foreman and one of the oldest, he'd be last in line, and have to watch the rest of them suffer, watch them die in terror, the children screaming, Marcellina's eyes condemning him to an eternity of guilt and regret.

"In fretta! In fretta!" the soldiers were yelling, gesturing with the points of their automatic rifles. Hurry! Hurry!

A phrase from the end of the Ave Maria, one Paolo had repeated countless times, echoed in his brain: *Nell'ora della nostra morte, Amen. Nell'ora della nostra morte, Amen.*

At the hour of our death, Amen.

He recognized the soldier who appeared to be in charge—the bespectacled SS officer from the house in Montepulciano, the one who'd bothered Vittoria. Pistol on one hip, wire-rimmed spectacles flashing in the afternoon light, tall, thin, with narrow palms and wiry sinews showing on the inner side of his wrists, the man stood just outside the stable doorway until all the workers and families had crowded in against the hay bales and walls. When everyone was in place, the officer stepped into the room and stood facing them, booted feet spread. The only sound was the muffled sobs of the children and a snort from the far stable.

Paolo waited, listening for any noise from above them, counting the other soldiers in the barn—only three—and wondering if there was any possibility of fighting them. In the corner of his vision, he could see both mothers kneeling in the dirt, pressing their children's faces into their breasts. He expected the officer's first words to be about the deserters, then there would be the search, the punishment. But the German began this way: "A friend of the Reich was killed here three days ago." His Italian was terrible, and he spoke in a quiet voice, the words emerging slowly, one after the next, like bits of poison dripping into the air around him. *"Assassinato."*

Paolo watched the man's eyes travel across his captives' faces, saw the pleasure there, the power. He remembered the way the officer had touched Vittoria during the delivery, and he noticed that neither she, nor her father, nor either of the house servants had been summoned. For a moment, he wondered if Umberto would see the German vehicles on his property and rush to the defense of his workers . . . but then another thought came to him, hard and cold as a January wind: What if Vittoria's father, furious at the loss of his friend, had himself called the Nazis? What if, at this minute, he was lying in his luxurious bed, waiting to hear the machine guns erupt?

The officer pushed the spectacles back against the bridge of his nose with one finger, sniffed, said, "We have come here to solve that terrible crime."

Silence. Antonina scuffed one hoof and whinnied. Ottavio whinnied back from the courtyard, still in the traces, waiting to eat.

"Who has something to tell?"

Silence.

"No one?"

Marcellina made a sound, a stifled grunt, and for one moment, one horrible shaking breath, Paolo was sure she was going to try to save herself by telling the officer about the deserters. The Nazi shifted his eyes to her. "No one knows anything about it," she squeaked bravely. "We're not murderers here. We work."

"We work," Gennaro Asolutto repeated dully from where he was sitting on a bale of hay in the far corner.

The bespectacled officer twitched his lips, reached down, and unsnapped the flap on his holster. "Really? You work. And who, which one of you, is in the charge of your work?"

Paolo felt the bottom of his stomach fall away. After a second's hesitation, he forced himself to raise a hand from hip to chest.

"Come here," the officer commanded, pointing to the dirt in front of him.

Paolo stepped forward and stood facing the man. They were almost exactly the same height. He stared through the lenses and waited. At first, his feet and ankles were trembling, but then, as if the back of his neck had been brushed by the hand of some braver spirit, he felt the fear suddenly leave him. Dirty water swirling out of a sink. The way this man had touched Vittoria. The way he spoke to them now. The continuous torment of their presence on Italian soil. Paolo could feel an inferno of anger in his cells, and barely stifled an urge to lift the German like a sheaf of wheat with both strong hands and fling him against the wall. He felt his fingers start to shake, small tremors.

"Who kills our good friend?" the officer demanded.

"No one, *Signore*. His car exploded. There is gasoline in a car, and a spark must have—"

The German reached out and slapped Paolo so hard across his face that the older man was knocked over sideways and fell to one knee. The children started crying louder. Behind him, Paolo could hear Enrico making strange sounds, very loudly, "Uh! Uh! Uh!"

"Stand up!"

Paolo stood. He could taste blood.

"I ask again. Who murders our friend?"

"No one."

The officer slapped him just as forcefully with the other hand. Paolo tilted over to his left but didn't fall. He straightened up, wiped a sleeve across his bloody mouth, kept his eyes fixed on the eyes behind the lenses. Nothing in them now. Circles of ice. *L'ora della nostra morte,* he thought. This was his penance for the deed he had done, for the taking of a human life.

The officer removed his pistol from its holster and placed the cold tip of it against the middle of Paolo's forehead. "Let me ask you last time."

From behind him Paolo heard a hideous "No!" screamed out into the air, felt a frenzied movement, and then saw Enrico flash past. The boy threw himself with all his weight against the officer's midsection. The pistol went off, the bullet flying up into the ceiling, causing a shower of splinters and dust to fall on them, and Enrico and the Nazi crashed hard to the dirt, arms and legs flailing. In an instant, all three soldiers had taken hold of Enrico, dragged him to the side, and begun kicking him—in the ribs, the knees. The boy curled into a ball and covered his face, grunting, shrieking. The officer clambered awkwardly to his feet, and pointed the gun at Paolo's face again, spectacles crooked, hat gone. The voice was no longer calm. His hand was shaking, and the words came hissing out between his teeth.

"For a German life," the officer hissed, "we kill you all. All of you! But since it was the Italian you killed . . ." He whirled, arm outstretched, and fired three quick shots into the neck of the horse. Antonina fell over sideways, her head cracking hard against the stable's wooden wall, blood spurting into the hay.

Chaos. Enrico, blood pouring from his nose, scrambling sideways away from the soldiers' boots and crawling over to the horse. Children screaming. Adults weeping. Gennaro Asolutto vomiting loudly into the straw. The officer straightened his glasses. One of his men was holding out his hat, but the officer ignored him. He spat forcefully into Paolo's face, said, "Next time I come here you have a name for me, or I shoot you one after the next, beginning with the idiot. Then the children.

Then the rest." He pointed to Marcellina. "You, fat whore, we shall leave alive. To clean the blood." And he stormed out.

Paolo wiped the blood and spittle from his face with the sleeve of his shirt and watched the soldiers leave. The children were crouching around Antonina, crying and rubbing her flanks as if they might bring her back to life. Enrico, nose dripping blood, lips swelling, was holding the horse's head in his lap, silent now, staring blankly out into the courtyard. Paolo felt Marcellina's eyes on him, and he turned to meet them but couldn't read the expression on her face. Defiance, surrender, hatred, he couldn't read it. He thought he heard the attic door open, a rumble of running feet above, but in another second he realized it was the sound of planes. The drone of Allied bombers. He wondered if the pilots—en route to the industrial cities of the North—would see the German military vehicles in the courtyard and release part of their deadly cargo. But the noise faded, the planes disappeared, and he was left standing there, face throbbing, hatred filling the place inside him where the guilt and fear had been.

Twenty

Three days after the ambulance came and carted away what charred pieces of Massimo's body could be retrieved from the wreckage of the black Ford, it seemed to Vittoria that her family's vineyard had been invaded. Late in the day she heard the sound of engines, stepped over to her bedroom window, and saw two Nazi vehicles careening onto the property. Soldiers climbed out and began summoning the workers—just back from the fields—and herding them roughly through the open barn doorway. Watching them, Vittoria realized with horror that her brother was among them, and that one of the uniformed men was the rail-thin Nazi officer with the wire spectacles. Tobias. She waited, watching the open doorway, feeling her heart thumping behind her left breast, clutching her hands, afraid to leave the manor house and try to help. And guilty at not having the courage to do so. For fifteen minutes there was no sign of anyone, and she stood there as if her feet were cemented to the floor. At one point she thought she heard a shot, or shots, and her whole body twitched violently at the sound. And then the soldiers reappeared, one after the next. She was squeezing her hands together so hard they hurt. Maybe the uniformed demons had shot every one of the workers, and her brother and Paolo and the others were bleeding to death in the stables.

After a few more seconds, the officer—the *demon captain* was the way she thought of him—stepped out of the barn and walked calmly across the courtyard. His men were standing around the flatbed truck that had brought them, but Tobias ignored them, stopped, ran his gaze over the manor house windows. She stepped back at an angle so he couldn't see her, and was sure he was going to march over to the main door and walk inside without knocking. Instead, he turned away, and strode past the mule's enclosure toward the large rectangular vegetable garden. As she watched, the captain unbuttoned his trousers and urinated on the tomato and pepper plants, turning himself this way and that as if wielding a hose. Then he buttoned his trousers and sauntered toward the house. As he came closer, because of the protruding patio roof, she could no longer see him. She heard the sound of planes overhead, glanced up, and then hurried away from the window. She pretended to busy herself changing the arrangement of silver candlesticks and a family photo on the top of her bureau, but her mind was a wild spinning circus of voices and thoughts that wound themselves around spindles of fear, and her hands were trembling. They could be dead, all of them. She'd made no move to save them. The spoiled princess. The would-be *partigiana*. A minute. Two minutes. Fifteen hideous minutes.

A tap on the doorjamb, a squeak of hinges. "He wants to speak with you," her father said behind her.

She turned and faced him. Fear there, also. "What for, Father? Who?"

"The German. He's spoken with everyone. Me. Eleonora. He's interviewing Cinzia now, downstairs. You next, he says. They believe it wasn't an accident, that someone planted a bomb to kill Massimo."

"I'm terribly upset, Father. I've been ill all morning. Surely they don't suspect me. Or you."

Her father stood still, staring at her, and at last said, "It was you who asked me to invite him, Vittoria. You said Massimo should visit again."

"Father! I asked as an apology, not in order to kill him! How can you think such a thing!"

Her father shrugged and, for a moment then, he seemed to her like a frightened boy, confused, grasping at any explanation. And for that moment, washed again by another wave of guilt, she wanted to cross the room and hold him in a warm embrace, hold him and rock him as if he were a child. He'd lost his wife, now his best friend. The daily reports from the South made it seem that their world—his world—so carefully constructed, so perfectly luxurious, so neatly labeled, was about to be shattered like a beautiful ceramic plate thrown against the wall. The Allies were moving north. How would they treat a man who'd been sending his finest wines to the SS? Whose best friend's factories had made uniforms and boots for the Fascist army? How would the Nazis react if they discovered that deserters had been hidden in his barn?

Her father's cheeks were bubbling, his blue eyes swinging side to side.

"They . . . I don't know. Who knows? Something is happening, Vittoria. They have apparently killed one of the horses!"

"What! Father, oh Lord and Savior. Is Enrico safe?"

Her father nodded as if in a trance. She did cross the room then and take him by both hands. "Please tell them I'm ill, that I've been vomiting ever since Massimo died. My own godfather. Look at me, I'm broken, Father."

It was all another act. The words seemed to lift out of a dark place, the throat of another person. A small, terrified, guilty person, but one who was capable of putting on an act in order to save herself.

"Broken," Umberto repeated, his cheeks shaking, and for a moment Vittoria believed that her act had worked.

But then her father swung his head from side to side, bent his lips in against each other. "I can't, Vittoria," he said. "The man, this captain. He's insisting. Who knows what else he'll do if we refuse. Kill the other horse. Set the house on fire. You must come downstairs. You must. Now."

He squeezed her hands once, turned and walked out of the room, and she saw no option but to follow. Better that than hear the sound of boots on the marble stairs and see the demon captain standing at the door of her bedroom, grinning, unbuckling his belt.

Before she'd gone even halfway down the stairs, she could see his black boots, then the trousers of his military pants, his hands clasped behind his back, and at last his head, uncovered by the usual military cap. He held the cap in one hand, and she wondered if, after pissing on their vegetables, he could possibly have taken it off out of respect for the house.

Two more steps and she saw the man spin around and lock his eyes on her, then run them from her face down to her feet and back again, as if assessing a farm animal he was thinking of buying.

Her afternoon *merenda*, tea with a slice of bread and their own salami, was pushing up against the back of her throat. She stopped in front of him and waited. Without a word, he reached out and took hold of her arm, and led her across the foyer into the small sitting room where her mother had often sat sewing, and where she'd sometimes breastfed Enrico when her husband wasn't around to forbid such a "public display." The captain said nothing, not a word, just kept holding her with his fingers tight on the back of her right arm, as if she might try to run away. Vittoria was doing her best to pretend she was unafraid, but her breath was coming in short gulps and she could feel rivers of perspiration running down her sides, trickling along her ribs.

Still grasping the back of her upper arm, the captain led her with a peculiar gallantry to a brocade sofa and gestured that she should sit. He pulled up a straight-backed chair—too close—and sat opposite her, adjusting his wire-rimmed spectacles, setting his hat (she noticed a piece of straw clinging to it) carefully on the coffee table, brushing back with three fingers what was left of his thinning brown hair. All in all, he was a particularly unattractive man, his face thin, centered by a blunt nub of a nose, his eyes slightly asymmetrical and the irises a pale-brown color with yellow streaks. With the first word out of his mouth, *"Allora"*—all right now—Vittoria remembered his awful Italian.

"Allora," he repeated, and then stumbled along with his mutilation—understandable enough but painful to the ear—of her language. "As you know, a friend of the Reich was murdered on your father's property three days ago."

What it sounded like to her was, "So, as you knows a friend from the Reich and to your father last week killed on the land."

She summoned as much confidence as she could, kept her eyes fixed on his, and nodded, once. *An accident,* she wanted to say, but the words wouldn't come.

"We just now questioned all the workers, and your father. A certain price had to be paid."

"You murdered one of our horses."

The man let out a short laugh. *"Murdered,* yes. Even then, of course, no one says to know anything about the tragic death of a man."

"Nor do I," she said. "Massimo was a great friend of the family, for many years, and my father is grieving terribly."

"And yourself?"

"I've been vomiting for three straight days. I've barely eaten. We had a peaceful life, always, until—"

"Until the war arrived and the German forces occupied your beautiful lands, yes?"

Vittoria squeezed her lips together, drew and released a breath. "Please don't speak for me. We've had a peaceful life. Nothing like this has ever happened to us. This man was my godfather. I loved him like an uncle."

"Yes, an uncle. Why was it that one of the serving girls just now claims you were screamed when he was found in your room late in the night?"

"I was having a nightmare. He was sleeping in the guest room beside mine. It was natural for him to come to my aid."

"A nightmare about what?" The captain slid his chair an inch closer, so that his knees were touching hers. "About the German officer?"

"About my mother. She died not long ago. I was dreaming that she was out walking in our fields and a wolf spotted her and was approaching. I was trying to warn her."

"You're lying."

"Why would I?"

"Because perhaps you kill our friend, your so-called godfather."

"Why would I do such a horrible thing!"

"Because perhaps he shows the interest on you, like I do, the interest on a beautiful young woman. The sex interest. And came into your room in the night and caused you to screaming for help. Perhaps his sex interest makes you disgusted."

"And then I did what?" Vittoria said, her voice rising and cracking and echoing out into the foyer. "Found a bomb in our house and put it inside his car in the middle of the night? Or mined the road leading to the city? Turned suddenly into a murderer? An expert with explosives!"

The captain was peering at her, burning his eyes into her. He reached across the small distance and put his hands on her knees. Vittoria flinched and pulled herself back against the sofa, but his hands followed her, crept upward a bit. "You are having the problem when men touching you, I think," the captain said.

The second his hand touched the cloth of her dress, Vittoria's courageous act abandoned her. She couldn't speak.

"You know, of course," the man went on quietly, "that I could taking you into the bedroom upstairs and do whatever I am wanting with you. Now. This minute. Have my men doing whatever they wanting. You know this, yes? Who is going to stop us, your father? The old man in the barn? The idiot?"

From the neck down, her body had turned to stone.

The captain held his hands on her for a long minute, then squeezed once with his fingertips, released her, and leaned back. "But your father was been kind to us, and perhaps even support our presence here. Who knows? Who can say about Italians?"

Roland Merullo

She watched him, heard voices outside the door. Paolo's calm voice. Her brother's, not calm at all.

"Plus." The captain reached for his hat, and flicked the piece of straw onto the floor with one finger. There was a loud commotion now on the front steps. She could hear Enrico's high-pitched wailing. He was calling her name again and again. *Vita! Vita! Vita!* "What I wanting to do with you," the captain said, grinning, "what I imagining to do, I can do anytime. Anytime that I want. We can be here for years, drinking your father's wine, and there are many women now for us for the time. Women come to us of their own reason, to show their gratefulness."

To have something to eat, Vittoria thought, and very nearly said it.

"So for now, stay here in your peaceful wine palace with the idiot and the old man. But, if we know that you have anything to do on the death of our friend, or that you are helping to our enemies in any way— any way—then you find yourself in our house in Montepulciano, in the upstairs room, begging us to kill you. Begging us. You understand?"

She could manage only a frozen nod.

"Good," he said, sliding the chair backward without standing up.

For a moment, her legs wouldn't support her. She heard "Vita, Vitaaaa!" from the front porch, and Enrico's voice gave her the strength to stand. The captain reached across and tapped the side of her face, once, lightly, with the back of his hand, as one might tap a disobedient child.

Then, in a blur, he was gone, there was the sound of engines beyond the windows, and Enrico had burst into the room, wrapped his arms around her, and pushed her back down onto the couch. "They hurt me, Vita. He killed Antonina, Vita. They made her dead! I'm going to kill him the way he killed Antonina. I will. I'm going to, when he comes to the barn again."

"He won't come again, Rico. I'm sure he won't."

"We have to take her now, Vita. Paolo said so. To the place. The . . . the . . . we have to take Antonina, can you help, can you?"

112

Twenty-One

When the two Nazi vehicles had driven out of the courtyard, and the wailing and weeping in the barn had settled into an undercurrent of miserable murmurs and sobs, Paolo's mind cleared enough for him to realize that something had to be done with Antonina's body. They couldn't leave it in the stable to be swarmed by flies and gnawed by rodents. After thinking about it for a few minutes, he sent young Gaetano to a nearby estate to ask for help. It was a decision he made with reluctance, because the workers there—on the six-hundred-hectare hazelnut and semolina plantation owned by another noble family, the DellaMonicas—would be as tired as he was after a day of labor, and soon to sit down to their evening meal. But there was a thousand-kilogram dead horse in the barn and less than two hours left of daylight, and for centuries there had been an understanding among the workers of various estates that there were times when one group or the other would need assistance with a difficult job, repayment guaranteed.

Within half an hour, Gaetano returned with six of the ablest workers from the DellaMonica property—four men too old for military service, and two strong young women. While he waited, Paolo had tied the sturdiest canvas tarpaulin he could find to the back of the wagon and fed Ottavio a handful of hay. Enrico had returned from the manor house, and Paolo tried to gently peel him away from where he sat: in the stable with Antonina's bloody neck across his lap.

Tugging, half lifting, using lengths of wood as levers, the six visitors and Paolo, Enrico, Gaetano, Marcellina, and Costanza were able to pull and push and slide Antonina's corpse onto the canvas sheet. Paolo driving, the others walking alongside, they slowly dragged the dead animal out of the barn. There was no question of trying to bury or butcher her: it would have taken a day to dig and then refill a grave so large, and Enrico, already so upset, would have been pushed to the edge of sanity by seeing his beloved horse cut into pieces. The only reasonable option was to drag Antonina to the ravine along the flattest route they could find, and somehow slide her down into it. So they went along, Paolo guiding the horse, the heavily loaded tarpaulin scraping across the dirt, Enrico wailing, and the others marching somberly behind as if in a funeral procession for a human being.

By the time they reached the great cleft that marked part of the southeastern boundary of the Vineyard SanAntonio, most of the light was gone from the day, a gentle, cool rain had begun to fall, and Vittoria, summoned by her brother, had joined them. She wore the same expression as everyone else from the vineyard: a reflection of terror, an electric wariness, as if the Nazis might return at any minute. But there was something else there, something in the way she held herself, in the way she walked, and Paolo, with a piercing soul-pain, wondered what had been done to her in the manor house.

His face was swollen, one tooth loose. He was hungry, burdened by guilt, soaked in a cold fury from the events of the day, but he was still able to appreciate the incredible sight of Umberto SanAntonio's children, two members of the famous family, working alongside *contadini* to try to slide the dead beast over the edge of the steepest part of the ravine. Enrico was letting out a symphony of grunts and wails broken by quick, loud sentences of grief—*I love you. I'll save you. I love you.* The rest of them were grim and silent, struggling. At last they managed to push the horse's midsection far enough over the lip that gravity drew her down into the stony underbrush. Side over side she went, stiff legs

swinging up into the air, then snapping beneath her as she crashed through the bushes and came to rest a few meters from the trickling stream at the bottom.

"Oh! Oh! Oh! Oh! Oh!" Enrico was crying out. Vittoria had her arm around his shoulders and was pulling him tight against her. The rain began to fall harder. Paolo thanked the DellaMonica workers, and they and the others went off to their meal and rest, but, instead of heading back, he stood there, one hand on Ottavio's bridle, watching.

It seemed to him that he'd reached the very lowest point of despair, a place like the one he'd known in the recent past, the bottom of a dark, bleak cave that felt as if it were beyond the reach of God. He had murdered a man; there was no question about that. And because of his sin, these two people were suffering. He wanted, more than anything, to go and stand beside Vittoria and Rico—the closest he had to family—hold them and comfort them, but a thousand-year-old wall, high as the tops of the tallest trees, stood between them. His mouth and jaw throbbed, the rain beat down, the cold wet night closed around his shoulders and the back of his neck. War. War had brought them here. War had swept away the fence between the territories of good and evil, what God found acceptable and what He did not, what good people would do, and what they would never do. In the wet darkness it seemed to him now, at last, that he'd come to understand the Gospel passage about the workers being paid the same for different amounts of work. Jesus was trying to tell them that there was no fairness here, on this earth. Good, bad, sinner and saint, if you inhabited a human body and lived on this soil, there was a way in which you stood absolutely unprotected. Anything could be done to you, no matter how good you tried to be. Anything. Even Jesus, purest of the pure, had been tortured and killed. Why hadn't he understood this before? Paolo listened to Enrico weep, and felt, suddenly, that his heart had turned into a dirt-coated stone. Whatever the beak-nosed man and Father Costantino asked of him now, he would do. No matter the danger, no matter the sin. If it might somehow free his nation from the yoke of Nazi evil, if it might somehow lessen the pain of the two people in front of him, the only two people he truly loved in this world, then he would do it.

That was no longer the problem. The problem now was asking Vittoria to do what Father Costantino had suggested she do: take the deserters to the convent. The problem was not his own sins so much as the further sullying of another soul, the risking of another life. But, as the priest had said: for him, for her, for all of them now—what were the options?

Twenty-Two

Next morning, Vittoria awoke in the grip of despair and lay in her bed for the better part of an hour, listening to raindrops tick against the windowpanes. The night before, after the horror of it all—Nazis in the courtyard, her interrogation, the gruesome disposal of Antonina's corpse—Old Paolo had taken her aside and asked if she'd be willing to bring the three German deserters to the nunnery in San Vigliano. Still half in shock from the encounter with the evil captain, listening to her brother's sobs as he trailed behind them, she could tell Paolo was hoping she'd refuse. The bottom of his face was hideously swollen, there was dried blood at the corners of his lips, and the words that came out of his mouth were slurred and muffled, as if being spoken by drunken little men crouching inside his cheeks. "It would be very dangerous," he said. "I have been asked to ask you. I'm sorry. I don't want to. I'd do it myself, if I could, or I'd ask Marcellina to do it, but I've been told—"

"It's fine," she said. "I'll do it." She reached out and put a hand on his shoulder, then touched his swollen face, gently, with two fingers, realizing, as she did so, that it was the first time she'd touched him since she was a little girl, riding beside him in the delivery wagon, or standing next to him in the barn as he showed her how they bottled the wine or how to brush the horses without startling them. "I want to."

Paolo squeezed his eyebrows down, shifted his eyes to the side and back. "It will be very dangerous," he said again. "And I'm sorry about asking you to . . . do the other thing. I ask you now to forgive me."

"I know, Paolo. Don't worry. Please don't worry. We're in a different world now than the one we lived in before."

The old man nodded, and, for a little while after that conversation, she'd felt like a warrior, a *partigiana*. For that short time, swept up in the emotions of what had been, after the day of her mother's death, the second most painful day of her life, and caught up in fury at the Germans for the misery they'd caused Enrico, and Paolo, and her, she'd felt as though she were cleansing the fine gold dust from her skin. Her mother had admired the workers. Enrico practically lived with them. She could almost picture her spirit leaving the manor house and migrating toward the barn to be with them, to be fighting for good instead of placating evil. To be risking some of the richness she lived with every day. To be joining with Carlo now—who must be afraid every hour of the day and night.

But the gray rainy light of morning cut through that fantasy and presented her with a cold reality: she was going to take the German deserters to San Vigliano and somehow sneak them into the convent there. And, no doubt, at some point soon, she was going to have to face Tobias again. The devil who'd murdered one of their horses and urinated on their vegetables, who looked at her as if she were a whore, and touched her as if she were his property.

She could feel the fear in her stomach, a cold serpent slithering, and all she wanted to do was slip back into her prewar luxury, sleep in fine sheets, be served a sumptuous meal while sitting on the patio, sip from a glass of her family's luscious wine.

She forced herself out of bed, dressed in her plainest clothes, braced herself for a conversation with her father. *I want to make a one-day retreat with the nuns, Father,* she'd tell him. *I want to pray for Massimo's soul, and for Mother's. I can take them their wine in the process. It's been ages since I've driven the wagon. I miss it. And they haven't had a wine delivery from us in a long while.*

But her father wasn't at breakfast. Eleonora said she hadn't seen him at all that morning. Stomach clenching and releasing, Vittoria had a few sips of coffee, a bite of bread, and went to find him. The bedroom was empty, the door to his study closed. She tapped on it once, twice, then heard a weak, *"Sì?"*

She opened the door to see her father sitting in an upholstered armchair holding a pistol in his lap.

"Father! What?!"

He looked up at her as if through a fog of dementia.

"What in the name of God are you doing?" She hurried over and pried the pistol from his fingers. His breath smelled of grappa. "What are you doing?!"

"Massimo," he said. Then: "The Nazis. The horse."

"Yes, and you were going to take your own life! It's a terrible sin!"

Her father shrugged his rounded shoulders. A helpless boy.

"What about me? What about Enrico? Do you know what that would do to us?"

Another shrug.

A hard truth reached her then, something she'd sensed for years, but only in flashes: her father lived alone inside a mirrored room. Her mother, herself, Enrico, the workers and servants—everyone else came and went like ghosts slipping quietly along the walls. Only *his* life was real. Massimo had been another mirror, a reflection. It wasn't Massimo's death that truly mattered, or her mother's. It wasn't the risks his children faced, or the feelings they wrestled with. What mattered was keeping the mirrors perfectly in place, the world labeled and in order, his reputation and comfort intact.

"Pieces of me are being taken away one by one," her father muttered, as if to confirm the theory. "Next it will be the wine. And then I shall be nothing."

"Nonsense. You have me, Enrico, your good name. The war will end one day. The radio says the *Americani* are in Naples already."

"The *Americani*," he said dully. "The *Americani* will despise me when they come."

"Nonsense, Father. I'm keeping this gun, and don't you even think of getting another one and doing what you were about to do! Go downstairs and eat. I'm taking wine to the nuns and spending the night there. I'll pray for Massimo's soul."

"It's raining," her father said, as if he'd just noticed, turning his eyes out the window and then back. "Let Old Paolo."

"Paolo can't go inside the walls, and Marcellina's boy is sick from what he saw last night, so she can't go, either. The nuns need wine for their Masses. It's been months since we've given them any. I'll pray for you, too, but never, ever, do this again!"

Her father turned his head to the side as if he'd been slapped. Vittoria realized after a moment that he was staring at the framed photo of her mother that he kept on his work desk. Another mirror. She thought, at first, that it might be love she was seeing on her father's face and in his eyes. But the look there was closer to anger, or resentment, or a bitter envy.

"I'm going, Father. I'll have Eleonora make you fresh coffee. Go downstairs now."

"Yes," he said distractedly. *"Sì. Va bene."*

She watched him for another few seconds, then left the room. The pistol was smaller than the pistols the Nazis carried on their hips, some kind of expensive antique weapon, perhaps from her grandfather's collection, but powerful looking all the same. A curved wooden handle, a short barrel. After several tries, she managed to tuck it awkwardly up into the tight-wristed sleeve of her dress. She took an umbrella from the foyer, keeping her eyes away from the room where the Nazi had questioned her, and crossed in the rain to the barn. Just inside the wide entrance she found Ottavio already hitched to the wagon, Paolo waiting for her there with a worker's waterproof jacket and a straw hat. He seemed disappointed when he saw her, as if he'd been hoping she wouldn't come. "The rain is good," he said, his face still swollen but the words a bit clearer than they'd been the night before. "A blessing. Easier to hide them, and not so many people on the road."

He gestured behind him, and Vittoria could see that a dozen cases of wine—given to the nuns regularly, free of charge—had been placed against the wagon railings, and a heavy green tarpaulin laid across bales of hay that formed three sides of a rectangle inside them. She heard footsteps on the barn stairs and saw Marcellina, and then, behind her, one after the next, three pale-looking young men dressed in workers' caps and clothing. One of them was wearing Carlo's jacket.

"We argued," Old Paolo said. "Marcellina thinks they should be visible, and ride along like workers. I do not. They can't manage the horse, can't speak five words of Italian, and it wouldn't make sense to have them on the wagon seat if we're taking it through the gates of the nunnery. I want them in back, underneath the tarpaulin. The priest said to take the Zanita Road, but I don't want you to. I had a dream that you shouldn't. The rain, the mud, the hills, I want you to go by the smaller road, the one along the river. It will take you longer, but very few Germans use it. Almost no one uses it who doesn't know it well. Leave one case out in the open, in front, and if you see Germans, offer it to them. I hope you don't. I pray you don't. You know I'd go with you if I could."

Vittoria pulled at the sleeve of her left arm and showed the pistol.

"This I never thought to see," Paolo said. He took the pistol from her, holding the rounded wooden handle in his palm, and snapped the barrel forward, revealing four filled chambers. He touched the backs of the bullets with one finger, shook his head in wonder, then snapped it closed again and handed it back to her. "So many things I never thought to see, *Signorina*."

"Where is my brother?"

121

"At the ravine. I accompanied him there early this morning. He stands on the bank and talks to Antonina. He wanted to climb down and kiss her. I stopped him. I tried to get him to return with me, but he wouldn't."

"When the Nazi touched me at their house, I merely hated him," she said. "Now I want to kill him."

Paolo slid his eyes sideways, away from her, shifted his weight. As she had a few nights earlier, when he'd told her about the deserters, Vittoria thought she detected something in his face, something in the wrinkled skin around his eyes, as if there were an encyclopedia of secrets there and he'd lifted the cover and was giving her a glimpse.

She watched as Paolo and Marcellina helped the men climb into the wagon and showed them how to position themselves on their backs, on a thin cushion of straw, between the hay bales and beneath the tarpaulin. Paolo tied the canvas securely to the railings, and then, before raising the back gate, set two more bales of hay in place to hide the bottoms of the men's boots.

"You remember how, *Signorina*?"

"Firm but gentle."

"*Esatto.*" A weak smile crossed Paolo's face. He handed her the waterproof jacket and placed the rain hat on her head with his own hands. She climbed up onto the bench as she had so many times as a girl, and took hold of the reins. She tapped Ottavio's hindquarters, heard Paolo say, "You've forgotten nothing," and then they were out in the rain.

People called the river road to San Vigliano "the witches' road" because of old tales that it was haunted. Vittoria didn't believe in such things and neither had her mother. "Pagan stories," her mother had called them. But, as she guided the horse into the trees and up and over the first rise, she did sense some mysterious spirit in the air. The rain and low gray skies, the nagging, bodily memory of the encounter with the captain, the awful moment with her father, Germans in the back of the wagon, the pistol now folded into a waterproof worker's hat at her feet, her brother standing at the edge of the ravine, mourning his murdered Antonina—it almost seemed that a living creature, some dark spirit, swirled in the wet air around her, whispering, taunting, telling her Carlo would never make it home, the country would never be liberated, the war would never end.

She went along in a hypnosis of doubt and fear, acutely aware of the silent men lying on their backs behind her, praying she'd get them—and herself—to safety. All the romance of the word *partigiana* had disappeared. Cold rain on her face. Rain drumming on the tarpaulin. Mud beneath the horse's hooves. She could understand her father's despair: What was there to live for? More torment? Surely, if the Allies were able to fight their way up the peninsula, the Nazis would grow more and more vicious . . . especially if they discovered, or even suspected, Italians conspiring against them. And, once the Nazis were chased north, who knew how the *Americani* would treat them?

But some frail hope drew her forward. She could feel it deep inside her, hidden beneath the fear and dark thoughts like the German deserters a meter behind her, lying still on a damp cushion of straw. Her mother seemed to be speaking to her, in that calm, soothing voice Vittoria had loved: *You can surrender to the evil or you can find a way to push back against it, that's the choice, Vita.*

As she went farther into the trees, Vittoria pretended it was a mild summer night, and Carlo was lying with her in the soft grass behind the smaller of the two barns. She imagined he was running his hands over her bare breasts, kissing her the way he did—a mix of gratitude and awe, of passion and gentleness, as if the early years they'd spent so close to each other had woven a fabric in which they wrapped themselves now; as if the enormous distance between their lives had been shrinking over those years, glance by glance, word by word; as if, when their bodies were linked, finally, in the heat and sweat and excitement, fifty generations of *difference* had become *same*. In the rain, in the cold, in the fear,

123

she clung to that image, to the memory of her mother's voice, fought back hard against the swirling spirit of negativity, insisted to herself that she and her lover would be together again, in peacetime, in some new arrangement—not in the manor house, and not in the barn, but something else, something she couldn't yet imagine. Yes, their adult lives had been lived in utterly different circumstances, but as little children they'd been able to connect with each other purely and simply as human beings, in a place beneath or beyond the roles in which society dressed them. Why couldn't she and Carlo find—or make—a grown-up life in such a place?

The ride would be short—less than an hour. She could have tea with the nuns, spend a night with them in prayer. She had Enrico to care for; the Good Lord would never let her be taken from him. And there had been a look in Paolo's eyes when she walked into the barn. Something different there. As if he were guilty at asking her, but also secretly proud that she'd agreed. As if they were connected in some new way. There had even been a hasty sign of the cross offered from Marcellina, a woman who'd always seemed to dislike her.

Caught in the hypnosis, lost in her dream, Vittoria didn't hear the police car until she'd turned away from the river and crested the last hill. The vehicle was slipping along, struggling up the muddy slope toward her, and the road was so narrow she had to pull to the side to let it pass. But, instead of going by, the car stopped, very close beside the wagon. A mustachioed man in uniform at the wheel. Another man beside him. The driver rolled down the window. "Going where, beautiful woman?" he asked. Without waiting for an answer, he opened his door as far as it would go, barely squeezed his big belly out, and stood there with rain plastering the hair to his head. He reached out to keep his balance and placed one hand on the wagon, close beside her left ankle.

"Delivering my father's wine to the nuns."

"Your father?"

"Umberto SanAntonio."

"A great man!" The policeman moved his hand a bit farther from her ankle, ran his eyes over the tarpaulin, seemed about to inquire further. Before he could say anything else, Vittoria reached down beside her and handed him first one bottle, then another. "I'm sure he'd want you to have these. As thanks for your important work."

The man's cheeks were soaked in raindrops. The ends of the wet mustache squeezed upward when he smiled. "This wine is famous," he said, holding a bottle in each hand and admiring the label. "Your father must be a genius."

"He is," she said. "Yes. A remarkable man."

"Why doesn't he have one of his workers make the delivery? Why, on such a day, would he permit his beautiful daughter—"

"Because I'm going to the nuns. I'm going to make a retreat there. No men are allowed inside the walls."

The policeman nodded somberly, glanced at the tarpaulin again. Vittoria kept her eyes on him until he looked back at her. "You'll be all right, going by yourself? You won't need us to accompany you?"

"Thank you," she said. "I know the way. I went many times as a girl. And it's very close now."

For just a moment, the officer seemed to suspect something. He squinted at her, shifted his eyes again to the strange arrangement in the wagon's bed. The puddled tarpaulin. Part of a hay bale sticking out.

"Really, I must go, Major."

"Yes, yes. I'm just a lieutenant, but yes. Thank you, *Signorina* SanAntonio. Go with God. Regards to your famous father. And everyone here still mourns your beautiful mother. We'll enjoy the wine, thank you!"

Another minute and she was alone again, wondering how much the German deserters had heard, how much they'd understood, what the Italians would have done with them if they'd been discovered. Turned them in to the local SS, no doubt, because those dozen or so men in the house in Montepulciano had terrorized everyone within an hour's ride in every direction, and because, most likely, the police were worshippers of their *Duce*, and perhaps of the madman, Hitler, as well. The old societal order, a severe and muscular manliness, the imaginary greatness of Italy—those were the guiding principles of their belief system, and those principles overwhelmed any human compassion, any at all. The fact that Mussolini had disappeared wouldn't matter to these men. He was a god, a Fascist icon, and if he sided with the Nazis, then so would they . . . until the end. The deserters would have been dragged from the wagon, driven to Montepulciano, beaten, tortured, and she and Paolo and the others the same. Tortured in hideous ways, then shot.

All along a slippery downhill stretch, and then onto a two-track path across open fields—she couldn't stop imagining it, couldn't stop thinking about what might happen to her when the Nazi captain returned, as he'd promised. The pistol lay carefully covered at her feet, and she realized how foolish it was to put any faith there. One small weapon she barely knew how to use, a few bullets, against an army of men trained to torment.

Another half kilometer, and behind sheets of driving rain the nunnery came into view, a plain, three-story, white-stucco building with crosses at each end, surrounded by gardens that fed the nuns; the gardens, in turn, were surrounded by high stone walls that kept the women from having any contact—even visual contact—with the people of the outside world. Vittoria knew that once a week the local priest went there to hear confession and say Mass, and the rest of the time the nuns lived behind those walls with very little contact with the outside world, eating simple meals, doing manual labor, waking early, praying, having no fantasies of a lover returning from battle, no dreams of freedom, no thoughts of an elegant dish of *reginette* enjoyed on a stone patio with a glorious bottle of wine. Never a pair of earrings, a bracelet, a new skirt or dress or blouse. Never a trip to the cathedrals of Rome or the palazzo-lined canals of Venice. Her mother had taken her here as a thirteen-year-old girl—they'd made a two-day retreat together before Easter that year, taken Communion kneeling side by side in the chapel, hands clasped, shoulders touching—and, in her teenage certainty, Vittoria had left the convent thinking it was a terrible way to live, that it was a sin to turn your back on all the beautiful things life could offer, a kind of selfishness. Now, it seemed, the coin had been flipped over. She drew up to the walls and felt she was looking through the bars of the gate from a kind of hell to a kind of heaven, a peaceful place, safe, unbothered. No partisans here, no heroism, no interrogations by lewd German officers.

A young nun, uncovered against the rain by anything more than her white habit and wimple, came and opened the metal gates, and Vittoria nodded to her and led Ottavio into the enclosure.

It was only when she was standing next to the young nun, untying the tarpaulin and helping the Germans climb out from beneath it, that she realized how foolish her thoughts had been. The nuns were risking torture and death, too, but without pistols, and without the SanAntonio name to offer protection. This young nun, apparently unsurprised at their arrival, told Vittoria that the mother superior would like her to come upstairs for tea. She smiled and led the Germans inside. Vittoria heard her ask, in Italian, if they were hungry, and the gentleness in her voice, the selflessness, the innocence—as if everyone on earth must understand Italian—sounded to her like a love song in the grayness of that day, a sweet hymn. For a moment, Vittoria could let herself believe the war would end, they'd return to the life they'd enjoyed, that her visions and fantasies about Carlo would be made into some kind of real, sane life. That the goodness of God would guarantee it.

Twenty-Three

Grimaldi, Rogliano, Aprigliano—day after day Carlo passed the small cities and towns on the instep of the Italian boot, skirting them when he could, worried he'd be seen as a deserter and shot on sight without being given time to explain. The food Violeta had given him was long gone. The patch Ariana had made for him had caused a circle of calloused skin to form around his left eye, the soles of his boots were worn through, the blisters on his feet had been opened and healed and reopened, but the more he walked, the more determined he became to get back to Vittoria. He would survive simply in order to see her again. Nothing else mattered.

In the town of Montalto Uffago, hungry again, he took a risk, ventured into the *centro*, and soon found the church—named Santa Vittoria, strangely enough—and saw a man he assumed to be Father Ascoltini, the priest Violeta had mentioned. He was at prayer in one of the pews, alone in the dim interior like a relic. When the priest finished his prayers, Carlo approached him, and the old man nodded and said there was some food and a bed, plus the sacrament of confession if he wanted it. Carlo asked if it might be possible to use the phone, but no. "My son," Father Ascoltini said, "the phones have long ago stopped working here. If you give me the number and a message, I can try to put a call through when I travel to see the monsignor in Cosenza in a few days."

In the dark safety of the confessional, Carlo unburdened himself. His hatred of Mussolini, his willingness to kill so as not to appear a coward; his leaving Ariana in tears and turning down the kind offer of the Sicilian family; his sense, increasing with every encounter, that he and people like him were little more than fuel for a machinery that could instruct its soldiers to hate and kill one group, then another.

And then, too, his guilt at having slept in the same bed with Violeta—"a woman near Reggio Calabria" was the way he described her, instead of using her name, so as not to breach her confidence.

"But how could Christ, the Prince of Compassion, judge you for kindness?" the old priest asked in the darkness, having listened quietly while Carlo declared his sins. "How could He mind that you left one woman because you love another, because you are seeking the true path for your own life? How could He condemn you for giving a lonely widow solace in her dark night?"

"I don't know, Father. I don't know so many things. The war, the . . . my wound, my face is so ugly now, my hopes . . . It feels like I'm in a confusing dream and I'm trying to wake up."

"This life *is* a dream, my son. For each of us. But, within that dream, we still must act in a way that pleases the Lord, so that, when we awaken beyond the river of death, we shall be rewarded with the peace of His presence. Let the light of goodness guide you in everything you do. Make your difficult voyage the walk of love, and God shall give you an interior peace while you live, and welcome you to eternal peace when your life is finished."

For penance, Carlo was asked to say one Ave Maria, slowly and sincerely. He thanked the priest, left the confessional, and walked on tired legs to the marble altar rail. He knelt there and said the prayer, remembering his mother teaching it to him, phrase by phrase, in the cold bedroom they shared above the barn. For the thousandth time he wondered who his father had been, and heard his mother saying, without a trace of bitterness at having been left to raise a child on her own, *You were conceived in love. You were a great gift to me in my loneliness.*

The priest had a pair of old work boots to give him, one size too large but whole, and three one-lira coins. After a night on the rectory sofa, a breakfast of weak tea and an apple, Carlo thanked him and walked on, trying without success to imagine the "light of goodness" in the ravaged landscape through which he traveled. At one point, on a road that cut through a stand of olive trees, he came upon a disabled German tank surrounded by a burst of yellow wildflowers, and he stopped and stared at it for a few minutes, said a prayer for Vittoria's safety, for Enrico and Paolo and the others, tried to tell himself it was a sign: something good would survive the war. Color, life, joy, rebirth. The vineyard, the people there, his beloved Italy—they would all survive.

That afternoon he caught a long ride with a field-worker in a farmer's cart, then another with a man in an automobile—something he'd seen only rarely on the roads. The man was wearing a suit and, even when Carlo inquired, avoided giving his name or saying what he did for work. "Four days it's been since the Americans passed through here and moved on," the man told him. "They're in Naples now. The Germans are running."

As they bumped along the road, Carlo watched the man's profile and couldn't tell if he thought the German retreat was a good or a bad thing, so he remained silent.

"You fought," the man said.

Carlo nodded. *"Sì, certo."*

"And deserted?"

Carlo shook his head and pointed to the patch over his eye. "By the time I healed, the war was far behind me."

The man grunted. "You didn't desert then?"

"I wouldn't," Carlo said.

Another grunt. An odd tension swelled into the air of the car, and Carlo didn't know how to break it. Italians were fighting against

Italians now, that was clear enough. People had chosen sides, rooting for Mussolini and his German friends, or for the Allies—the *Americani*. Loyal warriors or deserters. Italy the way it had been, or the way it might be.

The mysterious man took Carlo as far as Ercolano, near the base of the volcanic mountain at the southern edge of the metropolis of Naples, and dropped him there at the side of the road, nodding once, tersely, to Carlo's *grazie*.

Naples was a vision of devastation. For a few minutes, as he walked the rest of the way into the city, Carlo thought Vesuvius must have erupted at some point in the recent past because half the buildings had been reduced to rubble. The streets were choked with piles of debris, whole five-story *palazzi* looked as though they'd lost the will to keep standing and had broken apart and slipped—an avalanche of brick and mortar and stone and clothes and toys and furnishings—down across the sidewalks and into the alleys and narrow streets. A volcanic lava of ruin. One wall of a house was completely gone, exposing a large, untouched piano.

Everywhere, it seemed, there were American army vehicles and American soldiers. Some drunk and wobbling, roaring, grabbing at any woman they passed; others involved in spraying people with a white powder—against typhus, he heard someone say—or trying to maintain order in the endless lines that snaked along sidewalks and disappeared into doorways from which people emerged carrying tins of food and clutching loaves of bread to their chests as if they were children who'd just been given a precious gift at Christmas. Other soldiers, and other Italians—mostly older men—were working to repair the sewage pipes, the ruined piers of the port, the electrical lines. The faces of the people he passed looked more ravaged even than the faces he'd seen in the countryside. At least there, whatever the terrors from marauding soldiers, exploding shells, mines, and bombs, there were gardens and orchards and animals that might provide a little food. The family in Sicily had been eating three times a day, small meals, yes, but the shrunken faces and flimsy bodies he saw in line at the Naples food depots belonged to starvation, not hunger. Here and there street kids sauntered along, looking, it seemed to him, for something to steal. Some of them were shirtless in the cool afternoon, every rib showing.

His own hunger gnawed at him and seemed reflected in the faces of the people he passed. It must have shown in his face because an elderly woman going in the other direction stopped him, reached into a sack she was carrying, and handed him a quarter of a loaf of bread, part of her rations, he was sure. Ordinarily he would have refused—the woman didn't seem well—but it was as if his stomach were overruling mind, heart, and soul. "What happened here?" he asked, and for a moment the woman only looked up at him, confused. She offered a sorrowful smile, and Carlo noticed that one of her front teeth was chipped at an angle, and with a stab of pain he remembered Ariana's face—above him when he first awoke from his coma, and then streaked with tears as he bade her goodbye. "What happened to the city?" he asked again, though, of course, he knew what had happened. Somehow, he needed to hear the report from another human being, so it would be something less than utterly unbelievable. That people could do this to each other. That the God of Goodness could allow it.

"*I bombardamenti,*" she said.

"The Germans?"

She shook her head. "*Gli Americani. Gli Inglesi. E poi . . .*" The Americans, the English, and then . . .

"And then what?"

"And then the Germans came. They raped women, young and old. They made people stand in a group on the steps of the Ministry of Health and shot them, killed them. Children. Women. Men. Now the brave people here have chased them away, and the *Americani* have come to us." She gestured with her chin toward a passing jeep with a white star on its door. "Now, the war is gone. To Rome, to the north. But all our sins must still be paid for."

He and the woman were standing facing each other, surrounded by the wreckage of a city Carlo had seen once before, on a delivery of wine for the wedding of some important member of some important family. He'd been a boy, traveling in the truck with Gennaro Asolutto, but he remembered Napoli as being a glorious metropolis, filled with churches, palaces, and government buildings that looked as if they'd been constructed by angels in some heavenly stonemason's workshop and lowered gently to earth.

"I'm looking for the Recupero family."

"There are many Recuperos. It's not an unusual name."

"Near the Piazza Bellini, they live. I had a friend, from the war. He was killed. I want to find his parents."

The woman shifted the sack to her left arm. "Piazza Bellini is there," she said, pointing. "Very close. Ask there."

Carlo thanked her and went on, with mangy, hungry dogs slinking around his legs as he chewed the stale loaf, and a trio of American soldiers—policemen, they seemed to be—walking past, eyeing everyone around them. He had to ask four people on Piazza Bellini before speaking to a couple who said they knew the Recupero family, the one with a soldier son named Pierluigi. Although they'd been heading in the opposite direction, they turned around and walked two blocks with him until they came to an archway that led into a courtyard. The woman pointed, said, "Third floor," and, before leaving him there, added that she hoped God would send a blessing to him and his family, that Saint Lucy would soon grant him sight in the eye that was covered, that she would perform a miracle for a young man like him. "You were handsome once, I can see it," she said, and then realized what the remark sounded like and winced and turned away.

Two undernourished palm trees stood in the courtyard, leaning toward each other as if in whispered conversation. The heavy purple-black stones of the pavement—the size and shape of half a coffin—had been polished smooth by hundreds of years of foot traffic and seemed to have been recently swept. Carlo climbed to the third floor, knocked, was directed to another door, knocked again. It was opened by a man who looked so much like his late friend Pierluigi that, for a few seconds, Carlo couldn't speak. A woman appeared behind the man, leaning against the back of his shoulder, and she started to weep even before the one-eyed stranger at her door had spoken a single word.

They invited him in. The apartment, like the courtyard, was undamaged, with framed drawings of saints and the Blessed Virgin on the walls, and a vase with three yellow flowers sitting in the middle of a square kitchen table. The couple bade him sit, the husband poured three small glasses of Amaro—from a bottle they'd probably been saving for the return of their son. "Tell us," he said grimly.

Carlo went on at length: how he and Pierluigi had met in training and become fast friends, how they'd sat next to each other all the way south in the troop truck and on the train, how they'd been ferried across the straits and then ridden a train from Messina to Siracusa, and then another troop truck, west, to the hills above Licata. The heat, the days of digging, the Germans lined up behind them, giving orders. And then the appearance of the Allied flotilla near the end of that hot July day, the setting sun, the first explosions.

He left out the terror they'd both felt, and bent the truth slightly, saying that, when the order was given, Pierluigi had been the first one over the top of the foxhole. That he'd been extraordinarily brave, always. That he was a good friend and spoke often about his love for his parents. And, finally, that there was a family in southern Sicily, just west of Licata, the Buonmarino family, Bruno and Miracola, who'd given Pierluigi a Christian burial, and that, if Pierluigi's parents went to visit them after the war was finished, the family would show them the location of the grave. By this point, Pierluigi's mother had collapsed against her husband's side, and he had an arm around her back, both of them crying openly.

"Can we feed you?" the husband offered at last, and though the hunger seemed to be roaring in Carlo's belly, he shook his head, no.

Behind Pierluigi's father, he saw a telephone on a small side table. "Are the telephones working now? Here?"

"Qualche volta," the woman said, between sobs. Sometimes.

"Could I try to call my home? I have money. I can pay."

The couple nodded in tandem, refused payment, and Carlo found himself standing at the table, staring down at the heavy black phone, and remembering the way Gennaro Asolutto used to make him memorize the manor house number. "Six-four-six, three-one. Say it, Carlino."

"Six-four-six, three-one."

"Say it again."

"Six-four-six, three-one."

"And the region code?"

"Two-two."

"Good, if ever something happens to me on these deliveries, you are to go to the nearest church and ask them to call that number and tell the *Signore* where we are, and what has happened. Do you understand?"

"Sì, Gennaro."

"In the cities we go to, anything might happen. In life, anything might. If you are going to travel this far with me, this is the number you need to never forget. Two-two, then six-four-six, three-one."

"Sì, sì, capito."

He dialed it now, pressing the receiver against the ear on the undamaged side of his face, and looking out the window at an alleyway. On the fourth ring, someone answered. He couldn't make out the voice at first, and then realized who it must be.

"Eleonora, Eleonora! This is Carlo. I was wounded, I—"

"Pronto," he heard. *"Pronto?"* Hello?

"Eleonora, it's Carlo. I'm alive. In Napoli. Can you hear me?"

"Pronto?"

It sounded like a swarm of bees was filling the air between them. He heard Eleonora say the word once more, but it was very faint now, broken into separate syllables. *Pron-to.* Another few seconds and the line went dead.

He set the phone gently back into its black cradle and stood there, wondering at his foolishness. What had he been intending to do, ask Eleonora to call Vittoria to the phone? Did he really think Umberto would want one of his serfs calling the manor house to report on his status? To greet and send love to his daughter?

He returned to the living room but didn't sit down. All of a sudden, the apartment was oppressive to him, smelling of death and misery, of mourning, of the waste of so many young lives, the dirty trick of so-called patriotism. Suddenly, the war, with its starvation and ruination, its destruction of beautiful places, its crushing of the spirit of a mother and father, was too heavy and bitter a weight to bear. The injustice of it, of life, was too heavy. Pierluigi's death, his own deformity. He wanted only to be walking again, hungry and alone on the Italian countryside. Even if it meant—as he knew it would—drawing close to the line of combat and having to somehow find a way to cross it, he had to move on or else the sorrow in Pierluigi's apartment would eat out his heart. "They don't care about us. Our lives mean nothing to them," Pierluigi's father said in an echo of his son's words.

Carlo didn't have to ask whom he meant by "they."

Twenty-Four

Once Vittoria had guided the loaded wagon onto the wooded path and disappeared from view, Paolo stood for a long while at the open barn door, watching the rain splash and puddle in the courtyard. There could be no harvesting of the wheat in such weather, and that, he thought, was the second blessing. Not only had the rain made it easier to hide the deserters in the wagon, it also gave him and the other workers a chance to try to settle themselves after the events of the previous night, to be still and quiet for a few hours, tending to small chores instead of having to labor in the fields. Even now, the air of the barn seemed to echo with the broken Italian of the German officer, with the sound of his pistol being fired, the heavy thud and crack of Antonina's body against the stable boards, the shrieks and sobs of the children. That hideous quarter of an hour, coming not long after the explosion of the American car and the killing of the *Signore*'s friend, had dragged all of them—even the *Signore*, he guessed—out of their quiet country refuge and into the fiery pit of the war. Blood and death, killing and terror. He shook his head hard, as if to shake the sounds and sights from his mind.

After a time, he fetched a rag, reached it out into the rain until it was soaking wet, then used it to try to clean Antonina's blood from the wooden stable wall. Enrico had gone off alone—Paolo could guess where—and it wouldn't do to have the boy come back to the sight. When he'd done the best he could with that task, Paolo gathered up the straw that had been stained red and carried it around to the back of the barn. He'd burn it on a dry day, he'd scrape the remaining stain from the boards another time, or perhaps paint over it.

He finished the cleaning job, busied himself for an hour sharpening his knives and the scythe and adjusting a wheelbarrow wheel, made a desultory inspection of the kegs, and then realized that the weight bearing down on him was the weight of sin. The man he'd killed. The involvement of Vittoria and the risk to her life on this day and from this day forward. The way his actions had brought the rest of the workers he lived with, and the two house servants—people he was supposed to look out for—into the circle of danger with him. Guilt was eased by the sacrament of confession: he'd known that for a long time. But it wasn't Saturday, and it was still too early in the day for confession, and he was worried about Enrico, so he pulled a waterproof over his shoulders and, hatless, went out into the rain, searching for him.

He discovered Enrico in the first place he looked: at the section of the ravine where they'd left Antonina's body. The boy had found the sack with the Nazi uniforms in them—he'd most likely climbed down into the ravine to be with his horse and seen the burlap sack hanging there—and had removed one of the gray-green shirts and stretched it out in the mud. For a few seconds, Paolo stood still, watching. Enrico was gripping a stone the shape of a small melon in his left hand, kneeling in the mud and smashing the stone down again and again and again against the Nazi shirt, grunting, weeping, trying to kill what could not be killed. Paolo stepped closer and gently took hold of his arm. Enrico looked up, his face streaked with rain and tears. "I need someone to come with me to church," Paolo said. "You saved my life last night. I need you to come and protect me, now. Come on, stand up."

"It's not the day, is it, Paolo?"

"I'm going anyway."

When Enrico stood, Paolo had to pry the stone out of his grasp and toss it aside. He balled up the German army shirt and threw it down into the ravine, careful not to aim it anywhere near the horse's body, and nowhere it could be seen. "Come back and we'll put on dry clothes and go," he said, holding Enrico inside the elbow. For the hundredth time, as they went along side by side in the mud, Paolo wondered what purpose the Creator had had in mind when he fashioned someone like Enrico SanAntonio—born into a rich family, given a powerful body, a pleasant face, a sweet nature, and a mind that would never fully escape childhood. Surely he was destined for heaven, but what would heaven be like for him? Would he pass from this world and suddenly shed his mental condition? Would he live in a corner of paradise with others who'd suffered as he had while on earth? And was it suffering? Was he worse or better off than the rest of them, with their ability to understand things he could never grasp, to develop complicated skills like driving a truck and winemaking? Had he been sent to them like a kind of sun, pouring light into the world without asking for anything in return?

As they plodded along, Paolo sensed for a moment that everything—the gray clouds, the drops of rain, the tufts of wet grass, the bunches of grapes turning purple on their stems, the wet skin of Enrico's forehead and cheeks—everything was a piece of God, all of it soaked in mystery, its essence beyond the reach of the human mind. The professors in Bologna, the nobles in Milan, the generals in Rome, the nuns in the convent where Vittoria must be praying at this very minute, no one could understand it. No one. So why did a simple peasant like him even try?

The rain was easing. By the time he'd gone back to the barn and changed into dry clothes, it had stopped, but the sky was still dark with whirling, charcoal-streaked pillows of cloud. He met Enrico in the courtyard, and they set off. Using, at first, the footpath that ran through the forest, and then moving across nearby fields and pastures—instead of the muddy winding road the carriages and trucks followed—it was only eight kilometers from the Vineyard SanAntonio to Gracciano.

"We worked hard this week," Enrico said, and Paolo hoped he'd forgotten, for the moment at least, about Antonina and the Nazi captain and the shirt.

"Yes, we did."

"Bringing the wheat is hard work."

"Yes, it is."

"And it's good to work hard, even if my father is rich and important."

"Yes, very good, Rico."

"And my father's friend died. His car burned."

"Yes, that's right."

"And the man in the barn killed Antonina."

"Yes."

"Why?"

"I don't know, Rico."

They went on through rolling pastureland. Paolo glanced sideways at his companion. In the past year and a half, Enrico had grown in height and added muscle, and he was very strong, the size of a man now. It seemed to Paolo—perhaps he was wrong—that Rico had recently gained a bit in his understanding of life, too. He'd always had great patience for this boy and didn't mind fielding the same questions day after day, or having conversations that doubled back over territory that had been covered a few minutes earlier. It seemed to him that Enrico was making a heroic effort to understand the situation in which he found himself, to be good and kind, to behave in a way that seemed proper. The people of the barn accepted him to a degree that seemed beyond the capacity of his own father. Enrico ate with them often, and sometimes slept there, spreading out an armful of straw not far from the horses and falling into a sleep so instantaneous and peaceful that the old man envied him.

"We're going now to the church."

"*Sì*, Rico."

"Father Costantino works there."

"*Sì, sì.*"

"We're going to say our sins."

"Exactly."

They walked on for a bit, Enrico working his lips, furrowing his brow, reaching up and massaging his right ear as he did when something puzzled him. "A sin is doing something bad."

"Yes."

A few more steps, more puzzlement. "But I didn't do anything bad."

"You did something good, something very brave. You saved my life."

Enrico pondered this for a moment and then said, "But today I went down there to touch Antonina when you told me not to. She was cold."

"That's not a sin, Rico. You loved her."

"I loved her, Paolo . . . What do I say to Father Costantino?"

"When you kneel down you say, 'Father, I have no sins. Please give me a blessing.' Then you go up to the altar rail and say the prayers he tells you to say."

"I will. But why doesn't my father say his sins? Why doesn't the soldier in the barn who, who . . .'"

"Maybe your father goes to confession at the cathedral in Montepulciano, before Mass. Maybe he has no sins. About the soldier, I don't know."

"He hurt you. In the face."

"Yes."

There was a quick smattering of rain, the storm's afterthought. The droplets, carried on a gust of wind, held the wet scent of sage. A rabbit dashed across the dirt in front of them.

"Have you done something bad, Paolo?"

"Many times."

"Why?"

Paolo shrugged, allowed himself to remember the sight of the smoking metal and what remained of Brindisi's body. The latest and worst, it seemed to him, in a long line of transgressions. "Because I thought, at the time, that I was doing something good."

"Oh."

Another shower.

"Paolo?"

"What?"

"Why did the soldier make Antonina dead with his gun? The blood came out of her mouth. Why did he?"

Paolo walked along for half a minute without answering. It seemed to him that he could *feel* Enrico working through the trauma in the barn, a subject he'd already raised many times that morning.

"There are things only God knows, Rico. We can't know them until we die."

Enrico nodded somberly. They were most of the way there before he spoke again. "Paolo?"

"Yes?"

"What do I say to Father Costantino?"

Paolo repeated the instructions. They stepped onto a paved road and climbed a last serpentine kilometer into the village.

The nave was empty except for Father Costantino, who was dusting pews outside the confessional. Wide-shouldered and strong, with a rectangular face that seemed cut from stone, he smiled when he saw them, and then, when Paolo asked for his sins to be heard, the priest obliged without complaint and ducked into the middle part of the wooden confessional. Paolo and Enrico took their places to either side, the old kneelers squeaking beneath their weight. Paolo could hear the boy working hard to pronounce the sentence he'd just been taught, twice. "Please give me the blessing. Then go up to the altar rail, Father. I haven't done anything bad."

"Yes, my son, I know. *You* go up to the altar rail, not me. You say one Ave Maria, and then you sit in the front pew and wait for Old Paolo, and think about something that makes you happy."

"Yes, Father."

The Latin absolution followed, and then Enrico said, "I can go now?"

"Yes, Enrico. Go with God."

"And you go with Mary, Father."

Father Costantino covered the screen on the other side, and half turned, and Paolo felt the words flow from him like a river in springtime. Quietly, one syllable tumbling upon the next. "First I broke one commandment, Father, and now another. Now I am a murderer. And last night the Germans came to us and killed the boy's favorite horse. I am paying for my sins."

"They didn't find the deserters, I'm guessing."

"No, Father."

A long silence followed. Paolo could hear Father Costantino clearing his throat, swallowing, breathing, but he could see only a shadowy profile through the metal screen between them. "Two of the most important commandments," Paolo added.

Father Costantino coughed. "Paolo," he said, then paused again. "My understanding is that those sins of long ago have been confessed and forgiven in this very church. Am I correct?"

"Yes, Father."

"Then to speak of them now, again and again, is the same as cutting your arm, having the wound heal, and then cutting it again on purpose. God doesn't want that. God isn't interested in guilt. Do you understand?"

"Yes, Father."

"Then stop mentioning them."

"Yes, Father."

Paolo could hear Enrico at the altar rail, praying as loudly as if the sound of his words had to reach up past the stars and into heaven. "PRAY FOR US SINNERS, AMEN. AT THE HOUR OF OUR DEATH, AMEN!"

"And the most recent, Father?"

"Say three Hail Marys and imagine the world at peace."

"Not enough, Father, for what I—"

"Paolo," the priest said sternly, "we are as imperfect as this world. In a time of war, the imperfections are magnified. I tell this to myself every day. My own imperfections are magnified, too. They seem larger, but only because of the situation, do you understand?"

"I think so, Father. But he was . . . a man. Not a soldier."

"You have no idea what he was, Paolo. Or what he knew."

"Yes, Father."

"Then listen to me." Paolo could see the priest leaning in closer, so he leaned in, too, resting his forehead against the screen, so close he could detect the scent of wine on the priest's breath. Tobacco, wine. He found himself wondering what Father Costantino had eaten for lunch. "There's another assignment now. It is also part of your penance. A compensation. For the taking of guilty life, you will save many others who are innocent. Can you hear me?"

"Yes, Father, if I turn to you my good ear."

"Do you know the train line that runs through Chiusi?"

"Yes."

"Do you know, just north of the city, the place where the line runs near the River Chiana?"

"Yes, as a boy sometimes, I would fish there. And later I would take Carlo and the others fishing there. I know it well."

"Do you know the place where there's a hillside close to the west side of the tracks, very steep? And a dirt road?"

"Yes. That's the fishing place. We—"

"That train line runs from Rome, through Orvieto, to Firenze, Bolzano, and north across the border into Austria. The trains that use that route now, in the night, are taking Jews to the camps there. Did you know that?"

"No, Father."

144

"Did you know the Jews are being taken?"

"I've heard people say that, Father. I thought it was a rumor."

"Not a rumor. Do you know any Jews around here?"

For a second, Paolo had Eleonora's name on his tongue. But he remembered his promise to her, pressed his teeth together, shook his head. "No, Father."

"You're sure?"

"Yes, Father."

"Then listen to me. The person you met behind the rock will have another parcel, like the one I gave you. Tomorrow night, he'll come to the barn, late, and you and he will take it to that part of the train tracks, just before the steep hill. Make sure it's exactly at that place and nowhere else. You will set it there in such a way that it will destroy the tracks. Detonated by a timer this time. You'll be able to get away. Understand?"

"But, Father, how will I get there in the night? It's far, I—"

"He'll take you."

"But how? I—"

"Sleep near the barn door. He'll come for you and take you. Make sure you go to the right place, and nowhere else. Understand?"

"I think so, Father."

"Go in peace then. Go with God. For your penance, do this task, and perhaps you will keep some of our Jewish friends and Christian brothers from going to those camps."

"But if the train is blown up?"

"Not the train. The tracks. The train will come off the rails there, in a place where it should be going fairly slowly, so none of the passengers will be hurt. We'll have men ready. The Germans will be shot, the Jews and the others will escape."

"The Germans, Father, they'll be shot? Then other Germans will kill many of us for revenge."

"We have plans for that, too, Paolo. Just please do what I've asked you to do."

"Yes, Father."

"And a priest from the South called here on a terrible connection. I believe he said one of your workers had been there."

"Which one, Father? Carlo?"

"I'm not sure, and I have no other information."

"Thank you, Father."

"Go then."

"Vittoria took the deserters to the nuns."

"I know that."

"How could you know?"

"I just know."

"What will become of them? The three Germans?"

"They will be fed and then sent on in the night. From the nuns to another priest. From there, I hope, to safety. Now accept your absolution and say your penance."

"Yes, Father."

Paolo listened to the quiet run of Latin syllables, catching a word here and there that sounded like a word in his own language. Then he made the sign of the cross, ducked out into the nave, and spent a moment rubbing his kneecaps.

Walking the short distance from the confessional to the wooden altar rail, where Enrico was now sitting quietly in the first pew, Paolo felt caught in a swirling cloud. He'd lied to the priest—not once, but twice—about Eleonora. Unforgiveable. Why had he done that? And he'd meant to ask the priest more questions: Why did it have to be Vittoria who took the deserters to the nuns? Why couldn't the man who was going to take him to Chiusi carry the parcel himself and set it against the tracks? Why couldn't the tracks be damaged another way, with a pickax, a sledgehammer? And what if someone saw him leaving in the middle of the night, or returning just before dawn? It must truly be his penance. It must be. He'd taken a life, now he must save lives. "DELIVERY US FROM EVIL," Enrico started shouting at the crucifix above the altar. "DELIVERY FROM EVIL! US FROM EVIL!"

Paolo studied the sculpture of Mary for a moment, imagining what she must have felt, watching her own child be tortured and killed. He winced, sat next to Enrico, put a hand on his arm, said, "Quietly now, Rico. God hears when you whisper."

Enrico raised his eyebrows and stared at him as if he'd been shouting to block out the priest's words, his own thoughts, Paolo's sins. He kept his eyebrows up and said, "Paolo, what if Carlo doesn't come home?"

Twenty-Five

The mother superior's office was on the convent's second floor. Walking slowly, almost shuffling, apparently in pain, an older nun led Vittoria up the steps and along a spotlessly clean tiled corridor, knocked twice on a closed door, and then shuffled away without having spoken a word. Vittoria heard a voice from inside and opened the door into a large room, five meters square, the walls and ceiling painted white. One desk, two hard chairs, one crucifix and a painting of the Virgin Mother on the wall behind the desk. Nothing more. A woman in a white habit rose to greet her and gestured to the other chair, and when Vittoria sat, she felt the contrast between this place and the surroundings she was accustomed to, the upholstered armchairs, the walls hung with framed paintings and colorful fabrics, the vases, picture frames and velvet swags her mother had collected in better times from the markets in Pisa, Milan, and Lucca.

"My feet are soaking wet, I'm sorry," she said.

The mother superior waved her comment away, white sleeve flapping. "You're Vittoria SanAntonio. I remember when you visited with your mother, years ago. I'm Sister Gabriella. It's a pleasure to see you again."

"I'm surprised you remember us."

Sister Gabriella's tight smile pushed her cheeks into the sides of the wimple, and Vittoria could see fine white hairs there, dusting the woman's skin. "We don't have so many visitors. I remember your mother well. She had a lively spirit. And a compassion that is very unusual in her class. In yours, I mean. She was a radical in many ways."

"She spoke to me only rarely about those things."

"Perhaps out of modesty. Or perhaps she was waiting for the correct moment. In any case, you seem to have inherited some of her spirit. Sister Tomasina told me what you've done. It was very kind. And brave."

"What will happen to them now?"

"We'll send them off tonight. We have contacts. Partisan women. Some are laypeople, some are nuns."

"And Father Costantino? Does he help you?" Vittoria couldn't be sure, but at the mention of the priest's name, Sister Gabriella seemed to wince, almost imperceptibly. The nun recovered quickly. Her face settled back into a perfection of calm, a stillness it seemed no emotion could ever trouble. There was a knock on the door, and a nun Vittoria hadn't seen before brought in a pot of tea and two cups on a tray. She set the tray on the almost bare desktop—an open Bible there, a few sheets of paper, nothing else—poured the tea into both cups as precisely as any trained servant, and left. *They must believe it's sinful to speak,* Vittoria thought.

"I'm sorry. No lemon. No sugar. The war has made our simple lives even simpler."

They each took a cup and sipped.

"Do you have many encounters with Father Costantino?" Sister Gabriella asked, and again, there was the slightest touch of discomfort in the nun's eyes. So slight Vittoria wondered if she might be imagining it.

"Not really. We go to Mass in Montepulciano, not the village, though since he arrived, he's been to the house a few times to counsel my father."

"And you trust him?"

Emerging from the calm face as it did, the question hit Vittoria like a slap. "I barely know him. He visits on occasion, as I said, and he and my father take walks and have long conversations. He never stays for a meal. The workers—Old Paolo, Marcellina and the others—they see him every Sunday. I was under the impression that Paolo had been given . . . I don't know the right word, *instructions* from him."

"Paolo, yes," Sister Gabriella said, as if she'd heard the name but didn't know the man. She was peering at Vittoria now, reading her face.

Looking for sinful thoughts, Vittoria imagined. As if what she saw before her was a spoiled, unmarried woman, fond of sex behind the barn with a handsome worker, insufficiently grateful for her lovely life. "Why do you ask if I trust him?"

The nun took refuge in her tea again, sipped, swallowed, blinked, set the cup back on its saucer, every movement as deliberate as a choreographed dance step. There was a tiny flex across her shoulders that might have been a shrug. "In the work we're doing now, one has to be exquisitely careful. And we're entrusting the lives of these men to him. Along with our own lives."

"The Nazis came to the vineyard last night. The SS. They shot one of our horses."

"Searching for the three men you brought here?"

"No. For another reason, I think." Vittoria described the explosion, Massimo's death. The nun seemed interested, but said only, "I see," as if the explosion confirmed something she'd already suspected. *I see,* a sip from her cup, and then, "So much death, so much sin, so much betrayal." She moved the Bible a millimeter sideways with one finger and met Vittoria's eyes. "Your mother came here often, you know."

"I didn't know."

"She came by horseback. Alone."

"She loved to ride."

"We had several important conversations. Spiritual and political, both, though I don't really make that distinction."

"I'm surprised. Not about the conversations, about the visits. I didn't know."

Sister Gabriella nodded and shifted her eyes to the tea.

"You're keeping something from me, Sister."

Another tight smile. The pale eyes lifting again. "You were not bred to shyness, I can see."

"I try to be honest."

A flicker of a smile. Sad, bitter, wry. "How much do you know about your parents' marriage?"

Another slap. "I . . . I suspect that my mother wasn't happy."

Sister Gabriella's tiny smile flickered again and disappeared. "And you don't know why?"

"My father's . . . eccentricities, I suppose. The strain of my brother's illness. Tell me, Mother Superior, if you know more than that."

"It's not my place, child. It would be a grievous sin to betray her confidences."

"Even though she's gone? Even to her own daughter?"

The nun raised her eyebrows, lowered them, watched Vittoria with what almost seemed like pity. Shook her head once.

"Then who will tell me?"

A long hesitation, and then, "I know that your mother kept a diary of sorts. Perhaps she wrote something there."

"I haven't seen it. I wouldn't know where to look," Vittoria said, but the second she spoke those words, she realized that, if there were a journal or diary, it would likely be found in the bedroom where her mother had died. Neither she nor her father nor either of the serving girls ever entered that room now. Keeping it undisturbed had become a ritual of mourning, one of the few things she and her father agreed upon.

The mother superior pushed back her chair and stood up rather suddenly. Vittoria stood, too. Her cup was still half-full. "Thank you," she found herself saying. For no particular reason.

"We thank *you*," Sister Gabriella said, stepping around the desk and escorting her to the door. "For your courage. As you make your brief retreat tonight, please pray for those men, for the end of the war, and when the war is finished, come here for a longer stay. We'd welcome you. Perhaps we can talk in more detail then."

Vittoria opened the door and found the old nun there, waiting just down the hall. The nun led her downstairs to the dining area, telling her that the horse was being fed and watered, that the back of the wagon had been cleaned and "put in order again," the men "treated kindly." "Eat something, *Signorina*," she said, "and then you can pray with us in the chapel if you like."

Twenty-Six

Carlo walked north from Naples for three more days before he heard the first sounds of fighting. The weather was changing, and the cool fall rain was a torment, soaking him from hair to toes. North of Naples, with the sun out again, he came upon a German lorry with the bodies of two dead soldiers inside. There were heavy woolen blankets in the back, one of which he took, and a tin of food he managed to open with his knife. He found a field of tomatoes, ripe to the point of rottenness, unharvested. He ate three of them so quickly that the juice looked like blood on his hands and shirt.

The next day, avoiding the main roads with their mines and patrols, he passed through an apple orchard, gorged himself on the fruit, and was sick to his stomach. He drank from streams, shot at and missed a fleeing deer, was given shelter in the barn of a woman so terrified by whatever it was she'd seen or experienced that she couldn't stop shaking and couldn't speak. He tried reaching out to touch her and soothe her, but she recoiled like a beaten animal. She had food, though, and left a plate of cooked white beans just inside the door of her lopsided barn. By the time Carlo found it, next morning, it was covered with ants, but he picked them off one by one and ate the beans and drank the glass of sourish water she'd put beside the plate. When he tried to thank her before leaving, she wouldn't answer the locked door, wouldn't show her face at the window, so he left two of the coins the priest had given him in the empty glass as a thank-you.

On he went, and at moments now he could hear the sounds of war in the distance. He passed Teano and then, near Pontecorvo, noticed thin twisting towers of smoke in the northern sky, and heard the faint *tat tat tat* of machine guns and the thumping *boom* of artillery fire. He had no idea how he was going to cross the battle lines. Somehow, in the deepest part of the night, he'd find a way to slip through. He'd stay in the central forests, he'd travel only in darkness; he'd steal clothing from a line and food from a garden if he absolutely had to. The soles of the work boots the priest had given him were worn paper-thin, his feet were cold, and he felt feverish, hungry, so weak that, in the middle of the afternoon, wrapping himself in the German blanket, he lay down in another apple orchard—this one with half the trees charred and withered—and couldn't make himself stand up again.

He lay there, trying to cling to a vision of Vittoria's face, staring at the nearest tree's gnarled trunk, telling himself he'd rest for an hour, regain some strength, head toward the sounds of fighting, and trust, as the priest had suggested, in the light of goodness. Somehow, he'd make his way home, another few hundred kilometers. His childhood had toughened him, and it seemed to him at moments that his entire life had been a preparation to endure what he was enduring now.

He fell asleep staring at the gnarled tree trunk, remembering what it had been like to make love with Vittoria.

Blanket wrapped tightly around him, he didn't awaken until he felt the morning sunlight on his face. He opened his eye, shivering, and turned it upward to see a soldier in a German uniform, the black turtle helmet on his head, the gray-green cloth. Tall, broad-shouldered, the man was standing there pointing a rifle down at him, bayonet gleaming in the sun.

Twenty-Seven

Although his work varied with the seasons—pruning, weeding, harvesting, helping Gennaro Asolutto and then Carlo with the different stages of the winemaking, tending to the equipment in winter months, and performing so many other jobs—Paolo's morning routine was almost always the same. On Sundays, he'd spend a few happy hours in the fields with his shotgun, then walk back to the barn, wash and dress for Mass, and make the trip into Gracciano. The other six days of the week he'd rise, dress, go downstairs, use the toilet and wash his face, then take his seat at the head of the low table and eat whatever the women had prepared. Coffee, bread, eggs, sometimes prosciutto or mortadella or a piece of hard cheese. Sometimes a plum or a peach.

Before the war, his duties had been clear, the rhythm of the days predictable, the hierarchy rigid—from temporary traveling workers upward through the house and field staff and all the way to the *Signore* and *Signora*—dating back five hundred years, impossible to alter. War had taken away the younger men—Carlo, Gianluca, Giuseppe—and changed, to some extent, the working arrangements of those left behind. But his mornings remained what they had always been.

This morning was no different, though the wagon wasn't sitting in the barn, and one horse was dead, the other off with Vittoria at the convent. Face and hands still slightly damp, Paolo had taken his place at the table and was waiting for his food when he heard a commotion above him, and then a strange kind of noise echoing down the stairs and into the other first-floor rooms. *More trouble,* was his first thought. The horse was dead and rotting in the ravine, the deserters gone, Enrico miserable, the *Signorina* and the wagon still with the nuns—safe there, he prayed. The grapes were almost ready. The rest of the wheat had to be taken in. Now, something about that unusual noise made him think: *more trouble*.

Another minute and, one after the next, every person who lived in the barn stepped into the eating room. Marcellina and Costanza, Gennaro Asolutto, the five children. This wasn't so unusual. What was unusual was that Cinzia, the house servant, was with them, and that all of them were carrying some kind of pack or bag. Marcellina had food for him, at least: she set a cup of tea in front of him, then a plate with a heel of bread, two fried eggs and two thick blood sausages. But she didn't sit down.

"*Che cosa?*" Paolo asked her, gesturing toward the others. What's this?

"This," Marcellina said, facing him, hands on hips, her big round cheeks flexing angrily, "is . . . we're leaving. Leaving the barn, the vineyard. Going away."

"Going away where? What are you talking about?"

"We're leaving this place," Marcellina said. One of her children, the girl, Filomena, burst into tears.

Paolo looked at the only man among them, his oldest friend. "Gennaro, what—?"

"We're leaving, Paolo!" Marcellina almost shouted. "Today. Now!"

Paolo stood up. "You've gone crazy."

"Staying here is what's crazy! You heard the Nazi! He's coming back! What do you think he'll do then, play cards with you? He killed our horse. He would have killed *you* if Enrico hadn't saved you. He promised to kill all of us, except me. And you want us to stay? And what?

Wait to be raped? Tortured? Murdered? It's because of the Germans you kept in the attic, that's why!"

"He didn't mention the Germans. He—"

"We had a meeting!" Costanza yelled. Both her son and daughter were weeping now. "Without you!"

"Who'll do the work? The grapes . . ."

"Let the *Signore* and the *Signorina* do it!" Marcellina had started to cry, too, rivers down her cheeks, her mouth a shaking circle of grief. "You can come with us or stay and do it yourself, you and Enrico. We're not going to wait here to die!"

"You're crazy, Marcellina. *Pazza!* This is all crazy." Paolo looked from one face to the next, searching for someone who'd agree with him. Costanza's son, Gaetano, eleven or twelve, had his arms folded stiffly across his chest, and his lips pressed tight, but he was teary-eyed, Paolo could see it, and moved his eyes back to Marcellina. "And you'll go where?"

Marcellina swung a heavy arm behind her, accidentally striking her daughter in the face, which only made the girl weep more loudly. "To Costanza's sister. She works on a farm. North of Siena. They can keep us. Their men are gone, too. They need workers. It's a three-day walk."

"And Gennaro? How can he walk that far?"

"We're taking the *mulo* for Gennaro."

"Stealing it."

"*Taking* it. When the war's over, if we survive, we'll come back and bring the mule with us."

Paolo felt a furious hot rumbling inside his belly and chest. His whole body started to shake. He slammed both fists down so hard on the table that his mug of tea went over sideways. Tea on his eggs and bread, tea dripping onto his work boots. "I forbid it!" he yelled. Neck muscles, arm muscles, chest muscles, all tightened as if they would snap. "You're betraying the family that feeds us, that has fed us forever. I won't let you go! I'll get my shotgun, I'll—"

"And what?" Marcellina demanded. She'd stepped close to him now, so close he could have reached out and slapped her. "Shoot all of us?!" She pointed a thick, trembling finger at him. "*You* killed the *Signore*'s friend. Or you know who killed him. And look what trouble that brought us! Tell me I'm wrong."

"You're wrong," Paolo said, but his voice betrayed him, so he said it again. "Wrong."

Marcellina laughed. A horrible sound, three harsh notes that erupted from her mouth in a spray of spittle. "You can come, Paolo," she said from between her teeth. She wiped a sleeve across her lips. "Or you can stay here and die for your *Signore*. We gave everything for him, we're not giving our lives."

She glared at him for another two seconds, then whirled around and pushed past the others and out the door. Loaded down with their belongings, the rest of the workers followed. Only Gennaro Asolutto remained where he was, a cloth bag hanging by its strings from his gnarled left hand.

"How will you live, Gennaro? What will you eat?"

The old man shrugged, lifted the bag as if it contained a year's worth of meals. His eyes were steady, but he seemed dazed, under a spell. For one long moment he stood facing Paolo, unblinking, and then he smiled sadly with just the corners of his lips and said, "Come with us, my friend. We work for an evil man."

"I can't, you know I can't."

Gennaro watched him through rheumy eyes. "These are ugly times," he said, *i tempi brutti*, and he turned and shuffled away.

For a few minutes Paolo stood there, alone, listening. Out in the courtyard he heard the mule bray, as if, at last, after years of servitude, it had been granted its freedom. Someone came back inside and sprinted loudly up the steps, and he thought that maybe one of them—Gaetano, Costanza—had realized the foolishness of the plan and decided to come back. But then the footsteps pounded down the stairs. Paolo heard a woman's voice call out, a child answer. Then silence.

He sat down hard in his chair. He stared in a dull trance at the hay bales, the stone-and-plank walls, the spilled tea, the eggs, the worn wooden handle of one of their pitchforks leaning in the corner. Crazy though she might be, Marcellina was leading the barn family in a way that, as foreman, he should have been leading them. But he had reasons for staying that they didn't have. He would pay a price they didn't deserve to pay. The long-disappeared old priest, Father Xavier, had been right: Sins are seeds. You plant them, then eat the fruit they produce.

Twenty-Eight

Vittoria sat down to dinner with the nuns—a simple, silent meal, all of them at two long tables. Afterward, she joined them for an hour of evening prayer and then was shown to one of the rooms that had been set aside for women who wanted to make a silent retreat for a few days. It had been nine years since she'd stayed in this building with her mother, and what struck her about the convent now, in contrast to the frenzy of the outside world, was the complete absence of drama. Three German army deserters had been brought to them—men within the enclosure! The risk involved!—and the nuns had acted as if Vittoria had brought nothing more than the cases of wine in the back of the wagon, or a few kilos of wheat.

True, the conversation with the mother superior had been charged with things unspoken, with secrets and allusions, but even that talk seemed to have been held against a background of quiet steadiness, of cares larger than those of this world. From what Vittoria could see, the nuns' emotions had been set aside, or so deeply buried they could never reach the surface. Their lives were as bland as the small, bare-walled room in which she lay herself down to sleep, as bland as the polenta and greens they'd eaten for dinner, the tepid well water they'd drunk. As an adolescent visitor, she'd felt nothing but pity for these women, who were sacrificing every one of life's pleasures in the hope of moving closer to God. Now, though she knew she could never trade places with them, Vittoria had at least a small appreciation for what they'd gained. She thought of the tension that filled every room her father sat in. She thought of the sometimes-fierce arguments she'd overheard between him and her mother, the fits of emotion she'd heard in the kitchen, or among the people who lived in the barn. She thought of her own foolish worries: what to request for dinner, how to have the meat cooked, what to wear, in which part of which room to place a new divan, lamp, or painting. All of that was missing from this whitewashed stone building, and the absence made all of it seem so petty.

She had an urge to write Carlo a letter, even though she knew it could never be sent. She longed for a true, open conversation, heartfelt, honest, free of secrets. Talks like that had been one of the gifts he'd given her, brief and quiet and so rare in her life, more valuable than diamonds.

The day had exhausted her, but before she fell asleep, she was visited by a memory of bringing her mother four peeled slices of pear on the last day she was able to eat. Propped up against the pillows, one of Vittoria's ink drawings framed on the wall behind, her mother took a slippery slice in her fingers and laughed quietly when it twice fell back onto the plate. Eventually she was able to bring it to her mouth, chew and swallow it, and then she wiped her fingers on the blue silk napkin and shifted her eyes to Vittoria. So much love shone there. Love, and something else, compassion perhaps, fearlessness, a secret understanding. By then, the affair with Carlo had begun, and perhaps her mother sensed that, or had somehow found out about it. But her mother, also from a wealthy, landowning family, had been bred to silence and propriety, as if, in Italian high society, it was undignified to speak openly about life's more treacherous subjects. Love, sex, death, disappointment. But on that afternoon, her mother studied Vittoria for a moment, blinked, swallowed, and said, very quietly and deliberately, "My beautiful daughter, until you have your own children you may never understand how having a child opens your heart to the deepest possible love. There are so many things I haven't told you. My political views, my past, my secrets."

"Tell me, Mother. Tell me now, please."

Her mother shook her head. "I haven't the strength. And, in the end, as I now see clearly, those things don't matter very much. What matters is what I feel for you and your brother. It is, I think, what religious people must feel for God. A sense of having been given an incredible gift, and of being willing to give anything and everything back in return."

Her mother closed her eyes tiredly. Vittoria waited, wanting more, but feeling that the air around them was as fragile as the thinnest glass. Any word might shatter the moment. She watched her mother's chest rise and fall, the plate with the uneaten slices tilting on the tops of her thighs. Vittoria reached out and took the plate and napkin and set them on the night table, waiting, watching. At last, her mother opened her eyes, and the gaze there seemed to contain both death and something beyond death. Vittoria felt a tremor pass through her. Her mother smiled, wearily, and said four words Vittoria had been pondering ever since: "The surfaces fool us." And then she closed her eyes again, too tired to go on.

Vittoria fell asleep thinking about her mother, woke up thinking about her mother, drank tea alone in the dining room (the nuns had risen long ago and were not to be seen), and then, with the help of the one young nun who'd greeted her the day before, she set off in the wagon, still pondering those last words. A hundred questions rattled around in her thoughts. How had she not known that her mother had come here "many times," as Sister Gabriella put it? Were those the times her father or one of the servants had told her, *Your mother has gone to see her family in Salò* or *Your mother and a friend are taking a few days by the sea*? Vittoria wondered if all their years together inside the manor house had been wrapped in a fine quilt of lies, pretty new patches sewn on day after day, all of them hiding a thin stuffing of truth. *How much do you know about your parents' marriage?* Sister Gabriella had asked. What a thing to say! What a question!

As she guided the horse along, Vittoria realized that her answer should have been: absolutely nothing. That she should have pressed harder for answers, for information, for the revelation of secrets. But she'd been so relieved to have gotten the Germans safely behind those walls, and so intimidated—a rare feeling in her life—by the mother superior, and the meeting had ended so abruptly . . .

She pushed the horse to go a little faster along the muddy road. Even though, beside the rolled-up and neatly tied tarpaulin (was there anything the nuns couldn't do, any kindness they failed to observe?), the back of the cart was now empty, she worried about meeting the police again, or, worse, a German patrol. The small pistol sat wrapped in the waterproof at her feet, a foolish thing, perhaps, but it gave her some comfort. She wanted to get home as quickly as she could and try to unravel the threads on the quilt of lies. To rip off the pretty patches, tear out the stuffing, see what was there.

Just as the cart emerged from the trees a few meters from the court-yard, the clouds swirled and parted enough to allow the sun to shine through in flashes. For a moment, Vittoria realized how beautiful the property was: the grand manor house and pair of barns, like a larger brother and smaller sister who'd grown old together; the wide slope reaching up to a stand of trees at its summit and covered with perfect rows of vines, with a small orchard of olive and hazelnut trees to one side, the unused cabin there, and a small copse of fruit trees to the other; the vegetable plot, the stone patio with its metal chairs and glass-topped table, her mother's flower gardens. Sunlight brushed all of it, the golden tint dancing and disappearing, chased by patches of cloud shadow, and for a moment there was no war, no Mussolini or Hitler, no Nazis, no dark family secrets, no absent lover. For that brief moment she understood why her father was so attached to the property, and so proud of his stewardship. He hadn't created the Vineyard SanAntonio, but he had preserved it, over decades, kept the luscious wines flowing from those kegs of Slavonian oak.

She drew the cart into the courtyard and tied Ottavio to the barn post, stepped inside and brought him a handful of hay and a bucket of water. The building was eerily quiet, the mule's enclosure empty. She assumed Paolo had summoned all the workers to the field to finish the harvesting of the wheat, and just as Eleonora stepped out of the house, Vittoria was wondering if she should free Ottavio from the traces herself and lead him into the stable, rather than waiting for someone else—Marcellina, Costanza, or Paolo—to come and do it. She could tell instantly from Eleonora's face that something was wrong. Her father, she thought it must be. Her father had found another pistol and finished the sinful job she'd interrupted.

But no.

"They left, *Signorina*," Eleonora said, before she'd even offered a greeting. "They all left."

"Who?"

"Everyone in the barn!"

"Why? What happened? Everyone?"

Eleonora shook her head, braids swinging. "Paolo stayed. Everyone else left. Even Gennaro. First thing this morning. Paolo and Enrico are in the field by themselves doing the wheat. The others were afraid the Nazis would come back. They had a meeting and left. Even Cinzia."

"Does my father know?"

"Not yet. I couldn't tell him, and he hasn't noticed anything. Are you hungry?"

"I'll eat later. I'll go see him. Can you take the wagon to the wheat field?"

"Of course, *Signorina*."

As Vittoria expected, she found her father in his second-floor study. He was sitting at his desk but not doing anything, not reading or going over his books, not writing numbers in the ledger or composing a note to some official or other about one of his many tax and property line complaints. Just staring.

"Father?"

He swiveled the chair partway around and motioned for her to sit across from him on the divan. "I see that you've come back safely," he said, with the same dull voice he'd used in their previous conversation. Almost, she thought, as if he were surprised that she returned. Or disappointed.

"Yes, yes. It went fine. The police stopped me. I gave them two bottles of wine. They said to give you their regards. And the nuns were welcoming. How are you?"

Her father didn't seem to understand the question. He looked at her without expression, puzzled, stumped. "I spoke with your brother at breakfast. He's . . . he's . . . They killed his horse. Our horse. Antonina."

"I know, Father. You told me that, day before yesterday. We pushed her body into the ravine."

"Ah."

She could see he was waiting for more, watching her, baffled. By life.

"There's something else I should tell you," she ventured warily.

No expression.

"The workers have left."

"Who?"

"The workers. In the barn. Marcellina, Costanza. Their children. Cinzia, too."

"The women?"

"Eleonora is still here. The others are gone."

"Where? How? Gone? What do you mean, gone? What's wrong with you?"

"They left. They're afraid the Germans will come back and hurt them, so they left us."

"How could they?"

Vittoria shrugged. "They did. Only Eleonora stayed. And Paolo."

Her father seemed to shrink even more deeply into himself. Confusion now, not puzzlement. It was almost, she thought, as if he were blind, and she were describing to him a painting. Yellow, blue, red, the colors made no sense. This news made no sense. "How will the work get done?" he said at last. "It's fall. The wheat. Then the grapes."

"I don't know."

He pondered a moment, swinging his eyes wildly around the room. "There's nothing to live for anymore."

"Stop that, Father!"

He was shaking his head from side to side and tapping his loosely closed left fist on the top of his thigh, as if in time to a marching song. "Nothing now," he said. "Nothing to live for. I spoke with Enrico at breakfast. He blames me for . . . the horse. What could I do? What could I have done? My friend was killed. My best friend. Murdered."

A thought seemed to have found its way into the room through the bottom of the open window, a terrible notion, as if a stink or an ugly shriek had wafted in across the papers on the desk and sullied the air between them. It took a moment for Vittoria to understand, and then she felt a cold shiver flutter across her skin. She couldn't take her eyes from the face of the man across from her. "Father," she said, and for a few seconds she could go no further. Her father's face—the thinning brown hair above a high forehead, the eyes pinched in confusion, the noble, straight nose and narrow mouth—appeared like a mask over something so awful she had to fight against an urge to keep the mask in place, to keep the lies in place. But the visit with Sister Gabriella and the muddy ride back had changed something in her, shoved aside the intimidation she always felt in her father's presence. As if listening to another woman's voice, she heard herself speak. "Father, did you call the Nazis to come here that afternoon?"

He stared back at her as if the answer were obvious, or should have been. "Someone killed my friend!" he shouted. "Killed your godfather!"

He stood abruptly, shoving the chair away behind him with both hands, and began to pace the room, going around behind Vittoria, then circling back, slapping the top of the divan as he went past, touching a hand to his forehead, straightening a pencil on the desk, making slow, nervous circles. One, a second, a third.

"They threatened to come back," was all Vittoria could manage.

"Threatened, threatened," her father said loudly, pacing. He switched direction and was going clockwise now, touching everything he passed as if to keep it in place. To keep his life from disintegrating, object by object. "I cannot believe they abandoned us. After all these years of feeding them."

How much do you know about your parents' marriage? The question echoed in Vittoria's mind. What she knew was that the comment her father had just made was precisely the opposite of what her mother would have said. Precisely. Her father saw himself as keeping the workers alive. Her mother saw the workers as keeping the family alive. "You called them and asked them to come here, didn't you?" Vittoria said. "The Nazis."

Her father didn't hear, or was pretending not to have heard. "No, no. No more," he was saying now. She wondered if he'd been drinking—which would have been highly unusual for him at this hour of the day, but then, there had been grappa on his breath the last time.

"*You* brought them here, the Nazis," Vittoria couldn't keep herself from repeating, more loudly now.

Her father stopped between Vittoria and the desk and looked down at her. His whole upper body seemed to wobble from side to side, as if the words, or her tone of voice, were gusts of wind threatening to knock him off his feet. He blinked, watched her. "I'll call them and tell them not to come again," he said. "They won't come again. I'll call them."

A sudden wave of the purest sadness cascaded over her, a vintage sadness, well-aged. Vittoria could feel her eyes filling with tears. There was pity again, for the man who called himself her father, but this time the pity was drowning in a vat of something else. There was no urge to get up and embrace or comfort him. None. Only a thin line separated narcissism from true evil, and she saw now that her father had crossed to the other side.

She stood, turned around, and hurried out the door without closing it. Instead of fleeing to her own bedroom, she fled to her mother's. A coat of dust covered the bedposts and chairs. Vittoria ran her hand across the books on the shelves, making a trail with her fingertips, searching for a particular volume.

Twenty-Nine

Carlo's pistol and knife were taken away, and he was marched down out of the field by two German soldiers pointing their rifles at his back. *As if,* he thought, *I have the strength to run.* From the direction of the apple orchard where he'd spent the night, he heard the harsh rattle of submachine gun fire—four bursts that caused his shoulders to hunch up to his ears. They weren't shooting rabbits or deer, not with those guns. They were shooting human beings—others hiding there, perhaps, an Allied scout, or a group of villagers who'd failed to turn someone in. He wondered if he might be the *someone* those villagers had been falsely accused of hiding.

Step by dusty downhill step he went, exhausted, hungry, thirsty, expecting at any moment to feel bullets ripping into his back. Even before being called up to the army, he'd heard the horror stories about what Nazis did to their prisoners, heard that sometimes they'd force victims to dig their own graves before being executed, so there would be less work for the captors afterward. He'd always wondered why people would bother to obey. Why not just throw down the shovel, say a prayer, and let yourself be killed?

Now he understood. He wanted to stay alive. He wanted to see and hold Vittoria again. He clung to the hope—however thin—that the Nazis wouldn't kill him, that someone or something might intervene.

An American sniper, a merciful German commanding officer, a bolt of lightning. Something. Anything.

Step by step they marched him down the hill. At a huge, flat-topped boulder—it made him think of the stone they called *l'altare* on the SanAntonio estate—the path took a sharp left turn, and below them now he could see a gravel road and beyond it parallel ranges of green hills descending to the west. A German truck waited at the shoulder, the kind of vehicle he'd been seeing on Italian roads since 1940: large cab and railed flatbed with a swastika flag flying at one corner. Except this truck was painted in mottled green and light brown. Desert camouflage. After a moment, he realized it must be a survivor of the disastrous North African campaign. Another soldier stood at the tailgate, rifle pointed lazily at the ground. Carlo saw a man in the bed. Plain work clothes, Italian he guessed. The man was sitting calmly with his back against the cab, tied hands resting between his knees, and an expression on his face that would have fit a peasant boy about to head off on an outing to the circus.

Carlo's hands were tied in front of him with a length of wire that bit into his skin, and he was pushed unceremoniously up into the bed. Two soldiers joined them there, the third slammed the tailgate in place, climbed into the cab, and the truck started off.

The other prisoner seemed blissfully unworried. "Carmine Alberti," he said. "Napoli."

"Carlo Conte, Montepulciano."

"If they haven't shot us by now, it means they won't. They'll take us north. To make their bombs. They'll rough us up a bit—you look like you can take it. We won't eat much up there, but we'll get home after the war, you'll see."

You're so confident, Carlo wanted to say, but he only leaned forward a little to keep his backbone from slamming against the metal cab every time the truck went over a bump.

Dirt had gotten between his eye patch and the empty socket; he was able to move his bound hands and wipe some of it away. The tires raised a plume of dust behind them. He watched it balloon and settle, watched the hillsides go past, rows of olive trees, a few hectares of grapes—close to harvest. The famous *vendemmia*, or bringing in of the grapes, had been a glorious festival in better times, and it pained him to remember those days. It had been hard work, yes, but eased by a sense of togetherness, of receiving a wondrous gift from the earth. Afterward, after the new wine was bottled, there would be celebrations—two days off in a row, music and dancing in Gracciano, then a feast.

No doubt, this far south, the *vendemmia* would take place a week or two earlier than in the hills near Montepulciano.

After half an hour the roadway changed—paved now—and he could see that they were entering a town or small city. Brown-and-gray stone-and-stucco houses stood close to the side of the road, a few of them pocked with damage from the Allied bombing and strafing. Women walked along with bags dangling from one hand, or a pitcher on their head. One boy went by on a bicycle that looked like it would fall to pieces at the next turn of the pedals.

"Pietramelara," Carmine said. "I know the place. Had a beautiful sweetheart here at one time."

Another two minutes and the truck jerked to a stop. "The police station," Carmine said, and he let out a laugh. "I spent a quiet night here years ago."

They were pulled roughly down from the back of the truck and shoved inside the building to a cell with two wooden plank beds and a smelly hole in the floor. Their hands were untied, the barred door slammed closed behind them. They sat across from each other. Carmine, Carlo noted, was that rare creature—overweight in wartime. Round body, round face, curly black hair. His thick lips formed themselves naturally into a smile, as if the world amused him, as if even the war amused him. They exchanged stories. Carmine had been a chef by trade in one of Naples's most famous pizza places—an honored profession there—then he'd been conscripted and become a shipping clerk in Mussolini's army ("Puzzolini" he called him, from the word *puzza*, for a bad smell). "The stupids. I'm a chef, I could have made them and the troops great pizzas, but the idiots forced me to scratch numbers on papers all day. No wonder they're losing the war." He chuckled at the foolishness of it, burped as if he'd just eaten. "Once the clown, *Il Duce*, disappeared, I said to myself, 'This is ridiculous, Carmine.' I walked away, changed into clothes I stole, hitched a ride home, and set off a few days ago, heading north. I have a sweetheart in Rome. I was going to see her. Stupid of me. I thought the Allies would be north of Rome by this point, and I was all excited to get laid. Now—" He threw up his hands, raised his eyebrows, and pinched his cheeks tight in a gesture of resignation. "Now, *chissà*?" Who knows?

When Carlo told him how he'd been wounded, Carmine said, *"Ooh, minchia,"* a comment one might make after stepping in a puddle or bumping an elbow on a doorjamb. *Ooh, mienke.* Oh, shit. The remark wasn't in any way offensive, just strange, especially at a time when everyone else Carlo had met since leaving southern Sicily had been shocked by his injury, revolted, full of pity. Maybe he didn't look as terrible as he thought he did. The idea made him feel more hopeful about how Vittoria might react. If he ever made it home to Vittoria.

When Carlo told him about Ariana, Carmine asked for her family name and the exact location of their farm in southern Sicily, as if he planned to go courting her after the war.

A barred window had been cut high up in the concrete wall. After they'd sat on their beds for a long time, talking, the afternoon light softened there. A silent German minder brought them bowls of gruel—no spoons, no crust of bread—and Carmine gulped it down and actually smacked his lips as if it tasted like something other than machine oil. *"Andrà tutto bene,"* he said. All shall be well. And then he lay himself down sideways on the bed, pressed both palms together beneath his cheek, and was asleep within thirty seconds.

Carlo studied him for a time, then lay on his back and stared at the darkening ceiling. In the front office, the Germans had turned the radio volume up very loud. It was blaring Fascist propaganda from EIAR, the *Duce's* radio station, and Carlo realized after a minute that the volume had been turned up, not so the soldiers could hear it, but so the prisoners couldn't sleep.

Carmine seemed unaffected, snoring away, but the news blared on, the announcer claiming in a stern voice and formal Italian that the Allied advance had stalled in Calabria (something Carlo knew was impossible. If the advance had stalled in Calabria, Naples would still have been occupied by the Germans), that the Russians were deserting by the tens of thousands and cursing Stalin, that the demon Churchill had suffered a stroke and hadn't been seen in weeks. There was no mention of Mussolini. All of it, Carlo suspected, was untrue. The Fascists must still have control of the radio station in Rome, that's all it meant.

It was warm in the cell. He took off his shirt and wrapped it around his head, dimming the noise but not shutting it out completely.

He turned onto his stomach, the gruel sitting poorly there, his feet aching, and forced his thoughts back to the vineyard.

From the time they'd been children, he and Vittoria had enjoyed a kind of telepathic connection. He'd be in the stables and somehow sense that she'd come out onto the manor house patio, and he'd step outside and catch her looking for him. Before her father had forbidden her from coming to the barn, she'd somehow know if he was in the keg room, or with the horses, in the smaller barn, or out back gathering chestnuts, and she'd find him wherever he was and help him with whatever he was doing, or just sit beside him and draw (something she loved to do) and talk. Later, they were separated—her father ruled over her and the workers like another *Duce*—and Carlo had felt her absence like an ache, so much so that, at times, he'd make a point of not looking at her across the courtyard, not looking down from the vines, trying not to think of her. But then, later still, when they'd started to arrange their secret meetings, all it would take was a nod, a certain kind of glance, and they'd know where and when to meet. Once he'd learned to read—so much later than she had and with her help—Vittoria would leave him short notes, often with a sketch included, and hide them in various places around the property where she knew he'd find them. *We were put together by God,* she'd say, and at those words, written or spoken, he'd feel a thrill go through his arms and down into his fingers.

Listening to the harsh notes of the radio broadcast, and, in moments when it paused, to the equally harsh, if quieter, notes of an animated conversation from the office (were they deciding whether to kill their prisoners?), Carlo wished he possessed Carmine's easy confidence, the certainty that he'd be with Vittoria again, see that land again, that he'd go walking through the mountains with Enrico, or hunting pheasant, rabbit, and boar with Old Paolo. But a cloud dimmed the light of those memories. He was a prisoner; he and Carmine had made the same mistake. Their hopes—not so different—were confined now to a smelly concrete room in a dusty little town in the sorrowful interior of Campania.

The radio was kept on all night, and he slept fitfully. Even Carmine was eventually awakened by it; Carlo could hear him cursing on the next bunk. In the morning Carlo was exhausted to the point of delirium, his belly throbbed with hunger, his tongue felt as dry as paper, and by the time a soldier came, unlocked the door, and led him down the short hallway, he was thinking it wouldn't be so awful to be shot.

Shirtless still, he was led into a small room with an empty wooden chair in front of a table, and a German officer with a huge head sitting on the opposite side. "Sit," the officer commanded in good Italian. "Water?"

Parched to the point of being unable to speak, Carlo nodded. The officer poured him half a glass and pushed it across the table with an enormous, fat hand. Carlo drank it in two gulps and, though the pitcher was clearly not empty, the Nazi offered nothing more.

Carlo was asked his name, and provided it. Asked what part of the country he came from, and answered, barely able to sit upright and completely unable to keep himself from staring at the empty water glass and the pitcher. The man opposite him had a perfectly shaved face, and the hands and head of a monster.

"You fought?"

Carlo pointed to the patch over his eye.

"With us?"

Of course, with you, he wanted to say. *Who else was Mussolini going to make me fight with, the Algerians?* He nodded.

"Sit up straight. You deserted?"

"I didn't desert. I was wounded in the first battle, at Licata. The man beside me was killed. I was unable to move for many days. A family cared for me."

"And now what? You're returning to your regiment?"

Carlo felt too tired to lie again. He shook his head. "Going home."

The officer let out a short, bitter snicker through his nose. "This," he said, "this is why we're having the trouble we are having with our brave Italian allies. They don't fight. They want to go home, eat pasta, drink wine, play music, have sex. Meanwhile, my men are being killed."

Carlo shrugged, slumped again.

"Sit up!"

"I wouldn't be of much use now, fighting," he said. "Could I have more water?"

The officer ignored the question. "Hold your right hand on the table," he said.

Carlo placed his hand there and the officer took it, as if in some bizarre ritual, soldier to soldier. "Squeeze as hard as you can," he said.

Carlo squeezed. In spite of everything—the exhaustion, the hunger—he hadn't lost all his strength, not in his hands, at least.

Fifteen years of scything and shoveling and clipping vines six days a week had made them into steel tools. The officer was clearly trying to break his hand, but Carlo squeezed back, squeezed back, refused to surrender or cry out, and held eye contact, as if the very last bit of pride inside him was making a final stand. After a full minute, the Nazi grinned and let go. "You won't fight," he said, "but you still have strength. Which is lucky for you, because if you didn't, I'd have you killed. Today. This minute. You're strong. We heard your friend say he can cook. Lucky for both of you because we have a pile of your dead countrymen behind the building, rotting in the sun, too cowardly to fight, too weak to work. You and your fat cellmate will have the honor of building the weapons that will ensure the victory of the Reich. Say thank you, and I'll give you water."

"Thank you."

The man laughed again, made no move to refill the glass, but instead called out in German. Carlo was taken back to the cell, where, through a parched tongue and lips, he gave Carmine the full report.

"No torture?" Carmine asked. "No pulling out fingernails?"

Carlo shook his head.

"What then?"

"You were right: we're going to be sent north to work."

"We'll work," Carmine said quietly. "You watch how we work. We'll work like the old men on the benches in Napoli work. We'll make bombs that fall apart while they're still in midair."

Thirty

Once all the other workers had gone, Paolo's mind was overtaken by a frantic whirl of fear and worry. He sat at the low table in the barn and very slowly ate his tea-soaked eggs, sausages, and bread. When the meal was finished, he carried his cup out to the well—the water there so much better tasting than the water from the indoor tap or the cistern— and stood at the edge of the courtyard, taking small sips and staring at the vines. In a little while, Enrico burst out of the manor house's side door and trotted across the gravel toward him, and Paolo could see that, magically, most of the sadness had disappeared from the boy's face. His drooping mouth and wide-set eyes carried, again, the light Paolo was used to seeing there. *The light of heaven* was the way he thought of it, as if what had been taken from Enrico in the womb had been replaced with the promise of an afterlife free of pain. As if sorrow couldn't stick to his skin for more than a day. Many times Paolo had seen it. Many times he'd been grateful to Enrico for reminding him that there was more to life than worry and duty, that there might be something to hope for at the end of these six or seven or eight decades of struggle.

"Can we work, Paolo?" the boy asked happily, coming up close beside him and putting one hand on Paolo's shoulder in imitation of the way he'd seen men act with each other. Almost everything Rico did, Paolo thought, was a mirror of what the people around him did. He said things he'd heard other people say; he did things he'd seen other people do. That wasn't so different from the way everyone behaved, but it was as if Enrico had a special talent for holding on to the good and filtering out the bad. He didn't complain, wasn't lazy, never spoke badly of anyone, was as kind to the animals as if he knew they had souls. And, no matter how his own father ignored him, Rico always greeted the man with a happy *Papà!*, as if he were joyously surprised to see Umberto, or as if the *Signore* had ever once been affectionate toward him in return.

"*Sì, sì, certo,*" Paolo said, but it was painful to look into Enrico's face, to bear witness to the happiness and hope there. On this morning, with the rest of the workers gone and the threat of the Germans filling his thoughts to the point where he kept expecting to see their trucks coming through the gate, Paolo knew where Enrico's happiness and hope were headed.

"I'll go get Gaetano!"

Paolo wrapped an arm around the boy's shoulders, and steered him toward the hillside. "Let's you and me do the work today, Rico."

"And Gaetano. And the others. We need help because people are at the war. Men. The men are at the war and will be home soon, so everybody has to work."

"We do," Paolo said, leading Enrico along the path between vines, trying to decide what to tell him and what to hold back, how far into the future to put off his disappointment. "But the others had to go away for a while."

"Where? To church? It's not Sunday now."

"It's not Sunday, you're right."

"Where, then?"

"They went to the sister of Costanza, near Siena. She has a farm there and needs help."

"We could help, too."

"We could, but somebody has to stay here and finish the wheat, so you and I will do it."

"Okay. Yes. We'll finish the wheat, you and I will finish it. Can we finish it today?"

"No. It will take a few more days."

"Good. I like doing the wheat, Paolo. I like it."

"You're a good worker."

"We can take the wagon there and put the wheat on it and bring it to the other barn."

"Your sister has the wagon. She went to the nuns. She'll bring it back soon."

"I want to see her. I miss her."

"She's a good sister."

"And when she comes back with the wagon, we can load the wheat on and bring it to the other barn."

"Right."

"And we won't finish it today."

"Right, Rico. *Esatto.*"

As they crested the hill and went along the edge of the forest, and then down into the field where the wheat was grown, Paolo could see with a painful clarity just how much there was still left to do. With only the two of them working, it would be impossible to get the wheat in before it was time to harvest the grapes. And how were they going to harvest all those grapes, in any case, one old man and one helper? Bad enough that the three strongest men were away in the army and might never return. Bad enough that the itinerant workers who usually came through the area for the *vendemmia* were most likely also at war. If Marcellina and the others had stayed, he might have decided to leave the last of the wheat in the field and do the more important work: preparing for the cutting of the grapes. There was so much to do before the *vendemmia*. Once the preparation was finished, the grapes would be ready, and would have to be gotten in before the rain came and turned the clay hillside into a slippery swamp. They'd pick the grapes by hand, painstakingly, then load the fruit into reed baskets, carry the baskets on the wagon or on the mule's back to the large, open container where the grapes could be crushed. The stems would be separated out, and if, as he did in certain years, the *Signore* wanted some white wine as well, the skins, too, would be taken away at this point from certain batches of the purplish-green soup. Paolo wasn't an expert like Carlo or Gennaro Asolutto, but he knew that it was important, at least for a time, to let the yeast of the skins mix with the sugar of the pulp. That was where the alcohol came from, where the taste and richness came from. Working together, they all could have managed that much, and gotten the wine into demijohns and bottles, and then gone on to the olive harvest in November, and if there was a hectare of wheat left in the field, or a few kilos of olives or hazelnuts left on the trees, it wouldn't be tragic.

Now, walking beside Enrico, making the calculations he always made about how long each job would take, Paolo felt the shadow of impossibility sweep over him. He was tired already, wearied by the drama of the early morning. How was he going to find the energy to complete the *vendemmia* and bottle the wine? And then he thought, *What does it matter?* If the Nazis came again, they'd steal every case they could load onto a truck, then kill him, smash the rest of the bottles, shoot holes in the kegs, and burn down the manor house. Producing the next SanAntonio vintage, the goal that had pushed him out to work every morning of his life, would never happen. It was something he'd always been proud of, producing the vintage and then driving the truck with SANANTONIO painted on its side to shops in the great cities, the shopkeepers, workers, and ordinary people watching for him, looking on as he and Carlo or he and Giuseppe carried in the cases. Sometimes people would line up to buy the wine before the truck had even been emptied. Gone now. Finished. All ruined, and why? Because he'd listened to the priest and the man with the beak for a nose and killed the *Signore*'s friend with some kind of homemade bomb. How could he have been foolish and evil enough to do such a thing? And why had the priest needed to have it done?

For a moment, he stood and looked at the unharvested wheat, and then he and Enrico uncovered the scythes they'd left there and set to work.

Just after noon, Paolo saw Eleonora driving the wagon down toward them from the crest of the hill. She looked nervous with the reins in her hands but was doing a capable job. Beside her on the seat was a basket with a napkin over it, and, held tightly between her knees, a pitcher he hoped was filled with cool water. She brought the wagon to a stop, and Enrico went over and rubbed his hand along Ottavio's flank, talking to the horse in quiet tones, as if they were both mourning his lost stablemate.

The three of them sat together in a bit of shade and ate and drank. Bread, cheese, the good salami that was usually reserved for the *Signore*'s table, well water so beautifully cool on the humid day that it caused a film of droplets to form on the sides of the clay pitcher. When he was finished eating, Enrico wandered off for a time, searching for nuts in the woods, or peeing there, or praying, or seeking out the spirits he claimed he saw and listened to. He lived by imitation, yes, Paolo thought, but from time to time his own beautiful uniqueness broke through the mask, and Enrico would do something no one else did: he'd walk the fields toward Cortona, singing, always finding his way home by nightfall; he'd pound a stone on the shirt of a deserting Nazi; he'd break open walnuts in his strong hands, use his teeth to remove the meat, and end up with walnut oil on his face and fingers and have to be reminded to clean it off with the juice of a lemon.

Eleonora was sitting in the grass not far from Paolo, her legs bent sideways beneath her, with the skirt pressed down between her knees, and a crumb of bread clinging to one side of her mouth.

"Why did you stay," Paolo asked her, "when Cinzia and the others left?"

She shifted her dark eyes to him and brushed the crumb from her face with two fingers. "Antonio."

181

The boyfriend. She was risking her life for love. It made him like her even more. "I've never met him."

"Yes, you have, Paolo. He said he spoke to you. Behind *l'altare*." She hooked her second finger and put it up in front of her nose and smiled at herself.

"Ah, yes. He terrified me."

"He said how brave you seemed. And how strong. You frightened him, as well."

Paolo laughed and looked at the sheaves they'd been able to collect. Six of them. In four hours of work. Harvesting the rest of the field would take them until Christmas. "I see from the wagon that the *Signorina* returned."

"One hour ago. She's with her father."

"Yes. Her father," he said sadly.

"He was shouting. She was shouting back."

"Ah."

"After I serve them, I'll cook you supper and bring it out to the barn. Cinzia's gone, so it will take me a long time."

"You're not afraid? That the Germans will come back?"

"I am, yes," she said, twirling a braid in one hand, flipping it back over her shoulder, then fixing her eyes on him. "I have a favor."

"Ask."

"Antonio wants to stay in the barn tonight. With me. Maybe for a few nights. Then we'll decide, you know, what to do."

"Of course," Paolo said, but if Eleonora left, too, how would he live? Cook for himself, something he'd never done. Serve the *Signore* his meals?

"And you'll be staying?"

Paolo nodded helplessly, and tried to hold himself back from asking Eleonora to reveal some of her secrets. Her Jewish mother had been taken by the Nazis, and she'd been brought up by the nuns in

Bolzano—that much she'd told him. But how had she escaped her mother's fate? And why had the nuns taken in a Jewish girl and then sent her to this estate, so far from them? And why had she arrived just at the time when the *Signora* had fallen ill? Coincidence, or part of some larger plan? And how had she met Antonio? And how had the priest recruited her? And why had she been the one to suggest that he, the simple old foreman, speak with the priest about the secret work? She was entitled to her privacy and her past, Paolo thought, just as he was, but he could sense, again, that an entire other world lay hidden beneath the world he understood. The vines, the wheat, the grapes, and then . . . something else bubbling below the surfaces of things. He was about to venture a question to her when he heard Enrico behind him, singing a Christmas carol, of all things, stopping to run his hand down the white slash on Ottavio's face. "The little Lord Jesus lay down his sweet head," he sang quietly. "The stars in the sky . . . the stars in his sweet head. The stars in the sky . . ."

"As long as the *Signorina* stays, I'll stay," Paolo told Eleonora. "Where would I go?"

"If they come back, they'll kill you."

Paolo didn't answer. Until that moment, he realized, the commotion in the barn had made him forget about the new assignment the priest had given him. Tonight, it was supposed to be. Eleonora's boyfriend would come to the barn, late tonight, carrying another explosive. If the Germans returned and killed him, they'd have reason to do so. He thought of what Eleonora had said, that her boyfriend had found him frightening. An unarmed old man. He wondered, briefly, what he looked like to other people—to the priest, to Eleonora's Antonio, to the Germans, perhaps. To Vittoria. He wondered if the killer inside him, that hidden beast, was visible.

He grunted and climbed to his feet, thanked Eleonora, and went back to work.

The girl hadn't climbed even as far as the crest of the hill when Paolo heard a series of muted thuds in the distance. *Boom . . . boom . . . boom* echoing in the hills. "The Allies," he said, before Enrico could ask him. "The *Americani*. Bombing the Nazis."

"The war will be over soon!" Enrico said. "Soon it will be over, Paolo! And then we'll all be happy!"

Thirty-One

On the hard bed of the jail cell, Carlo fell asleep after a time and dreamed of Vittoria yet again. They were in the keg room, opening a bottle of the wine saved for the manor house, the good wine. Vittoria had brought cheese and bread and was holding the food up to his mouth, holding out a glass of water . . .

He was shaken roughly awake. After a few seconds of confusion, he focused his eyes on a smiling, round-bodied man on the plank bed across from him, and then on the soldier who'd pulled him from sleep.

No pointed rifle, no tied hands now, this new German soldier—quiet and businesslike—led him and Carmine outside into the bright morning and gestured for them to climb into the truck. Another soldier with a holstered pistol sat there, watching them, and, until yet another soldier appeared and climbed in, Carlo wondered if it might be possible to overpower him.

Off they went. A five-minute ride with the sun rising over the hills. "The beginning of our vacation abroad," Carmine joked, and Carlo just glanced at him and shook his head. What would it take, he wondered, what amount of misery would it take to dampen the man's spirits?

When the truck stopped, Carmine laughed his joyful laugh and announced, *"Stazione,"* as if to a group of passengers sitting on a tour bus.

They were marched through the empty train station, its waiting room, hallways, and unused café dimly lit by the sun and by a lamp left on in an empty office. One soldier ahead of them and one behind, they passed the toilets and the ticket window and two closed kiosks. There were propaganda posters glued to the walls on either side. The usual scenes: Mussolini with his chin thrust out, smiling peasants working the fields. Carlo had seen them many times on the deliveries, sometimes explaining to the other workers what the words meant. He went tiredly along, thirsty, hungry, weak, wondering if there would ever be a propaganda poster that showed a hungry peasant, a victim of the Blackshirts, a soldier who'd lost an eye in the war, or parents who'd lost a child.

The only trains he'd ever ridden were the ones that had taken him from Padova to Reggio Calabria, and then, after the crossing of the strait into Sicily, from Messina to Siracusa. The station reminded him of those rides, which reminded him of Pierluigi, which reminded him of Ariana and her family and the life he'd chosen to leave. Regret was an emotion alien to him. Like everyone else who lived in the barn and worked the SanAntonio estate, like every other *contadino* he'd ever met, he lived in the moment, neither remorseful about the past nor holding to great hopes for the future. Once in a while, with a word or a few words here and there, Paolo had alluded to an old flame, the love of his youth; other than that, they worked, they slept, they inhabited the moment, they took their small pleasures and endured the rest of life in silence.

The train station, with its sense of some unfamiliar destination, made him realize that it was Vittoria, with her kisses and their moments of lovemaking, that had broken apart the shell of the present moment in which he'd always trained himself to live. He'd made love with other young women, but those experiences had been purely physical, a brief release from the monotony of their days. Those encounters had never pointed toward any future dream, any destination along a rail line; they'd never moved him to imagine a life different from the life he led. He had no lust for wealth or property, none at all, no fantasy of marrying Vittoria in a church ceremony and inheriting the vineyard. But he did imagine spending the future with her, and it was impossible to picture that future as being lived in the upstairs room of the barn. So, after each of those times with her behind the secondary barn, tentatively, half-afraid, he'd allowed himself to imagine *something*, to hope for different days, perhaps a small house and a few hectares of their own vines somewhere. The dream was vague, the particulars blurred by the confinement of the ancient cables that bound each of them to their separate lives. But it was a dream all the same, and it had lifted him up through the hardest days of his service, pulled him away from Ariana and Sicily, sustained him through all the hours of walking, the hunger, the fear.

Now, though, as he was marched onto the platform by Nazi soldiers, it seemed that the dream had shattered into a thousand pieces and those pieces were crunching like ceramic shards beneath the worn soles of his boots. Maybe the war would end, eventually. Maybe the Nazis would lose. Maybe Mussolini would disappear forever, and some enormous change would come over Italy. And maybe, as Carmine had stated with such confidence, the two of them would survive the work camps and return home. Maybe Vittoria would also have survived, and maybe she'd have held on to her feelings for him and would be willing to turn away from the beautiful life she lived and make another, more modest life with him somewhere else.

A freight train, six or eight blood-colored cars behind a huffing locomotive, sat before them on the tracks, and, studying it with a tired eye, Carlo imagined the endless ride north into Germany, all the things that could happen to him there, all the *maybe*s that had to turn into facts in order for him to even see Vittoria again, never mind make a life with her. The last of his hopes seemed to break apart then; he could feel himself releasing them. It was best to live in the moment, try to survive, not torment himself. *I had to let go of that love,* Paolo had said to him once, as they walked back from the Gracciano festival where they'd shared a couple of bottles of wine. *I had to turn my eyes from it.* Carlo hadn't asked for details, but now he felt that he understood.

The soldiers marched them down to the next-to-last car and pushed them inside, into a crowd of shadowy figures, sweaty men, like animals being taken to slaughter. The car smelled horribly of urine. The door was rolled closed, and clicked loudly, and they were encased in complete darkness. Carlo and Carmine managed to find a piece of dry floor, and they sat there with their backs against the wall, listening to murmured conversation in the language of exhaustion going on around them. There was a brief wait, then the train whistle sounded up ahead, someone in the group burped, someone spat, someone sneezed. For a moment it reminded Carlo of the barracks at night—snores and grunts and burps and whispers—and the feeling of being sent off into a deadly future. There was a clanging yank, the car jerked forward, tilting them sideways, and they were rolling north.

Thirty-Two

Vittoria sat at the desk where she liked to draw, resting both hands on her mother's unopened journal and watching dusk throw a blanket of gray over the property. For the tenth time in the last few hours she sorted through the conversation with Sister Gabriella. What a strange, truncated encounter that had been! She wondered if somehow the mother superior had sensed the sins—the sexual sins—of the young woman sitting opposite her and had been either so revolted or so terrified that she'd chased her out of the office like a demonic spirit.

Or if it was something else. A tainted spiritual inheritance from her father. An evil inside her that was visible only to a woman of God.

Vittoria lingered over the memory of those "sins" for a few minutes, almost feeling again the soft, cool grass beneath her bare body, Carlo holding some of his weight just above her, every part of her alive and singing, the need to be silent battling with the urge to cry out. Afterward, the sense of complete ease in her limbs, in her spirit, the sense of him lying against her, breathing with her. *What a gift*, Carlo had said to her. *What a gift you are.*

She shook her head gently, setting the memory aside as if it were too painful to hold. She removed the pistol from her dress pocket and slid it carefully to the top of the desk, still within reach. She took a long, slow breath, whispered a prayer, and opened her mother's dusty diary to its first page. The handwriting immediately brought tears to her eyes—so elegant, all swirls and curlicues and unique *s*'s. She remembered having an argument with the nuns in her fourth year at school, insisting that the way she wrote her *s*, with a little twisted squiggle at the top, had to be correct because it was the way her mother wrote it. It took Vittoria less than a page to realize that the book she held in her hands wasn't really a diary at all—not a record of her days, but more like a collection of musings. Her mother setting down her thoughts in ink on parchment, as if to see them more clearly and enable herself to penetrate life's mysteries.

~

I look back on the wondrous childhood I had, running across the fields of my parents' estate, riding horses, swimming in the river, making trips to Milan and Venice and Rome and Paris, and I wonder why I wasn't able to pass on a life as enjoyable to my own daughter and son. I suppose the political surroundings (and now, of course, the war) made things more difficult. But there's more to it than that. My choice of a husband, my evolving feelings of guilt—or, at least, discomfort—with our great wealth. The condition of my lovely Enrico. Over time, an enormous distance swelled between the life I imagined when Umberto first took me to this place as his young wife, and the life I've actually lived here.

I can sense now, and Dr. DeMarco confirms it (though I can't yet bear to burden Vittoria with the news) that I'm moving—too soon!—into the last stage of my time on earth. These are my last few months, perhaps my last few weeks. I wonder at times if, via some evil magic, the strains and dissatisfactions of my days here have broken this body, the way the strain of overwork can cause a mare to sicken and die.

I have so much, and yet, so many regrets. It's almost the opposite of the workers' lives—or the way I imagine them to be. They have so little. They exist in a cage of blunted dreams, fed scraps of pleasure. And if they try to break out of that cage, what dreams they have are soon crushed beneath the wheels of the great societal machinery that has given me the enormous house in which I sit and write this.

And yet, despite their limited lives, one hears them singing as they work the vines and fields, and laughing in the barn in the evenings. No wonder Vittoria enjoyed spending time there with them, until Umberto forbade it. What a row he and I had over that issue! "You don't know the men of the barn like I do!" he shouted—such a strange irony there, for me. "To them, the sight of a girl like Vittoria is like the sight of an apple to a hungry horse! Would you want her to have one of them as a husband? To bear his child?"

"Perhaps she'd be happier than I am!" I shouted back, which hurt him, of course, and was wrong. But it seemed that Vittoria's movement toward adulthood brought into focus the crushed dreams in each of us, Umberto and I both, the betrayals, the distance, the deep ravines of dissatisfaction across which we could no longer really see or hear or speak kindly to each other.

Sister Gabriella said to me in one of our marvelous conversations that perhaps all the trouble in the world has, at its root, our insistence on denying others their full humanity. Surely the Germans are doing that with the Jews (what would they do to me if they knew I was part of a chain of Italians working to hide and save them?! If they knew about Eleonora! About the nuns!), but we all do that, albeit in smaller ways. We were raised, Umberto and I, to ignore the full humanity of the people who keep us alive. And it's always seemed to me that he can't even see the full humanity of our Enrico.

The people I'm involved with in Montepulciano—another secret; I hold so many now that at times it wearies me—see the workers and servants as human beings. Their urge for a new system is based on that, and I agree, of course. And yet their views are so rigid: all landowners bad, all peasants good. Father Xavier joined us the other week. I don't know who invited him, and I don't know what he thinks, because he said little and only listened. I confess to wondering for a moment if he might be some kind of spy—the Vatican made its sordid peace with Mussolini years ago. But perhaps his silence reflected only the difficulty of his position. On the one hand, the young radicals care for the peasant class as Christ certainly would have. On the other, they have little good to say about the pope or the Church, and most of them don't believe in God.

If I live long enough and regain some of my lost strength, I'd like to invite Vittoria to one of these meetings. I think, for the most part, she'd approve. I hope she would. I so hope that she has the courage to lead her life more honestly and openly than I have.

~

Absorbed as she was in the pages, eager as she was to read on, Vittoria reached that short paragraph and had to close the book.

If they knew about Eleonora, her mother had written! What could that mean? Was Eleonora Jewish? Was her mother, her quiet, intellectual, flower-growing mother, involved in hiding Jews?!

And: *the betrayals, the distance.* What did that actually mean? Vittoria lowered her head and began, very quietly, to cry. There was so much she'd never know about her own mother, so many secrets hiding in the stone walls of this house. Part of her was afraid to read on, afraid of what she might discover there. In that beautiful handwriting her mother had written: *I so hope she has the courage to lead her life more honestly and openly than I have.* It was a kind of motherly lesson she was offering: Don't make the kinds of choices I made, my daughter. Have courage.

Cinzia and the barn workers were gone. Tobias and his SS henchmen could return at any moment. The Americans were fighting up the peninsula—for the second time today she'd heard bombing in the distance, just as she closed her mother's journal. She didn't know where Carlo was, or even if he were still alive. *The courage,* she thought. *The courage.* She pushed back from the desk and sank to her knees and, leaning her forehead against the wood and clasping her hands together, prayed for her mother to send her a sign.

Thirty-Three

That night, after eating the supper Eleonora brought him, a delicious meal fit for the table in the manor house (a cut of pork stuffed with figs and wrapped in prosciutto, with rosemary potatoes and escarole), Paolo felt a wave of the most intense nervousness come over him. One of his teeth was loose, his face still sore. Tired from the day's labor, he lay down for just a moment in the straw and, in spite of his worries, immediately fell asleep. He awoke to see a figure standing over him in the darkness, and realized that the figure was a man, and that the man had kicked the bottom of his right work boot to awaken him. For an instant, Paolo thought it was the German officer, but then he saw the enormous nose. He sat up.

"Time," Antonio said.

In one hand he held a paper-wrapped package, the sight of which shoved Paolo back against a horrible memory.

"Yes, yes." Paolo held an apology in his mouth—how could he have fallen asleep at such a time? And for hours, it seemed! He stood, brushed the straw carefully from his clothes, by habit, as if he were about to sit down to supper, or head off to Mass. At this late hour, the middle of the night, he was unused to being anywhere but in the bed in his upstairs room. The single exception had been the night he'd sneaked out, in the early hours, gone stealthily along the edges of the courtyard, and crawled on his back beneath the black Ford.

He'd been alert then, hyperalert, but now his mind felt dulled, as if thoughts were slogging through it in knee-deep mud.

Antonio handed him the package—like the last one, heavier than it looked. Terrified of dropping it, still half-buried in sleep, Paolo held the small bundle against his midsection with both hands and followed Eleonora's lover out into the darkness and across the courtyard. It wasn't until they reached the place where the courtyard narrowed onto a dirt road and headed into the trees that he saw the cream-colored Fiat there, leaning a bit to one side as if on a bad leg. This Antonio, this mysterious associate of Father Costantino, this frightening lover of the sweet Eleonora, had access to gasoline, to an automobile! He must have rich friends, or powerful friends, or friends who were thieves. The sight of the old car at the edge of the woods made Paolo's hands begin to sweat. He and Antonio opened the doors, climbed in, and took their places—one of them, Paolo thought, a partisan, a soldier, young, strong, capable of finding an automobile and gasoline in wartime, and unworried, apparently, about driving a car along a lightless road with a bomb in the front seat.

The other, a tired old man.

The car seemed tired, too. When Antonio fired its engine to life, the noise echoed so loudly in the trees that Paolo worried every Nazi and Fascist in the entire province could hear it. They bumped away slowly down the road. At the first intersection, three roads converging, Antonio made a very sharp right turn and looped back, south, in the direction of Città della Pieve. Once they were on that road, rough and little-used, Paolo had the most terrible sense of being trapped. He'd been connected to the vineyard all these years, all his life in fact. Tied to it. Unable to leave. But in spite of that, and in spite of the unchanging work schedule, he'd enjoyed a certain amount of freedom. He could hunt on Sunday mornings, walk the fields or take the boys fishing on a holiday afternoon, sit up with Carlo or Gennaro or Giuseppe playing briscola after supper on Saturday. Now, he was trapped as surely as any animal ready for slaughter. The war had trapped him, trapped all of them. He watched the dark trees pass, and remembered Father Costantino gesturing him into the back room after Mass—when was it? Three months ago? He could picture the young priest standing very close, facing him, placing a hand on the top of his left shoulder. He could hear him saying these words, quietly, almost smiling, "Old Paolo, Christ would not want us to stand quietly by while the forces of evil are threatening our country, while others are being hurt and killed. Would He?"

"No, Father."

"Then will you work with us?"

"What kind of work, Father? Repairing the church?"

A laugh, almost a snort. Father Costantino closed his eyes for a moment, shook his head in a way that made Paolo feel foolish. "Secret work, Paolo. Against the Nazis. Against *Il Duce*. Will you join us?"

That had been the start of it, that "Yes, Father, if you want me to, I will."

Would he report what he saw on the roads when he made his deliveries? Yes, Father. Would he carry a note for a shopkeeper in Pisa and hand it to him when no one could see? Yes, Father. Would he let the priest know if he had any Jewish acquaintances, so the church could help protect them? Yes, Father, of course. Would he make sure to relay what people were saying about the bombing in Montepulciano? Were they upset at the Allies? Were they angry?

Yes, Father. Of course, Father.

The man was a priest, after all. A man of God.

But then: Would he take this package and, late at night, slip into the courtyard and tie it to the exhaust pipe of the visitor's fancy American car? Would he bomb the train tracks near Chiusi?

That first yes had caught him like a rabbit in a trap. One foot was enough. Every yes after that had dragged him further and further away from the simplicity and straightforwardness of his old life, the rabbit dragging the trap across a field, in pain, afraid of being killed. And now here he was, riding in a rattling Fiat with a stranger, at midnight, the barn empty of people, the vineyard waiting for another visit from the SS, a bomb wrapped in paper and tied with twine sitting in his lap.

They were deep in the trees now, enveloped in darkness, the road visible only because a slice of moon made the sky above them half a shade lighter than the trees to either side, and because the Fiat had one feeble working headlight. It wasn't a well-traveled route, not one Paolo had taken since the days when he'd brought Carlo and some of the other youngsters to a certain part of the River Chiana on fishing trips. A decade ago. On those trips, taken always on holidays when they had a full free day, a lot of people were out, and they'd been able to hitch rides in both directions. Then and now, there were no houses along this road, just stone walls and fences that marked the property lines of hidden estates. The headlamp blinked and went out, came on again. Antonio was spewing curse words under his breath, taking the Lord's name in vain, swearing in Italian and muttering in some dialect Paolo didn't know.

Antonio went along as quickly as the road and darkness would allow, trying to avoid the deepest holes and ruts, the windows open and the tires making soft splashing sounds in the wet dirt, crunching sounds where there was gravel.

"We are going now to damage the train tracks, yes?" Paolo asked, because the man beside him made him terribly uneasy. From the moment he'd first seen Antonio's face—the huge curved nose, the mop of hair, the big jaw, the narrowed eyes—he'd felt like he was looking into the mouth of a volcano, all fire and smoke and tremendous heat. He wondered what must have happened to the young man in order to have made him so incredibly angry. He wondered, not if Antonio had ever killed anyone, but how many people he'd killed. And he wondered how a girl like Eleonora could be attracted to such a person.

"Not exactly," Antonio answered after a few seconds, and in such a murderous tone that Paolo felt as if someone had taken hold of the back of his neck with freezing fingers. He thought about it for a few seconds, assessing the mood, the tone of voice, the strange midnight errand. And then he understood. It was a pretend assignment, an elaborate trick. The package in his lap, securely tied, could be nothing more than a piece of oak, a metal money box filled with sand, a square stone. So this was the way they were going to kill him: take him into the woods late at night, shoot or stab him, and leave his body to rot there by the side of the road in a place where no one would find it for weeks. Clearly, Eleonora had been aware of this plan and had fed him one last, exquisite meal as if in apology. So it must be then that she and her Antonio worked for the Nazis. Or that they suspected *him* of working for the Nazis. Either way, they'd decided it was time to eliminate him.

For a few seconds he considered jumping out of the moving car and running away. But where? Into the trees? And how was an old man going to outrun someone like this Antonio next to him? Paolo kept his eyes forward, fingers splayed on the tops of his thighs, package held between his wrists, and he waited as long as he could before saying, "If you're going to kill me, kill me now. Let me pray, and kill me while I'm praying. I won't fight with you."

He risked a look sideways, saw the man's huge nose, a dark blade, heard a nasty one-note laugh. Then nothing.

The motor muttered and skipped, the car splashed and skittered from one side of the road to the other. Antonio peered through the windshield as if searching there for the expected firing squad that would help him with his evil errand. Paolo realized that the tiredness in his limbs and the murkiness in his thoughts had disappeared, replaced by a strange burst of energy, as if he were required to remain absolutely alert now in order to have any chance at all of staying alive. He waited another minute, trying to hold it back, and then a river of words rushed out of him. "I understand nothing," he admitted helplessly. "Father

Costantino said there would be a train carrying Italians to the camps. Italian Jews. And that I was supposed to place this terrible thing"—he gestured to the package on his lap—"at a certain place, and send the train off the tracks so the people could be rescued. But it made no sense to me even then. There's a river there, and steep banks. How would I save the Italians by sending the train into the river? And if the Nazis driving the train and guarding the Italians survived, how would they let anyone go? How would I fight them with no weapon? How would the Italian prisoners fight them? With their bare hands? And why am I the one who has to use the explosives, when you could do it, anyone could do it? Why was I the one who had to put the bomb under the American car? Why was Vittoria the one who had to take the German deserters to the nuns? Why are she and I being put in danger this way?"

Silence.

In all his decades of spending time around working people, Paolo had known many men who spoke only rarely—Gennaro Asolutto was a perfect example. But, so far at least, this Antonio seemed like the most tight-lipped of them all, the king of silence, as if words had to climb an icy mountain path in order to reach his mouth, and then slip out between his lips one at a time. Paolo turned to look at him again. Nothing. "Explain to me what you know," he said at last. "Or I'll open the door and jump out and you can shoot me if you want to shoot me."

Antonio grunted skeptically. "First, tell me," he said, and then there was another dark stretch with no sound in it beyond the slip and slop and bump of the tires and the irregular struggles of the Fiat's old motor. "Did you do something to your *Signore*? Did you steal from him? Cheat him on the weights when you took the olives to the mill the way all the *fattori* do?"

"I'm not a *fattore*. We don't have that system on our vineyard. The *Signore*'s father changed it long ago. We have a wine boss—Carlo now— and a foreman—me—that's all. And no, no, no, never! I never cheated!" Paolo shouted at the windshield. "I never did anything wrong to him!"

So the *Signore* was the one who suspected him, who'd decided he should be killed! The word "wrong"—*scorretto*—echoed in the small car. "I'm sixty-four years old! I lived on this vineyard all that time! Sixty-four years I worked here. Every day but Sunday. I never stole one bunch of grapes, one bottle of wine, one ax, one hammer. Nothing. Never. I never cheated anyone in my life! Why do you even ask me? Does he speak badly of me? Has Eleonora heard him curse me?"

Another grunt. Antonio retreated into his silence and wrestled with the wheel.

But then, in the moonlit darkness, with the seat of the car shifting and bumping beneath him, Paolo understood that Antonio's remark—*Did you do something to your* Signore?—had been not merely a question, but an answer: he began to suspect that what he had *done* to his *Signore*, in some ways the worst thing one man could do to another, might very well be root of the harvest of troubles he was reaping now. Depending on what the *Signore* knew of the past, and how he had come to know it, the man who controlled Paolo's life might have been nurturing a ferocious bitterness inside himself all these many years, biding his time, planning a complicated revenge.

Once that understanding struck him, layer upon layer of lie and half truth, years of the most terrible, impossible, agonizing pretense began falling away from him like scales of diseased skin. After a few minutes he felt as though there were no clothes on him at all, no skin; his flesh was raw. The touch of the cool night air was like the cut of a blade. The war, the secret work, the Nazi officer tormenting Vittoria, the priest with his odd, superior smiles, the murder of the *Signore*'s friend, the Nazi slapping his face and putting the gun to his head, the killing of the horse, the screams and weeping, Enrico's misery, the tears of anger on Marcellina's face as she broke open a thousand years of obedience and subservience—all of it had scraped from him every last bit of pretense, everything that was less than perfectly true.

Antonio held to his silence, and that, too, was like a sharp blade on flesh, scraping, scraping, ripping the pretense away, exposing the raw truth. *"Io,"* Paolo managed to say into the terrible silence. I. And then, though he tried to hold them back, something in the middle of him pushed hard against the memories buried there. His mouth opened, and no flex of muscles or act of will could close it again. "I . . . with the *Signora*, Umberto's wife . . . *alcune volte* . . . A few times. Many years ago. We were still young. She and I in the field . . . several times. She was unhappy, and I thought . . . and we . . . And then we stopped, we had to stop. She had to make us stop."

That was as far as he could go. Amazed at himself, he buried the rest of it, the most important part. All the laypeople he'd known and kept the secret from since those days, more than twenty years! Now, half-broken by the series of horrors he'd been living through, he'd chosen this person to hear it! His legs were trembling from the knees down.

"Who else have you ever told?"

"No one."

"No one?"

Paolo's hands were squeezed into fists. The package, held between his forearms, was shaking back and forth. The truth, the truth, the truth now. "I told the priest who used to be here, who left. Father Xavier. In confession."

"And this priest? Costantino?"

"Yes, also in confession. He's forbidden to tell anyone."

A curt laugh. Antonio shifted his weight but kept his face forward and his mouth pressed into a grim line. "Costantino is no good," he said quietly after a time.

"How, no good? He's a priest!"

"He told someone. That someone must have told someone else—your *Signore*, maybe—who told someone else, who told me."

"But . . . in confession! How could he?"

Another one-note laugh, mean as sickness, then a shake of the head. "And you, an old man," Antonio said quietly. "To say something like that."

"Yes, old, old, and a sinner! But I don't understand. I don't understand anything. Kill me, if you're going to kill me, if you work for the Germans. Or if you think I do. Or if the *Signore* wants me dead. Let me start to pray, and then kill me."

"The priest works for the Germans, not you. Not me. Not Eleonora. And your *Signore* cares about no one but himself. He's a Nazi sympathizer, and always has been. A stupid devil."

Paolo squeezed his eyebrows down, closed his eyes, tried to force his brain to function. "The priest?" he managed to say. "But if the priest works for the Germans, then Brindisi, the *Signore's* friend . . . the man we killed—"

"*You* killed him. A good man. It was a mistake, a trick."

"How? Who?" Paolo was slamming one fist down on the top of his thigh. The parcel was knocked sideways, and he barely caught it before it fell to the floor.

"You might be careful with that."

"Tell me!"

"The priest works for the OVRA."

"Mussolini's police? The torturers? How do you know?"

"I know, that's all. I have a very tall friend who figured all this out. And, as I hope I don't need to tell you, the OVRA works with the Germans. Did you ever wonder why a brilliant Milanese priest was sent to serve the little church in Gracciano and its uneducated parishioners?"

"Sometimes, yes, I—"

"Your good priest was sent there, to that little place, for a reason. Your vineyard is on their bad list."

"But why? But how can that be?"

"Perhaps because your *Signora* was friendly with the communists from Montepulciano, also on the bad list, some of them now dead.

Your priest was sent here to spy, to see who was loyal to *Il Duce*, and who wasn't."

"A communist?! She wasn't a communist! She told me she wasn't. She cared about us, that's all. She was the one rich person in my life who cared about us. And I talk to the *Signore* maybe one time in a year! Always about the wine, the grapes, the olives."

Antonio spat to his left out the open window and turned his face forward again. "You live on the surface," he said. "The grape vines, the hazelnut trees, the tomatoes, the peppers, the olives. Underneath that surface there are moles, mice, rats, worms, beetles, snakes. You try to be *good*. You do what you're told. The moles and mice and rats and snakes don't care about being good. They're doing things you can't see, chewing the roots of your goodness, eating holes in the walls of it."

"Speak plainly to me," Paolo demanded. "Where are we going? What are we doing? Who is bad and who is good?"

"Your priest was sent here to pretend to be a *partigiano*. And he's very good at it. Very, very good."

"How do you know this?"

"Because he made one mistake."

"What mistake?"

Silence.

"Tell me!" Paolo demanded.

"This Brindisi was driving home in Montepulciano after visiting your *Signore*, his good friend. He took a side road because the main road had debris from the bombing. And who did he see coming out the back of the house where the SS stay?"

"Father Costantino?"

"Exactly. And he made the mistake of mentioning that to your *Signore*. Eleonora was serving them food. She heard him. Maybe your *Signore* mentioned it to the priest, possibly in passing, by accident, or maybe on purpose, who can say? Possibly he said, 'Father, did you go to the SS house in Montepulciano?' And the priest said, 'No, of course not. Why do you ask, Umberto?' And he said, 'Because my friend Massimo said he saw you there. Were you giving confession?' 'No, no,' the priest said, 'I never went there, to the Nazis. Why would I go there, Umberto?' But by the time of that conversation—if there was such a conversation—the priest already knew Massimo Brindisi had seen him—which would be dangerous for him—and so he'd already arranged to have the man killed, and he was happy to have you be the killer. The conversation with your *Signore* was only a confirmation, something that made him certain it should be done. You see now how things work?"

"No. I don't see. I don't understand! How can a person be so evil? A man of God? He holds the host in his hands. Christ's body! He gives confession!"

"Lots of priests are with *Il Duce*. The Vatican is with him. Maybe your good priest was drinking with the SS that day. Maybe he went there for the women, who knows? Happy, a little drunk, he came out of the house with his face uncovered, before dark. That road was hardly used. He made a mistake. Brindisi saw him. He saw Brindisi see him. Perhaps Umberto confirmed it. The priest understood that his disguise as a *partigiano* was in danger of being ripped away, which meant he would then be killed if certain people—me, for example—found out."

"Does Father Costantino know that you know?"

"That's the question, isn't it? I don't think he knows, not yet."

"But why would he have us kill the Germans on the train if he loves the Germans?"

"He hasn't killed any Germans so far, has he? Think about it. This is a fake plan. A plan that will get you and me—two *partigiani*—to an isolated place in the middle of the night. Your priest tells us we're going there to damage the train tracks. But why would he send us to such a hidden place?"

"I don't know."

"Because he's arranged for his friends from the OVRA to ambush us there, kill us, and throw us into the river where we'll never be found."

"But why?"

"Because the *Americani* have taken Sicily."

"I heard they were fighting there."

"The fighting there is over. They took Sicily. And Calabria. And Napoli. Soon they'll be in Roma, then here. *Il Duce* is gone, no one knows where. The Nazis and the OVRA are losing. They're panicking. They're trying to kill everyone they think is an enemy, but they're doing it in a sly way. The priest recruited you so he could know which side you're on. If you had said no when he asked you, he would have left you alone."

"Vittoria."

"Yes, exactly. He wanted Vittoria to take the deserters so he'd know which side *she's* on. Now he knows. I'm surprised he didn't arrange to have her killed on the Zanita Road or something."

"And Eleonora? And you?"

"The same. If he knew Eleonora was Jewish, she'd be dead by now, or on her way north. Why do you think he's sending you and me together to be met by the OVRA in the darkest, most remote place he could think of? He'll leave Eleonora and Vittoria for the next SS visit. The devils will have their fun first, then kill them."

"I don't understand. I don't think this way. I— Why are we going then?"

"Because I'm one step smarter than your good priest. The OVRA men waiting in the car there are dead by now, killed by my men. And there is, in fact, a train that comes along that route and takes Italian Jews and others to the work camps. And we are, in fact, going to send it off the rails and save the people in it and make sure the trains can't run there again for some time."

"Won't some of the people die?"

"Not if we do it right."

"And the Germans driving the train? The guards?"

"A handful. My men will take care of them. You and I will be gone by then. You'll place the explosive, set the timer, and we go."

Antonio reached behind him with one hand, took hold of something there, and lifted it over the back of the seat. He rested it across Paolo's knees, just in front of the package. Black metal.

"A rifle," Paolo said.

"An automatic rifle, American-made. We have these now. The OVRA bastards learned that too late. The Germans in the train will learn it."

"And the explosives? Why me? Why not have your men do it?"

"Because you are one of my men now."

Paolo moved his hands so that he was holding the automatic rifle in place and keeping the package between his forearms. His fingers were trembling. He felt as though every dark tree they passed was pointing at him, announcing his sins, promising punishment.

"Your problem," Antonio went on, the words flowing out of him now, as if a dam had broken, "is that you want to be pure. A pure man. In war you can't remain pure and you can't remain neutral. You're fighting with us now. You've made your choice."

Paolo was shaking his head back and forth, back and forth, trying to clear it. "Then it's you I have to trust."

Another mean laugh. "Not really," Antonio said. "We'll get to the train tracks in another few minutes. If you see a car there with dead OVRA killers inside, and a group of my men with guns like these, and if, tonight, you get back to your barn alive, then I think you'll understand who you should trust and who you shouldn't."

Thirty-Four

The boxcar was completely dark, savagely dark. Carlo couldn't tell how many other men were in there with him and Carmine—twenty, he guessed, from the brief glimpse he'd had when they'd first been shoved through the open door at the station in Pietramelara. All of them had moved to the far south end of the car because the north end was where several of the men had already relieved themselves. On the plank floor near the side wall, he and Carmine sat in silence, in darkness, the train rumbling along, the air filled with the stink of sweat and urine and the sound of nervous conversation. They'd gone less than an hour when Carlo felt the train slowing down. The wheels squealed against the tracks. He and Carmine were jostled sideways, there was the screech of brakes, and the car slowed still further and lurched to a stop.

"Roma," Carmine said.

Someone nearby exclaimed, "*Sì, sì,* Roma!" as if he thought Rome was the end of the line and any minute the big door would slide open and they'd all be greeted warmly and let out for a meal of spaghetti and Chianti.

But the door didn't open. A few minutes passed, an hour passed, two hours. Men stood and stretched their legs, or apologized to the others and went and pissed at the far end of the car, tracking the smell back on the wet soles of their shoes.

A third hour passed in the darkness. Carlo was beginning to sense an angry, frightened restlessness in the low voices around him, and feel the same emotions in himself.

"When they open the door," someone to his left said, "we should rush them all together and overpower them."

The suggestion was met with silence at first, and then, another voice in the darkness: "They have guns. We'll be slaughtered."

"It's either that, or be worked to death in the cold," the first man said, but those words only echoed against the metal walls and drew no response.

Carlo was horribly thirsty, and very hungry. A strange state of mind had taken hold of him. Not defeat, exactly, but what felt like the leading edge of a vast resignation, a prisoner's patience. On some of the wine deliveries with Gennaro Asolutto and Old Paolo, he'd ridden past big lakes—Bolsena, Trasimeno, Bracciano—and, though he was a poor swimmer, having learned only by jumping into the deep sections of the Chiana on fishing trips, he'd find himself dreaming that he was required to swim across those lakes. In the dreams, he'd be struggling for breath after a few dozen strokes, arms and legs already growing heavy. It would be impossible to turn back: he'd either make it to the far shore, or give up, breathe in water, and let himself sink. As a teenage boy and young man, he'd had that same dream many times. He remembered telling Vittoria about it. She couldn't swim well, either, and found the dream terrifying.

He remembered the dream now, in the dark boxcar, started to mention it to Carmine, but Carmine was quietly snoring.

Carlo felt now that he was stepping into the lake of his dreams. The water was cold, the other shore too far off to see, the idea of making it all the way across—of surviving the work camp and eventually getting home—next to impossible.

It seemed likely that the Nazis were going to ship them all the way to Germany without giving them anything to eat or drink, and then keep them in the prison factories or camps, making bombs until the war ended. Days, the ride could take. Years, they could be kept prisoners. Some of the men would die en route, he was sure. And more of them would die in the northern cold.

As if she were standing there, just outside the boxcar, pounding on the door, Carlo could sense Vittoria at the edge of his thoughts. He turned his mind away. If the odds of making a life with her had been small before his capture, they were minuscule now. He wouldn't give up, wouldn't let himself sink to the bottom of the lake. Not yet. But he felt he had to steel himself against the future. From this moment forward, he'd have to live minute by minute, wrapping the dream of her into a tight ball and pressing it down into the depths of his thoughts, keeping it there, out of sight.

Three or four hours they'd been waiting when the door finally slammed open. The light from the station blinded him for a moment, but with his eye closed, Carlo could sense a commotion at the door, German and Italian voices. When he could open his eye, and stop the fast blinking, when he'd adjusted to the light, Carlo was amazed to see a crowd of people climbing into the car. Women, small children, and then men, some of them white-haired and frail. Almost all of them were carrying something—bundles, small boxes wrapped in twine, books. One man was holding what appeared to be a case for a musical instrument. Behind them, Germans in uniform were yelling in a tone of voice that Carlo had never heard used on a human being. Even the vineyard animals weren't spoken to that way. Half the children were crying. The teenage girls, the women and men, every one of them had terror painted on their faces. By instinct, Carlo stood, but he would have had to stand anyway in order to make room. They were all pushed in close to each other, and by unspoken agreement, the men sidled toward the north end of the car and let the women and children stand in the cleaner south end.

Carlo didn't understand. How on earth were old men and women and small children going to work in a factory?

Through the open door, he saw a sign hanging beneath the station roof:

ROMA TERMINI

A German voice, commanding. The door rumbling sideways and crashing closed. He could hear a lock snap into place. *"Questo,"* Carmine said beside him, *"non è giusto."* This is not right.

They waited there for several more hours, crowded body to body, breathing the putrid air, children weeping. And then, at last, a loud whistle, a violent jerk, and they were moving again.

Thirty-Five

Vittoria fell asleep with her mother's journal open across her breast, and awoke with it still on the bed, but closed now, buried between the soft pillows. She'd dreamed of Carlo—no specific scene, just his face, his presence, and the vague sense that he was in danger. For a few minutes she lay there looking at the ceiling, the fingers of one hand on the book, wondering if the dream meant he'd just been killed. Her father's pistol lay beside her on the night table, and she turned her head and stared at it for a time, as if it were the opposite of a saint's statue. A satanic relic.

It was very early. Her bedroom was lit only faintly; the sun had not yet risen above the hillside to the east. She forced herself out of bed, washed, dressed, brushed her hair, and then, instead of going downstairs to find something to eat, she sat at her desk and opened her mother's journal again.

~

As I move closer to death, it seems that my worst sins, so far in the past now, are being brought into sharper relief. At the time, of course, they didn't seem like sins, but actions that were natural and just, as if God had presented me, not with a temptation, but with a gift, a reward. There are many moments now, many many moments, when they still seem that way. A reward.

But for what? For my patience with Umberto, I suppose. I felt it was a chance to in some way reset the balance of our marriage. I had an abundance of evidence of his many betrayals—I can't bear to list them here. Those things were perhaps not so unusual among Italian men, but they began so early in our married life, crushing the flower of my young dreams.

And then there was the group in Montepulciano, those thrilling afternoon gatherings, the talk and wine, the radical ideas being discussed. These were at Olivia's home, a woman in our social circle, someone we knew from church. I'd gone there at first because I knew what Umberto was doing—the echoes of his lies followed me around the house—and I needed some escape from it. I knew, too, that he didn't want me to go to those gatherings—his politics were far to the other side. So I went to find solace, and, perhaps, sinfully, to spite him. I think the ideas there took hold of me in the same way Mussolini's ideas—so very different—had taken hold of my husband. That the peasants were human beings and should be treated as such. That women should have some of the same advantages and opportunities as men. In Italy at that time—even now—those were radical ideas, an impossible challenge to the social order.

I was young then, Umberto twelve years older. My body sought the ordinary pleasures, though perhaps not often enough for my husband. At times we enjoyed something of a physical connection, but it was rare and fleeting, and without any spiritual dimension. During the day, I rode the horses, spent time in my flower gardens and around the barn, made a point of talking with the people there, something members of a noble family almost never did. Umberto was often away on his business ventures, no doubt enjoying his illicit liaisons. I was young, angry, not averse to physical attraction. I walked the property alone at times, and God presented me with a certain opportunity. Conversation at first, with one man in particular, a kind, good, somewhat older man. I felt, perhaps we both felt, a strange, forbidden sense of connection, shadowed by guilt. It was I who pursued it, I confess to that freely. I indulged myself, both began and ultimately ended the physical aspect of it. Ended it too late, of course. And I've lived with the consequence—or, more accurately, the gift—all these years. The incredible gift. But then I watched the hope on that man's face change to torment—his penance and mine—and then to resignation, and then to a stolid hopelessness, a peasant hopelessness.

He won't be at my deathbed, I know that. It would never be allowed, and I couldn't bring myself to ask for it. I wonder, though, if, after these silent decades, I might find the courage to speak with him, to humbly apologize. Would that tear the scab off a brutal old wound? I watch him now, with the horses, working the vines, speaking with Enrico. He never looks at me.

I wonder if Umberto knows, and whether I should tell Vittoria before I die. Enrico, of course, I would never tell.

~

The writing ended abruptly there, as if her mother had grown too sick to write, or as if her courage had deserted her. Vittoria paged hastily through the book all the way to the end, twice, but the remaining pages were empty.

She sat there, staring blankly out the window, her thoughts as still and heavy as stones.

No wonder, she thought. *No wonder Old Paolo and Enrico enjoy each other's company so much.* She stood, reached for the pistol, and dropped it into the pocket of her dress.

Still dazed, but with other thoughts—dark, unformed—appearing like thin vines at the edges of the stones, she was drawn by hunger and habit to the breakfast table. So distracted was she by what she'd read that it dawned on her only when she saw Eleonora that the others were gone. Eleonora's face was like a mirror of her own, washed in astonishment and worry. She brought coffee, pastry, one egg boiled hard, the way Vittoria liked them. Without speaking, the young woman set the cup and plate down, and then, from the pocket of her apron, she brought out a small sealed envelope with *V.* written in ink on the front.

"Your father asked me to give you this," she said. "He woke me very early and handed this to me." Then she fled to the kitchen.

Thirty-Six

Once it left Roma Termini, the train picked up speed and hurtled along at such a pace that people were continually falling against one another, being held upright by a neighbor, or by a hand pressed against a metal wall. From the deliveries he'd made, Carlo guessed it would be two or three more hours until they passed close to Montepulciano. That city was set too far up on a steep hill to be served by the main rail line—which ran through Orvieto, Città della Pieve, and Chiusi—so there was no chance the train would stop there. But, full as this boxcar was, others might not be full, and there was a chance the train might stop at Città della Pieve or Chiusi, not so far from home, and in the confusion and darkness, he might try to slip away.

Another fantasy. He'd be shot within seconds, and how would he open the door in any case? As he had when being marched down the hill by the German soldiers, he realized that, even in misery like this—the stink, the hunger and thirst, the terror—he and the others wanted to live. There was some deep force inside them, not the fear of death so much as the insistence on living out their allotted time, grasping another hour, another week, another year, taking their last breath in a less hideous setting.

Minute by minute, the situation grew more difficult to bear. The thirst, the hunger, the crowded darkness, the wailing of kids and weeping of women, the putrid flood swinging back and forth against his feet with every shift of the train's center of gravity. He himself had added to the stinking puddle. They all had, or soon would.

Two hours north of Rome, Carlo was startled out of his standing half sleep by the sound of a man at the end of the car, singing a phrase in a strange language. To his surprise, Carmine, pressed close beside him, answered in what sounded like the same language, and then almost everyone in the boxcar was chanting together, some kind of sorrowful hymn or prayer. It took Carlo a few seconds to understand what language it must be, what kind of prayer. *But women and children and old men!* he thought again. *Of what use will they be in the Nazi factories?*

The prayer concluded, and in a short quiet moment, Carmine said, "It's Friday night, Carlo. Our Sabbath." And then someone started praying loudly again, in Italian this time.

"Benedetto sii Tu, o Signore, nostro Dio, Re dell'universo, Tu che ci hai santificato coi Tuoi comandamenti e ci hai comandato di accendere le luci di Shabbat."

Blessed are You, Adonai our God, Ruler of the universe, who has made us holy through God's commandments and commanded us to light the Sabbath candles.

Carlo could see that two men at the other end of the car had ignited their cigarette lighters—he'd seen such a device only once, held by his *Signore* to light a cigar—and were holding them high above their heads.

Less than a minute after the darkness was broken by those two frail lights, Carlo felt a terrific jolt, and the car tilted violently sideways, as if the God of these people had been called upon to save them, and was responding. In a ghastly chorus of screams the world tipped over sideways, and the wall to his left slammed hard against the earth, throwing him and Carmine violently down against it. Carmine's body cushioned him, the world seemed to bounce slightly, and then the whole car was skidding downhill, their bodies sliding unstoppably toward the ceiling, people crushed against each other, the air filled with screaming. The car slammed hard against something, and in the mad crush Carlo realized

215

that the ceiling and wall close to him had split open and Carmine had disappeared. A horrible mass of bodies pressed on him, a jagged edge of metal passed just in front of his face, water poured in through the opening. He was pushed out and through it by the weight behind him, the eye patch ripped from his face, and the shirt and skin of his left shoulder sliced away as he went. Another second and he was up to his neck in cold water, a mass of bodies behind and around him in the darkness, complete chaos, then gunfire, machine guns, men screaming in German, what sounded like a battle raging on the other side of the ruined train.

Everyone was caught in a state of panic. He thrashed his arms, his feet slipping on rocks. His head went under. There were bodies against his legs, a current tugging at him, gunfire when he surfaced, shots returned, a spotlight shining on the other side of the train, throwing eerie shadows. It was worse than any nightmare. He pushed on madly, blindly, at one point circling his left arm instinctively around a small girl to keep her head above the surface. A second later he went under himself and swallowed water, and she slipped out of his grasp. He reached for her in the darkness, but she was gone. He swam a few strokes, blindly, crazily, coughing and gasping, and finally felt the bottom beneath his feet. A few more bursts of gunfire well behind him, people yelling everywhere, frantically calling out names in the night. He reached the far bank and clambered up a short distance on his hands and knees, turned back to pull two women and one old man up after him. The spotlight had been turned off or destroyed in the gun battle, but in the moonlight, he could see bundles and packages abandoned everywhere, shadows running toward a dark line of trees, a few men calling out, a few stumbling back, searching for a child or spouse or brother. He looked for Carmine and didn't see him, watched a dark body float past, face down, yellow dress matted above bare lower legs. From the other side, where the exchange of gunfire had now ceased, he heard one shouted *"Viva Italia!"* He stumbled toward the river, calling,

"Carmine! Carmine!" but didn't see him among the scrambling crowd. He tripped and fell onto his chest, slipped down the bank and went face-first into the water, clambered up again and crawled with the last of his strength into a row of bushes. He lay there, exhausted, soaked, bleeding.

~

He awoke at first light and turned onto his belly so he could look back at the river. The scene before him, still mostly in shadow with only the tops of the trees touched by a grayish light, was a vision from the paintings of hell he'd seen on his one visit to the Montepulciano cathedral. A hundred meters to his right, the locomotive lay three-quarters submerged. Behind it, eight train cars rested on their sides in the mud like sleeping animals, some intact, the rest damaged in one way or another. One of them—his, it must have been—was bent and broken almost in half against a massive oak tree, and there was a jagged split along the car's roof. There were bodies everywhere he looked, in the water, crushed and sticking out from beneath the cars. On the far bank, two light-haired little boys, twins perhaps, lay side by side, facedown, still as death.

Not one living soul was visible. Nothing except the water moved. There was no sound beyond the twittering of birds in the trees and the gentle plash of the river against the metal of the locomotive and the gray rocks. The doors of every boxcar stood open to the sky. He watched the light change, gray to pale yellow, and suddenly understood what every other survivor must have understood in the night: he had to get away before the Germans figured out where the train was and sent soldiers.

He got to his feet, slowly, painfully. The blood on his shoulder had dried, but his left sleeve was mostly torn away, and his clothes were still wet. The air felt cool against his skin, and against his eye socket. He could walk, though his knees ached. To his left, beyond the last train car, he saw a shallow rapids. He limped in that direction, made his way across. He was upstream from the bodies and so he knelt and cupped handfuls of water into his mouth, one after the next after the next.

On the far side of the tracks, he saw a different hellish scene: bodies—German soldiers, strewn in bizarre poses of death. They'd been stripped of their guns and lay in a ribbon of grass and weeds between the toppled train and a little-used farmer's road, two dirt tracks, that ran parallel to the river. An automobile rested on the shoulder there, windshield shattered, doors pocked with bullet holes. Carlo approached it warily. In the front seat were two dead men, faces mutilated. Hell, it was. He couldn't make sense of any of it, but by instinct he hurried along, limping, on the road at first, and then, as it turned away from the river, he realized the Nazis would have to use it when they came, and he angled immediately toward the forest. A few steps into the trees, he stopped and looked back. Again and again he ran his eye over the scene, held there by the horror of it, even as he listened for the sound of a car or truck engine in the distance.

After a minute he realized that he knew this place. As a boy, he'd fished this stretch of the river. He'd swum here. The Chiana. He recognized the cliff face on the far side. The way the river bent away from the old road and formed a deep pool before it disappeared into the trees. There was a gorge farther north, he knew that.

And he realized that he must be only about twenty-five kilometers from the vineyard, from home.

Thirty-Seven

Vittoria sat alone at the huge mahogany dining room table, holding between her hands the note her father had left her. It had been written on their own stationery: heavy, cream-colored paper with a design of one small bunch of blue grapes centered on top, and VINEYARD SANANTONIO 1887 printed beneath it. There was no salutation, only this:

> Enough gas in the truck. Leaving to stay with Vito in Viareggio.
> All responsibility is yours now.
> U.

U., she thought. *Not "love," not "be safe," not even "your father." Just U.* For a moment, until she checked and saw the *V.* on the envelope, the tone of it made her wonder if Eleonora had misunderstood, and the note had been meant for someone else. Vittoria read it over a second time, a third, then set it flat on the tablecloth and turned her eyes out the window.

A loathsome idea occurred to her then, a whispered possibility that might as well have been a viper crawling between her feet. She tried, without success, to kick it away. Her father had sent her on the delivery to the SS house in Montepulciano when there had really been no need for her to go. When she'd told him what the Nazi captain had done, he'd seemed unsurprised, unconcerned. Then, after Massimo was killed, her father had called that same captain to come and investigate, and had said nothing to her about it, given her no warning. When she returned from the nunnery and went to see him, he'd seemed surprised, almost disappointed, that she'd made it back alive. Now he'd abandoned her without warning, left her there unprotected, knowing that the captain would almost certainly return. She imagined her father being stopped on the road to Viareggio and giving the Nazi salute to a pair of German soldiers, all thoughts of his daughter and son having already been left far behind.

The idea was so gruesome that she felt physically ill. Her whole being recoiled against it, but she couldn't seem to escape the suspicion that her own father had wanted her dead, or worse. Or, a slightly less horrible option, that, involved in his own troubles, consumed by them, her father simply didn't think about what might happen to her and Enrico, didn't really care.

She answered a question or two from Eleonora, then left the note and her untouched breakfast on the table and walked in a daze, in a kind of deep mourning, out of the dining room, along the hallway, and through the front door. She stood on the patio for a moment, then crossed the courtyard and climbed the slight rise to the smaller of the two barns. Her father had taken the truck and left the barn doors wide open. She went around behind the building to the place where she and Carlo had made love, and she sat down in the soft grass there with her back against the wall.

How much do you know about your parents' marriage? Sister Gabriella had asked.

She knew a little more now. A little more about who her mother had been, and a little more about who her father was. It seemed to her that they were the perfect representation of the rift in Italian society: change, however naive and vengeful, versus tradition, however unjust and rigid. Thinking about her parents' marriage, it occurred to her that human beings were always striving for power over one another, a murderous dominance. And that love was the only force in the universe running counter to that. She thought of Enrico, and how the last thing he ever seemed to want, the very last thing, was to have power over another person. And people pitied him!

She put her palms down flat on the grassy earth to either side of her, as if to take hold of the fleeting minutes she and Carlo had enjoyed there, a bond they'd forged against every unspoken rule of Italian history. How like her own mother she'd turned out to be! She composed another letter for Carlo in her mind but could not imagine finding the strength to write it.

She swore an oath to herself then: if the Good Lord would bring him back to her alive, she'd use every last drop of her strength to nurture and protect the love between them. They'd make a new nation of two—fair, generous, based on kindness and mutual respect, not dominance, not riches. She made the sign of the cross and swore the oath upon her mother's soul, and sat there imagining that love, that future, until she heard Enrico's voice and then the plaintive squeak of the wagon wheels.

Thirty-Eight

When Paolo awakened—later than usual—on the morning after his trip to the railroad tracks, his first thought was that, in spite of everything that held him to the vineyard, now was the time to leave. Marcellina had been right: the chances were good that the Nazis would return. It was impossible to forget what Antonio had told him the night before about Father Costantino, impossible to forget the feeling of the offi- cer's pistol aimed at his forehead, the spark of evil in the man's eyes, the way, without hesitating for an instant, he'd turned and shot three rounds into Antonina's body. Probably the only reason he hadn't killed all of them on that night was because he worried about who the *Signore* might know—a German general who loved his wine?—and what kind of trouble that might bring a lowly captain. But, if what Antonio had said was true, then the *Signore* sympathized with the Germans. And, if what Eleonora had told him was true, then the Nazis had executed twenty Italians because of an *insult*. So what was to keep the men from returning, lining him and Eleonora and Enrico up against the wall, and shooting them as if they were just more horses in a barn?

Still, as he dressed and went downstairs to use the toilet and wash, Paolo tried to tell himself it was possible the Nazis wouldn't come back. Possible they'd be busy with other duties, tormenting other people, investigating the wrecked train near Chiusi—if the explosives had worked as planned—fleeing the advancing Allies. In any case, he couldn't leave as long as Vittoria and Rico were there, he knew that. After all these years, it would be like tearing out his lungs. They were alone in the manor house now with the *Signore*; Eleonora and Antonio had spent the night in the attic hayloft, though he'd heard Eleonora get up early and tiptoe down the stairs. He told himself that he and Rico could work together, and that maybe Antonio would help. Eleonora could prepare their meals. Perhaps they could get in enough grapes to at least make a few kegs' worth of wine.

But by the time he'd finished washing his face, Paolo understood how foolish he was being. The choices were either to abandon the only people he cared about on this earth, or to go see the *Signore* and ask him to intervene with the Germans.

The first option was unbearable, the second as unlikely as finding white wine in the barrels of *vino nobile*. The barn was eerily empty—never, not for one day of his life, had it been that way. He fed Ottavio. Then, after standing still and staring up at the vines for several minutes, he took one of the scythes and headed out across the courtyard, telling himself the Good Lord would send him a solution as he worked. He picked a tomato from the part of the garden the Nazi captain hadn't poisoned, washed it at the well, and ate it as he climbed. The grapes were almost all purple now. Another week or ten days, depending on the weather, and it would be time to pick. It was a massive job, one that had required long days from him, Carlo, Giuseppe, Gianluca, a few traveling workers, and Gennaro Asolutto and the women as well. He couldn't think about that now. He couldn't think about what he and Antonio had done the night before. The only sensible option was to run. He'd work for a few hours, until Vittoria was awake and had eaten, and then he'd gather his courage, step into the manor house—forbidden territory for him—and ask her to leave with them, all together. The *Signore* would hate him for it, but, from what Antonio had told him, the *Signore* already hated him. And, Paolo thought, not without reason.

The day was cool. He'd been working barely half an hour, distracted, but swinging the scythe in a familiar, soothing rhythm, running the sharp blade through the stalks, when he heard Ottavio neighing, and then the squeak of the wheels. He turned and saw the wagon crest the rise, just as it had the day before, only this time Antonio and Eleonora sat in the bench seat, Enrico standing in the bed behind them. "Paolo! Paolo!" the boy shouted happily, a huge smile stretching his face.

And how could I leave you? Paolo thought. *How could I possibly leave you?*

Eleonora had brought him a breakfast of bread and cheese and water, and for a few minutes they stood with him while he ate. Enrico ran over and grabbed the scythe and started working. Paolo felt that his mind was a spinning motor, thoughts flying this way and that, a smoke of confusion and guilt circling over everything. "What if they come back?" he couldn't keep himself from asking aloud.

Antonio pointed to the *automatica* on the seat. "Then we'll kill them," he said. "Every one of them."

Paolo wanted to ask Antonio if he knew what had happened to the train, if the bomb had gone off, but he couldn't bear to look at him. On the previous night, Antonio had seemed so confident and mature; this morning, holding one hand tenderly on Eleonora's shoulder, he appeared strangely young. A boy who was going to take on a carload of SS killers with the help of his girlfriend, an old man, Rico, and one automatic weapon!

Eleonora checked to see that Enrico was too far away to hear, met Paolo's eyes, and said, "The *Signore* left."

"Left where?"

"Us."

Paolo shifted his eyes to Antonio, moved his head far enough to see Enrico, then looked back to Eleonora, as if she might be able to tell him what astonishing thing would happen next. Eleonora was watching him closely. "I brought breakfast to the dining room this morning," she said.

"Only the *Signorina* was there. I handed her the note her father had given me, and when I returned"—Eleonora demonstrated by moving her palms to either side of her face and holding them there, not quite touching her cheeks—"the *Signorina*'s face was puffy. Her eyes were wet. She was holding the note in her hands. I asked her what was wrong, and she looked up at me as if from a dream. 'My father went away,' she said. 'He took the truck and went away.'"

"But he'll come back." Paolo swung an arm toward Enrico, then in the other direction. "He has to come back. His children are here. His grapes."

Eleonora shook her head. "He went to his friend in Viareggio, the *Signorina* said. She said her father had left her in charge. She said she didn't think he was coming back."

Paolo couldn't make himself move.

Enrico let out a sound and shouted, *"Lepre!"* A moment later the hare he'd startled and nearly sliced in half came hopping past them and scurried under the wagon. "A rabbit, Paolo!" the boy called.

"Sì, sì," Paolo called back, but his mind was spinning.

Eleonora asked him exactly what he'd been about to ask her: "Now what do we do?"

Paolo raised his eyebrows and looked around. The fact of the *Signore*'s departure was settling in his thoughts and hardening there into a shape. The shape was like a concrete box with all the past in it. All the work, all the years. Leaving the wheat unharvested didn't matter now. Even the idea of letting the grapes rot on the vines no longer mattered.

He looked up from his trance and saw the young couple watching him. "We should leave, too," he said, "before they come back." The words were like blood in his mouth. Almost to himself he added, "But the *Signorina* and Enrico have to come with us. We have to convince them to come."

"Let them save themselves," Antonio said angrily.

Paolo was shaking his head. The rabbit sprinted out from its hiding place and went hopping across the harvested section of the field. Enrico watched it go and laughed.

"Maybe the *Signore* left because he knew the Nazis were coming back," Eleonora said. "We should hurry."

Thirty-Nine

Carlo barely had the energy to climb the thickly forested hills that marked the landscape east and north of Chiusi. He was unbearably hungry, dry-mouthed still, despite the few handfuls of river water, and he hadn't slept more than a few hours for each of the past three nights. He knew where he was. And he knew that, if he'd had enough food and sleep over the past month, he would have been strong enough to walk to the vineyard by nightfall. But, as it was, he could barely put one foot in front of the other on the uphill stretches, and his legs wobbled and trembled as he descended.

The sun had already moved up and over the treetops behind his right shoulder—he was using the moving shadows of the trunks as a kind of compass. To his left and far below, he could hear the occasional truck engine. In better times, he would have made his way down to the road, stood there and held out his thumb, and no doubt would have been home by supper. But he was certain the Germans had found out about the derailed train by now and would be scouring the nearby countryside for every escaped Jew they could find. So he stayed deep in the trees, grateful there was no open farmland here and wouldn't be until he drew closer to Pozzuolo. Having fished the streams that flowed into Lake Trasimeno, he knew the territory fairly well. Soon enough, he'd find water to drink, at least, and, if he had to, he could sleep for part of the night and cross the open fields—the last part of the walk home—in darkness.

At some point, weary beyond weariness and moving more slowly with each hour, he came upon a row of wild grapevines, so old and so evenly spaced he wondered if they might have been planted by the Romans. They'd turned color, mostly, but were a week shy of full ripeness. It didn't matter in the slightest. They were a gift, as if the fruit he'd cared for so lovingly all those years was coming to aid him in his hour of need. He sat and ate two bunches, swallowing the pulp and chewing all the bitter nourishment from the skins before spitting them out.

When he was done, he couldn't help himself—he lay back in the dirt and fell instantly asleep.

Forty

They rode back toward the barn together in the wagon, three of them silent, Enrico noisily confused. "We're supposed to work the wheat! We have to work the wheat, Paolo!" he cried out several times, and Paolo couldn't think of a way to tell him that the plan for the day had changed because his father had abandoned him without so much as an *arrivederci*. In any case, he knew Enrico well enough to understand that the emotion in the boy's voice had little to do with the interrupted wheat harvest. When something upset him—especially something as terrible as the days he'd just lived through—he'd shriek and weep and smash a stone against a Nazi shirt, or dig holes in the ground, furiously, in random locations. The emotion would sink deep into him, be covered over by an energetic happiness for a while, and then resurface, as it had now, in something apparently unconnected.

They crested the rise and started downhill, past the vines. Paolo was praying that they'd see Vittoria, because she was the one who should tell Enrico about the *Signore*, she was the only one who could really calm him when he was in a mood like this . . . and because Paolo was desperately hoping she hadn't decided to abandon them, too, and that he could convince her to quickly put together a bit of food and a change of clothes, and leave with the rest of them.

As they neared the base of the slope—Paolo with the reins in his hands, Eleonora beside him, Antonio next to her, Enrico standing in the bed, practically talking into Paolo's ear—he did see Vittoria. She'd come out from behind the smaller barn—the doors were open there—and was standing in the courtyard, watching them. She waited for them to pull to a stop at the doorway of the larger barn, Ottavio snorting and shaking his head, as if he, too, were upset at the change of plans.

The expression on Vittoria's lovely face made Paolo feel that someone was using a pair of shears to cut his intestines to pieces.

He told Eleonora and Antonio to get ready. Just that, *Preparativi*. Not *get ready to leave*, just *get ready*. He didn't want to have to explain to Enrico why they were leaving, and he was hoping against hope that Vittoria would join them. Eleonora hurried toward the manor house, Antonio pounded up the stairway of the barn, and Enrico, still talking, disappeared into the barn's ground floor, headed for Antonina's stable, Paolo guessed, a place that, along with the ravine, had become a kind of shrine for him now.

Paolo kept Ottavio hitched and tied the wagon just outside the barn door. Without a word, Vittoria went into the barn and brought out water for the trough and a handful of hay. Those errands done, they were left standing, facing each other, in front of the open doorway.

Vittoria was staring at him with great intensity. "I have something very difficult to ask you," she began.

Paolo nodded, a dozen possibilities flying across his mind like birds that had been startled in a pasture. Was she going to ask him to stay and see to the grapes? To leave and take her and Enrico with him? To accompany her to Viareggio—a trip of at least three days—to confront the *Signore*?

But, after a terrible, two-second hesitation, she surprised him by pronouncing a sentence he would never forget: "I've been reading my mother's journal." And then, before he could react in any way, she added quietly, but with an intensity he'd never heard in her voice, "Tell me, are you Enrico's real father?"

He stared back at her and could feel his whole body beginning to tremble, soles of his feet to scalp, mouth, hands, shoulders. A shaking man. *All this time,* he thought. *All this time.* He managed one word, *"No"*—she seemed to think he was lying—before they heard the awful sound of vehicles racing through the gate, then turned and saw them skidding to a halt in the courtyard dust. A German army truck—gray cab with the iron cross painted on it. And a military car with a familiar face showing through the windshield. Before either Paolo or Vittoria could move—and where could they have run?—the driver jumped out of the truck, another soldier climbed out of the passenger side. A third soldier, riding in the back, pulled three men there roughly to their feet—the deserters—and pushed them so hard that they jumped, hand-cuffed, off the back of the bed, stumbled, fell in the dirt, then staggered to their feet again. Hands behind their backs, faces bruised, blood on the clothes they'd been given during their stay at the vineyard, they looked like skeletons wrapped too tightly in battered skin.

At the same moment, out from behind the wheel of the jeep stepped the bespectacled captain, his perfectly pressed uniform making the trio of deserters look even more ragged, as if they were half-human, half-alive. He said something to his men in German and then switched to his pitiful Italian. "But we wait before shooting them. I have the business with the princess, and I want the others to listen." Two quick steps, and he had hold of Vittoria by her ponytail and was dragging her toward the barn. Paolo lunged toward him, got as far as putting a hand on the captain's shoulder before one of the soldiers struck him in the chest with the butt of his rifle and sent him flying over onto his back in the dirt. He got to his feet, clumsily, with an old man's movements, barely able to take a breath. The soldiers pushed him and the three deserters back against the barn wall, then stood two meters away from them, rifles pointed.

One of the deserters beside him began muttering what sounded like a prayer, spoken through sobs. Paolo was frozen, wanting to run into the barn and pummel the Nazi captain, but frozen, coated in terror. Half a minute passed. His legs were shaking so forcefully he could barely stay on his feet. The German deserter beside him was praying, sobbing, the others with their backs against the wall. One of the soldiers stepped forward and pointed his bayonet at Paolo's throat. The man was grinning. Five seconds passed. And then, from inside the barn came the most hideous sounds he had ever heard in his life. A piercing scream, then grunting noises. The deserter closest to him collapsed in the dirt.

Forty-One

Countless times since her first terrible encounter with the SS captain, Vittoria had imagined being assaulted by him. The vision had obsessed her, invaded her dreams, but in her imagination, the assault had always occurred in her bedroom, and she'd always pictured herself fighting him off, as she'd fought off Massimo. From the time she'd taken it from her father's fingers, she'd carried the small, loaded pistol with her wherever she went—to the convent, to the dining table at breakfast, even into the bathroom. Somehow, though, from the moment the captain had stepped out of his jeep and come toward her, nothing happened the way she'd imagined. It was the speed that caught her most off guard. Tobias was upon her in two seconds. She felt him take hold of her hair and yank her backward, she sensed Paolo trying to help, saw him being struck, but the Nazi was pulling her violently into the barn, and she thought only of trying to stay on her feet. He dragged her across the dirt and threw her so roughly down in the straw of Antonina's stall that all the breath went out of her. Another second and he was lowering himself on top of her. She did try to reach for the pistol then, tried to get her right hand into the pocket of her dress, but his weight was on her, his tobacco breath in her face, her dress already up over her knees, his left forearm pressing down against her right elbow. She fought, but she could tell how useless it was—he was so much stronger. She bit at his glasses and felt one lens crack between her teeth, but it only made him press down harder against her, tearing at the front of his pants now, spitting, grunting. Lips bleeding, she closed her eyes and started to pray, and at that moment she felt the captain's whole body go suddenly rigid, and heard him let out the most horrible scream. And then a series of grunts as if he couldn't catch his breath.

She felt something sharp against her belly, warm liquid there. She opened her eyes to see the captain's face contorted in agony, and, behind him, Enrico backing away, hands made into fists and pressed against his eye sockets.

She was able to slide halfway out from under the captain. He was gasping, spitting blood, grunting. She heard Rico let out a wail and only then saw the shaft of the pitchfork sticking out of the Nazi's back. He was struggling to stand, on all fours, impaled, blood leaking out past the protruding tips of the three sharp tines. Holding on to the wall of the stable with one hand, he managed to get to his feet, and was reaching around behind himself with one hand to try and take hold of the pitchfork. He gave up, turned, grunting for breath, dripping blood, and took four wobbly, drunken steps out into the sunlight.

Enrico rushed over and wrapped her so tightly in his arms that he nearly knocked the breath out of her again. "Vita! Vita! Vita!" he kept saying, sobbing, soaking the side of her neck with tears. "Vita, I—I—I . . ." From just outside the barn, she heard a rattle of gunshots, and she wrenched her face toward the door, expecting to see Paolo and the deserters on the ground, and expecting, any second, to die in her brother's arms.

Forty-Two

Paolo heard the scream, then the grunting noises—sounds a boar might make after it was shot—and he was torn exactly in two, leaning like a man wearing concrete shoes. He had risked one step, the bayonet centimeters from his throat, when he was stopped perfectly still by the sight of the German officer, glasses gone, face contorted, knees bending out crookedly to each side as he staggered from the barn. The man had barely made it into the courtyard when he fell straight forward on his face, a pitchfork—one of their own pitchforks—sticking up out of his back and wobbling like a tomato stake in a storm.

His men had turned, had started to move toward him, when Paolo heard a tiny sound above and behind him, a squeak of hinges, as familiar as the creak of the wagon wheels. He didn't have time to look up at the small attic loading window before there was a burst of shots, impossibly loud, and the three Nazi soldiers were falling backward and sideways in bizarre contortions. Rifles thrown into the air, chests, necks, and faces erupting in fountains of red. They fell to the ground, two of them twitching and groaning, one completely still.

Paolo looked straight up and behind him and saw, at first, only the barrel of the *automatica*, then Antonio's hands and arms, then the bottom of his jaw and his huge nose.

And then, as if in a dream, he watched Vittoria step out of the wide doorway, unsteady on her feet, straw in her hair, dress torn and stained at the front. Alive. Enrico was bent over double just behind her, weeping.

The officer was writhing on his face in the dirt, the pitchfork handle wobbling crazily. As Paolo watched, still frozen, Vittoria took three steps toward the man, put the small pistol to the back of his skull, and fired. Once. The officer's head disappeared in an explosion of flesh and bone.

Forty-Three

Carlo awoke at sunset, angry at himself for sleeping that long, and, in the twilight, made it as far as a stream he knew. It was more a narrow river than a stream, spotted with deep, cool pools where he'd fished and swum with Giuseppe and Gianluca, both of them at war now. *Il Sussurratore*, they called it, the Whisperer, for the sound it made as it lost some of its force in summer. He drank handful after handful of water, crept back into the trees, crouched there and made sure of his bearings while there was still enough light. Across the river stood an expanse of harvested wheat field, and then a wide, gentle slope covered with the DellaMonicas' hazelnut trees, planted in perfect rows. There was still that hill to climb—he could eat some nuts, at least, to give him strength—then more woods, then their own wheat field, and then a last rise, from the top of which he'd be able to see the manor house and the barn. Five kilometers, no more.

But as full darkness fell, the moon already high, he was struck by a deluge of bad thoughts. He would arrive back at the barn looking as filthy and ragged as a rabid fox. Enrico and Paolo would welcome him, Umberto would let him go back to work. Most likely the Germans and OVRA wouldn't come to the vineyard looking for him, not for a time, at least. But what would Vittoria think when she saw him? What if he ended up spending the rest of his life working the grapes while she lived in the manor house, married to another man?

He stripped off his clothes—the worn-out shoes, the too-short Sicilian work pants and rope belt, the shirt with one torn, bloody sleeve—and washed himself in the cold river. He tore off a piece of the hem of the shirt and tried to fashion some kind of covering for his eye, but it didn't work, and after trying it different ways, he threw the scrap of cloth angrily aside.

The bad thoughts had full hold of him then. Facing Vittoria, he felt, facing what might await him at the vineyard, would require more courage than climbing out of the foxhole beside Pierluigi. All this way he'd come, all these things he'd survived, and now, this close to the dream that had sustained him, he wasn't sure he could summon the will to start walking again.

He'd rest then, gather himself, start for the vineyard at first light.

Forty-Four

Vittoria would recall those moments in the barn and the courtyard only in broken-up flashes. Still photos, framed and set in a line on some interior side table, they would haunt her, to one degree or another, for the rest of her time on earth. It was one thing to feel the clinging fingers of guilt every time she thought about the role she'd played in Massimo's death, but something else entirely to have squeezed the trigger and blown Tobias's skull into bloody pieces. It was something else entirely to feel the savagery in her when she did that, the fury, the desire to eliminate him from the earth. She'd dropped the pistol immediately, almost as if she wanted to go back to her other self; it landed in a puddle of bloody sand and gravel. She was aware of Enrico—heroic, marvelous Enrico—sobbing violently, clasping her right arm in both his strong hands; she'd have bruises there for a week. He was half hiding behind her right shoulder, as if he worried the Nazi would rise from the dead and seek revenge, or as if he, too, were shying away from the person who'd wielded the pitchfork, that other part of him, like that other part of her—vicious, murderous—planted, watered, and harvested by war.

Second by second, Vittoria became aware of her surroundings: the pitchfork, standing there like a tilted, perverse grave marker, so close she could have reached out and taken hold of the smooth wooden handle. Paolo came over, touched her on the shoulder as if gently waking her from sleep. She turned, and saw everything there in his face, everything, all of it, the people they'd once been and the people they'd become, the terror, the horror, the awfulness of the scene. She hesitated one second and then took him in a tight embrace and held him and shook and wept. After a moment, she felt his strong arms encircling her, but even then she could sense the mix of tenderness and hesitation she'd always felt with him, as if, in daring to touch her that way, even now, even after everything that had happened, he might be banished from the property.

When Vittoria opened her eyes again, she saw that her lips had left bloody stains on the top of Paolo's shirt, and she saw that the deserters were standing in a tight knot, holding each other, and that the uniformed German soldiers were splayed out on the ground in grotesque positions, as if caught in the middle of some satanic ballet, arms bent backward beneath them, faces half-gone, bodies still as stone. She had to close her eyes again, and when she did, she heard Eleonora's voice, speaking in German, and one of the deserters answering.

It all had the feeling of a dream, photos, moments, voices, against a vague, timeless background. She let go of Paolo. Enrico had gone over to comfort the horse, who was pulling violently at its lead.

Eleonora turned to her, hands clasped in front of her chest as if in prayer, lips trembling. "*Signorina*, they are going to take the truck and go. They . . . look!"

Vittoria saw that the deserters were frantically stripping the clothes from their former comrades—boots, trousers, belts, even the bloody shirts. Another moment and they were stripping off their own clothes, down to the underwear, and dressing themselves in the uniforms.

"Tell them," she heard Paolo say to Eleonora in his foreman's voice, "that their own uniforms are hanging in a canvas sack in the ravine, hanging from a bush, or on the ground near it. Tell them to take these four bodies and dump them there, then they can take the truck and go."

Eleonora spoke to them. One of them spoke back. "They don't want to," she told Paolo, shifting her eyes to Vittoria. Then to Antonio, who'd just come down from the attic, still carrying his magical weapon.

"They say they're leaving. Now." Antonio stepped from body to body—the dead soldiers were half-naked—prodding them with the toe of his boot, silent, grim, satisfied that they were dead. "Tell them they have to, Eleonora," he said, without emotion. "They have no choice. Remind them that we saved their lives. Twice. Tell them to take the bodies and throw them into the ravine, as Paolo said, and then come back here and clean up before they leave. The clothes, the bloody dirt—tell them to clean it."

Another German exchange, this time more heated. When the deserters hesitated, Antonio raised his gun lazily, with one hand, and swept it across the three of them, as if he were all too ready to shoot them where they stood. A few bad seconds passed, and then one of them went and backed the truck over close.

One of the other soldiers yanked the pitchfork out of the captain's back, tossed it aside, and then spat loudly, one time each, on the four bodies. They loaded the bodies into the bed, Paolo pointed the direction, and the truck lumbered off.

"They said they were caught two kilometers from the convent," Eleonora said, "on the Zanita Road, it sounded like. At night. They were brought to the police station and beaten until they told we helped them, but they said they didn't tell about the nuns. They say that the other SS men—from Montepulciano—know they came here today, and they'll come back and— Are you all right, *Signorina*?"

Vittoria nodded, yes, then shook her head, no, and hurried into the barn. She ran to the toilet and sat there, lips bleeding into both hands, and it seemed that everything was leaking out of her, the past half hour already beginning to replay itself, vision after vision, detail after detail: the Nazi captain's furious strength, the lust and hatred in him like a force of nature, the smell of his face against hers, the horror, the complete sense of the most intimate vulnerability—how many thousands of women had experienced these things? Then the scream, his body going rigid. She looked down and saw three evenly spaced spots of blood on her stomach. The tines had gone through him and through the front of her dress, just barely breaking her skin. She turned her upper body sideways and vomited.

Soon, as Eleonora said, the others from the Montepulciano house would come looking for their comrades. They'd see the blood on the ground; they'd guess what had happened. Outside again, she saw Eleonora and Antonio hurrying toward the manor house and she wanted to call out to them to take all the food they wanted, to take the candlesticks and silverware, to take anything they thought they could sell. Enrico was trotting after them. Paolo was staring out over the vines.

"We have to leave," Vittoria said to him. "Now. Immediately. All of us. We can take the wagon. I know where we can go."

He turned to her, and in his face she saw again what she remembered seeing there from her earliest years. Arms hanging at his sides, he seemed different, however. Eerily calm, less servile, boring his eyes into her, intensely but tenderly, his lips pressed tight together.

"Why did you lie to me?" she heard herself ask, through the pain on her lips.

He blinked, stared back at her. "I did not."

"You had . . . an affair with my mother."

A pause. Old Paolo blinked again, lifted his chin almost imperceptibly. "I did."

"And in her journal she wrote—it wasn't clear—but it seemed she believed she'd gotten with child. By you. Was that true?"

Nothing moved on his old face. She waited, directly in front of him, their bodies a meter apart. She expected him to deny it again, or to tell her they had to leave, now, urgently, they could talk about this later. But Paolo only stood there, still and expressionless as the trunk of a tree, green eyes steady, face slightly swollen, her blood on his shirt collar. Seconds passed. He made a small nod, one movement.

She thought she heard the mutter of the truck engine, the deserters returning. Strangely then, she felt her own breathing change, as if, in the deepest part of her, one enormous thought was stirring from a long sleep. "But when I asked you earlier, you said no."

Paolo didn't move or look away. Now the truck had come into the courtyard. She could hear the wheels crunching on gravel. She didn't move her eyes from Paolo's face.

"You asked if I am Rico's father," Paolo said. "I am not."

It took one more breath, another three seconds, for the enormous thought to rise up fully inside her. Paolo didn't move his eyes. They were her eyes, she saw that now, green as a new leaf. She saw it, finally, after all these years, all these moments, all these conversations. The understanding swelled in her and climbed up past her heart and lungs, into her throat, and then it burst out of her eyes in an explosion of tears. She put both hands to her face and lowered her head and felt the tears dripping down her forearms, and she shook and shook. She felt two strong hands take hold of her shoulders, but she could not make herself look up.

Forty-Five

Paolo sat in the wagon, staring at Ottavio's chestnut-brown rump and feeling the cool metal of the pistol against the skin of his belly. Driven by a strange, cold, half-familiar resolution, something that felt, at once, both utterly alien to him and completely just, he'd taken the weapon from the ground where Vittoria had dropped it, carefully washed off the bloody mud at the well, loosened his belt and tucked the pistol, not even as large as his hand, into the top of his pants. He pushed his shirt down over it to hold it there.

Behind him now, sitting in the wagon's bed, he could hear Enrico singing softly to himself, going over and over the same part of a song the workers liked to sing in the fields, *"Il Cielo Azzurro Azzurro."* "The Blue, Blue Sky." There were four cases of wine beside Enrico, a small burlap sack with a few of Paolo's clothes in it. Against the old man's not very forceful objections—no, no, come with us!—Antonio had insisted on taking the German jeep. There were keys, gas, even an extra rifle in the back. *My men and I will find a good use for it,* he said, and, bringing Eleonora with him, he'd raced off into the hills to continue killing Nazis. *The priest!* was the last thing he said to Paolo, and he left it at that.

The priest.

Paolo had no urge to join them. He was done with that, or almost done with it. One more act was required of him, one more piece of what he thought of as the secret work. One more terrible thing, and then, he told himself, he would be done with that world forever.

Face streaked with tears, voice coming from far off, Vittoria said they could go and stay at her father's friend's vacation home at Lake Como—it belonged to the man he'd killed—and wait there for the end of the war. They'd grow food, fish in the lake. *I have plenty of money,* she said. *We won't starve.* Paolo noticed that it had taken her several minutes to recover from what had happened, to recover enough, at least, so that she was able to speak and move. She left a note, for Carlo she said, then went into the manor house to pack a few clothes for her and for Rico.

Paolo put together his own small travel bag, then took his place in the wagon and waited for her, nervously, eyes on the south gate. It would be at least a ten-day trip to Como, he guessed. If they could leave before the other Nazis came looking for their countrymen, if Ottavio could go most of the night without stopping, then they could get far enough away from this place, from these killings, that the Montepulciano SS might not catch them. He worried that they'd take revenge on other people, though, other workers, or the nuns, but there was nothing he could do about that. He'd leave that to Antonio and his men. If they did manage to get away, he wasn't too worried about the trip itself, as long as they traveled mainly on back roads and avoided the cities. Workers on other estates to the north would shelter them—helping each other was the tradition, the rule—let them sleep in their barn, water and feed the horse. They'd likely share their food, too. Of course, they'd know instantly that Vittoria wasn't one of them—her clothing, her hair, the way she spoke and held herself, her hands. And they'd see the SanAntonio label on the bottles and know which estate the strange trio was fleeing. He could only hope they'd keep that information to themselves.

Laden with bags, Vittoria came hurrying out the front door. She lifted the bags to her brother in the back, told Rico to secure them there, then went into the house a second time and reappeared with her arms full. Blankets, two candlesticks, a small book, more food. Without meeting his eyes, she climbed onto the bench seat next to him, and Paolo couldn't tell what she was feeling, what she thought of him now, what she thought of herself. Before he could even tap Ottavio with the reins, he saw Rico climb over the seat back and sit beside his sister, moving her to the middle so Paolo could feel the side of Vittoria's body against his own. He turned the wagon completely around, glanced once at the vines, fixing the sight of them in his mind, then forced his eyes forward. Into the trees they went, along the dirt road, away.

"I have to stop once," he said, when they'd gone along quietly for a few minutes. "It's Saturday. I have to stop at the church in Gracciano."

"To say our sins?" Rico asked. His voice wobbled. He'd stopped singing and had intertwined the fingers of his left hand with the fingers of his sister's right.

"*My* sins," Paolo told him. "You don't have sins anymore. After the brave thing you did, you won't have any sins for the rest of your life."

Paolo pushed Ottavio a bit, listening intently for the sound of a truck or jeep behind them, fingertips of nervousness running up and down his spine. He realized he hadn't asked Vittoria's permission to stop at the church, but she hadn't objected, hadn't said a word. From time to time, she turned and looked over her shoulder, but no one was following them. Not yet. It seemed to Paolo that, after telling him they should go to the house on the lake, and after gathering herself enough to pack the supplies, she'd once again lost the ability to speak, and no longer realized she was the *Signorina*, and he the lowly *contadino*. She sat beside him, working a loop of rosary beads in her free hand, holding to Rico with the other, occasionally swiveling around, but as silent as the earth.

They made it to Gracciano without incident. His insides twisting and leaping, Paolo tied the wagon in front of the church, asked Rico to join him, asked Vittoria to wait outside. She nodded silently. She'd become another person now, and so had he.

"Rico," he said, before they went through the door, "you go up to the altar like last time. Pray as loud as you want. Make sure God hears you, okay?"

"I'll pray for my father, Paolo. He's on a travel. I'll pray for him."

"Loud, okay?"

"*Sì*, Paolo. *Sì*."

Paolo found Father Costantino in his small back room, a Bible open upon his knees. The priest looked up, startled at first, as if he'd never expected to see Paolo again, but then the smile appeared. "Old Paolo," he said, "you have trouble painted on your face."

"No, Father. No trouble. Only a need to take from my soul a heavy weight. It's Saturday. Please confess me."

"You couldn't wait until this afternoon, the usual time?"

"We're making a delivery, Rico and me. We'll be gone."

"I can hear him praying."

"Kindly confess me, Father."

Father Costantino closed the Bible and placed the purple stole around his neck with such reverence that, for a moment, Paolo was brushed by a breath of doubt. It passed, and the other Paolo, last week's Paolo, yesterday's Paolo, this morning's Paolo, disappeared into the church's shadowed corners. He followed his priest to the confessional and knelt there, only thin wooden boards and a metal screen separating them. His stomach swirled, but there was almost no doubt now, almost none. He unbuttoned the middle of his shirt and took the handle of the pistol into his palm. Immediately, his hand began to shake. All of who he was, everything he thought himself to be, had fallen behind him, like rusty old tools falling from the bed of a bouncing wagon. Strangely, so strangely, he felt something like what he'd felt those times with Celeste in the darkness of the grassy field many years ago, as if the quiet, obedient peasant had floated away and a full man had emerged in his place. The feeling was so powerful then that he hadn't been able to speak. And he couldn't speak now.

Father Costantino coughed, waited. At the front of the church Enrico was shouting. "GOD! GOD! WATCH MY FATHER! WATCH HIM, GOD!"

"Paolo, did you destroy the train tracks?"

"No, Father. The car broke down. Antonio said we'll try again once he gets it repaired. I'm not here for that, though, Father. I'm here as a sinner."

"Fine then," the priest said in a flat voice. "Make your confession, will you? I have business to attend to."

"Yes, Father, but first—"

"Speak your sins, Old Paolo, please!"

"I'm worried about the deserters, Father. Are they all right? Do you have any word about them? Any news?"

Two seconds of a thumping heart, Rico's loud prayers, Paolo pointing the barrel of the pistol forward, away from him, at the height of his chest, just below the screen. And then Father Costantino said, "As a matter of fact, I do. I just heard from a fellow priest in the North. The three deserters made it safely to Switzerland, crossed the border last night, very late. The Lord will bless you for helping them."

Paolo took one deep breath, raised the pistol to the middle of the screen, and squeezed the trigger three times. The sounds echoed around him, three *pops* banging against his ears. He dropped the gun there. Stripped by the war of his old skin, filled to bursting with sinfulness, and yet, somehow, feeling as if he had done what needed to be done, what the horrors of war had required of him, Old Paolo hurried up the side aisle, quieted Rico, and told him it was time to go.

Forty-Six

Carlo awoke in darkness, but, after lying still for a few minutes, he could begin to sense the first faint gray light in the eastern sky. He drank from the river, washed his face there, found a shallow place where it was easy to cross, then, worried he'd already slept too long and there would be too much light, made his way warily uphill through the DellaMonicas' hazelnut trees, hyperalert. At the top of the hill he rested, but there was a stretch of woods ahead of him, downhill now, and there was little chance of encountering anyone there. Beyond that, he'd be on SanAntonio property, at last.

The sleep and the familiar landscape had restored some of his confidence. He told himself Vittoria was too kind a soul to love him any less because he was lacking an eye. And that the chances were slim she'd have met someone else in the months he'd been away, and already gotten engaged or married. He'd wash again, shave, find clean clothes in his room. It might take them a day or two, but they'd meet behind the small barn again and be able to talk again, and touch. Just the idea of that was enough to carry him forward. In the warm morning he could let himself believe that a guardian angel had been protecting him all along: by some miracle, he'd survived the assault on the Licata beach and ended up with Ariana's kind family; he'd slipped out of the house of the *Duce* supporter, managed not to be reported by the mysterious man who'd asked—twice—if he were a deserter; he'd been given meals, a pair of shoes, money. Simply because of the strength of his right hand, he'd avoided being killed and thrown into the pile of Italian bodies behind the Pietramelara police station. Most amazing of all, the train had derailed, or been sabotaged, and he'd survived that, too, and hadn't starved to death or died of thirst between that gruesome hour and this moment.

Even so, there was still an open field to cross—Umberto's property, yes, but a place where he might be seen if there were soldiers searching. It wouldn't do to get caught now, after having traveled all the way from Sicily. He raised a prayer to Saint Christopher and Saint Jude, hurried past the small, empty cabin, through the wheat—not fully harvested, he noticed, which was unusual this late in the season—and ducked into the trees again not far from the stone they called *l'altare*. He crouched there for a moment and then crept forward silently. Full daylight now. Paolo and the others would have eaten their morning meal and, at this time of year, might already be harvesting the grapes, or at least preparing for the harvest, checking to see that the moment was right, that the small seeds inside the pulp had changed completely, not partially, from green to brown. The thought of seeing the people he loved lit a warm fire in his belly. He imagined the surprise, the greeting, Enrico nearly squeezing him to death and then running off to fetch his sister. Someone, Marcellina or Costanza, would remark on how thin he'd grown, and go upstairs to prepare a plate of food. Bread, cheese, salami, fresh vegetables!

He made himself go slowly, carefully, moving from tree to tree and standing behind each one for a few seconds, quiet as a hunter. Not far from the place where he knew the manor house would come into view, he heard voices. His own people, he thought at first, Paolo calling out the morning work assignment. But another step closer and he dropped to the dirt and flattened himself there: the words he'd heard were German words, not Italian. How could he have been traced here so quickly? Or were they simply checking every property within fifty kilometers of the ruined train?

He listened for a moment. Orders, they sounded like, but there was a bizarre joyful tone to the words. Sweat dripped from his face and neck. He couldn't stop himself from crawling forward, very very slowly, barely moving, then staying still, moving again, waiting behind tree trunks, behind large stones, staying as low as he could.

Eventually, he reached the point where, if he raised his head slightly, he could see the roof of the manor house, then, moving a little farther forward, the roof of the barn. Then the walls of both buildings, then the courtyard. At first, the scene below him made no sense. A German truck pulling away from the barn with what looked to be eight or ten cases of wine in its bed. Four soldiers who almost seemed to be celebrating a holiday. Until he saw them go into the manor house, and then appear again carrying various objects—an upholstered chair, a painting, a beautiful ceramic serving bowl—he wondered if the war had ended and they'd come to celebrate with the locals.

He watched. Four men going in and out of the manor house. One of them seemed to be in charge and directed others to load the stolen objects onto the bed of the truck in a certain way. The painting here, the bowl there, lamps over there, wrapped in beautiful quilts. Finally, the truck bed was nearly full—just enough room left for the soldiers to climb in. The man who seemed to be in charge disappeared through the front door, remained in the house for a minute or two, searching for a final treasure, Carlo supposed, then came hurrying back out again, empty-handed. For another minute they all stood silently in the courtyard beside the loaded truck. And then, to his horror, Carlo saw a puff of smoke come out of the open front door, then a tongue of flame licking out one of the first-floor windows. Two more minutes and there was smoke and flames everywhere. Windows were bursting open, glass shattering and tinkling. The men backed the truck away a short distance and stood there cheering hatefully every time there was a small explosion inside, or a larger tongue of flame showing at one of the windows. Soon he could hear the sound of the inferno, a subdued roar beyond the manor house walls. The soldiers backed the truck up farther, and he wondered if they were about to set fire to the barn, too. Then a piece of the tile roof collapsed, and a thick column of black smoke poured up and out through the hole. A huge cheer. Flames were coming out of every window, and suddenly the entire main roof of the manor house collapsed and caused smoke to puff out to the sides like the dirty exhalation of a sinful giant. One final cheer and the men were climbing into the loaded truck and it was slowly making its way south, off the property, through the gate there and over a rise. Gone.

Carlo waited a few minutes, then pushed himself forward and sat with his back against an oak tree, staring at the manor house as it burned. After the better part of an hour the flames could no longer be seen, but the entire roof was gone, wisps of smoke still leaking out the windows. Vittoria and her father and Paolo and Enrico and the servants and workers were dead, he guessed, dead or captured. Or maybe, if they'd had enough warning, they'd gone off somewhere and were safe. He felt that the last ounce of will had been drained from him. A thousand kilometers of walking only to reach an empty property and witness this.

Eventually it was hunger that made him get to his feet and start down the hill. There might be food in the barn, surely there would be. Gingerly, watching the place to his left where the truck had disappeared, he went down past the vines, picking off a bunch as he walked and eating one succulent grape at a time. Standing in the smoky air of the courtyard, he noticed what seemed to be patches of dried blood in the dirt. No mule. The barns were empty—no delivery truck, no wagon, no horses. He went from room to room on the ground floor—nothing—then climbed the steps and found, in the workers' kitchen, part of a stale loaf of bread and some prosciutto wrapped in paper. Dazed, caught by an almost unbearable sorrow, he took a glass, carried the food down to the keg room, and sat on a bale of hay eating the food, drinking wine from a barrel he'd never been allowed to sample, holding himself on the edge of tears. What was the point of living now? Where was he supposed to go? How was he supposed to eat? Stay there and live on grapes and vegetables and apples and wine? And what? Wait for the Nazis to find him, for the war to reach him?

When he'd finished the food, he wandered back and forth in the barn, slightly drunk, worn out, broken. He decided to go up to his room and see if he might have left some clean clothes there, at least, his almost-new work boots, a beautiful piece of polished white stone Vittoria had given him on his last birthday, too large to have carried off to war. He climbed the stairs, walked down the narrow corridor, the old boards squeaking beneath his sore feet. His door was open. He'd taken one step inside when he realized that something had been tacked to the door, at the height of his shoulder. He turned and saw a piece of paper there, folded in half. He tore it from the nail, unfolded it, and saw a strange sight. The paper looked as if it had been placed there recently, but on it was a sketch—done in haste, it seemed—not very different from a drawing Vittoria had made for him when they were small. He'd been eleven, she was eight. It was summer. The family had gone away for a month, and when they returned, she'd hurried over to the barn to see him, carrying a drawing she'd made of the house they'd stayed at near Lake Como. Her godfather's house, she said it was. The four columns, the fountain out front, it looked like a palace. He recognized it immediately, but this was an adult's work, not a child's. He stared at it for a full minute before he understood that she must have left it there for him. Lake Como was hundreds of kilometers away, but that didn't matter. Before leaving the property, Vittoria had left this sketch.

For him.

Forty-Seven

Vittoria didn't ask why Paolo had to stop in the church. Confession, she supposed, strange as that seemed at such a moment. Cinzia had told her once that, among the people of the barn, Old Paolo had a reputation as the most religious. During the few minutes he and Enrico were inside, Vittoria sat very still on the wagon's bench seat, her head tilted slightly downward, eyes open, rosary beads clutched in her left hand. She was no longer praying, no longer looking around to see if they were being chased by Nazi soldiers. She felt as though an enormous church bell were ringing inside her, shaking every organ and bone the way the cathedral bell in Montepulciano made the ancient pews tremble and caused the huge hanging lamps to sway slightly above their heads. As a girl, she'd been terrified that the oblong metal-and-glass lamps would come crashing down on them, and her mother would always rest a hand on Vittoria's leg when the bells were rung.

What she'd give now to feel that touch, to feel Carlo's. The incredible fact that Paolo had revealed to her an hour earlier seemed to be staring back at her, a pair of eyes, watching, waiting, filled with a pure, steely truth. A surprise, yes, but wrapped around the unsurprising. Behind those eyes, surrounding that incredible fact, the horrors of the day rang again and again inside her—violence was its own music: loud, discordant, ugly. She thought she heard two or three sharp reports from inside the church, like sticks being snapped. She looked up: no movement there, no other sounds, but small waves of fear were running across her skin. She thought of what Carlo's existence must be like, with the constant threat of death and injury, and she wondered if Paolo had gone into the church to ask for news of him. To see if the priest—what was his name? Costantino?—might have heard something.

After a short time, Paolo and Enrico stepped out into the daylight, hurrying it seemed. The pace of their movements threw more fuel on the embers of anxiety inside her. Enrico jumped up into the seat. Paolo untied the wagon, climbed up more slowly, took hold of the reins in both hands, and led Ottavio away from the church. Out through the north end of the town they went, then onto a quiet farm road, two dirt tracks with a strip of grass between them.

They rode until dusk, watered Ottavio in a stream, fed him a few handfuls of hay, ate something themselves, then pushed on in near-darkness. Toward Arezzo, her brother climbed into the back and fell asleep, but Vittoria didn't move to her right, away from Paolo. She sneaked a glance at his profile. There was a quarter moon, and in its light she watched him for a moment, studied his workman's face, his rough hands, and struggled and struggled to fully believe what she now knew must be true. She felt words in her mouth, but held them there. Ottavio's hooves clopped a quiet rhythm. The wagon shifted and bounced, wheels squeaking too loudly. The cool darkness, filled with terrors, secrets, and hopes, brushed against her skin, and at last she managed to speak. "All these years," she said. And then, after a long, slow inhalation, "All these years, after you saw my face, you had to live with what you knew. You couldn't speak of it. How terrible that must have been."

For a full minute Paolo didn't answer her, didn't even turn his head. She watched him in the moonlight, waiting. *La pazienza dei contadini* was a phrase one often heard. The patience of the peasants. Vittoria could almost hear her mother saying it, and she wondered what torments her mother had lived with, what kind of coldness or fear or societal chains had kept her from seeking out the man she loved and speaking with him, having one conversation at least, explaining, asking forgiveness. She wondered, over all those years, with Paolo so wounded that he eventually refused even to look in her direction, what measure of guilt her mother had felt. Guilt, doubt, confusion, shame, regret. She wondered if her father had sensed the truth, or discovered it.

She would never know.

At last, Paolo swallowed and coughed once. *"Sì,"* he said into the night, his voice tight with an old, long-subdued sorrow, *"dirlo non potevo. Ma ogni giorno potevo vederti."*

Yes, I couldn't speak of it. But every day I was able to see you.

He'd used the *ti* with her, the informal pronoun. A first.

Vittoria felt that *ti* echoing inside her. She shifted the beads, reached over and rested a hand on her father's arm, just inside the elbow. She squeezed once, then took her hand away and felt, in spite of everything that had happened on that day, and everything happening in the world around her, something that resembled peace.

Epilogue

Even though they'd been at Lake Como for the better part of a month, Paolo found that he still wasn't comfortable sleeping in the enormous house that had belonged to Vittoria's godfather. He'd killed the man, for one thing; the guilt of that act still tormented him. And, for another, the bedroom there was far too rich for his blood and bones. Vittoria seemed to feel perfectly entitled to it, almost at home there, and he was not surprised about that. It was a beautiful house, set less than a kilometer above a small town on the lake's eastern shore, with flower and vegetable gardens, columns and a fountain out front, and balconies on the second and third floors that offered views of the lake, and of the mountains on the western side, near the Swiss border. Vittoria and Enrico and the hired woman, Zenia, who cooked for them in exchange for her food, a place to live, and a bit of money, slept in a wing of the main house. Paolo took his meals there but asked to sleep in an outbuilding that must have been used by Brindisi's servants before the war. The room there was luxurious compared to his room at the barn, and he slept well. He spent his days tending to the vegetable garden and fruit trees to one side of the house (Vittoria worked in the flower garden to the other side) and taking long walks with Enrico up into the hills, or fishing with him from one of the piers that jutted out into the lake.

Since there was only so much work to do around the property, he found that he was spending more time in prayer. He prayed for forgiveness for the things he'd done; for the souls of the people he'd killed—directly or otherwise; for Vittoria's mother, Celeste, whose name he still had not spoken aloud, all these many years. The house was far enough away from any main road or important town that there was no Nazi presence, and so far, at least, the four of them had been left alone. Perhaps it had to do with the house's isolation, or with the reputation of the late owner of the property—a "friend of the Reich," the evil captain had called him, but who could possibly know if that were true? Or perhaps it was because, if Paolo understood the news correctly, at least some Italians were now fighting on the side of the Allies. All over Europe, Zenia told him, the German army was losing ground. So perhaps the Nazi soldiers had other things to worry about.

From time to time Paolo thought of the grapes rotting on the vines at home, an entire harvest, lost. And he often wondered what had happened to Marcellina and the others; where the men of the barn—Carlo especially—might be fighting if they were still alive; what Antonio and Eleonora were doing, and where. But he was coming to understand that it was the nature of war to ruin the earth and to separate people, to keep their fates unknown to the ones who loved them, and to fill the minds of the living with various kinds of fear, regret, shame, and anger, and deprive them of all but the most fleeting moments of peace. He prayed every day for the German surrender.

Whenever he sat with Vittoria on one of the benches that looked down over the lake, or took a stroll with her in the warm evenings (sometimes she'd hook her arm inside his elbow), he could feel both her love for him, and that a difficult conversation hovered around them, secrets swirling, questions tapping at their ears. He'd resolved to wait until she asked, and then he would tell her everything. Everything she wanted to know. Much of the time she seemed sad and preoccupied, and he understood that. Like all three of them, she was still recovering from the trauma at the vineyard, still hoping for news from Carlo. Although, if there were any news, how would it reach them?

On that late October day, sunny but with a cool breeze sweeping off the lake, Vittoria was on the far side of the house, choosing a selection of autumn flowers for the dinner table. Paolo had done what work he could do around the property—pulling out the tomato plants and using seeds he'd found in the shed to plant a cover crop of winter rye—and was sitting tiredly on one of the benches, looking down at the lake. He could see Enrico there, fishing patiently from the end of a pier, having no success. And then, for some reason, Paolo's eyes were pulled to the left, south, along the paved, unlined road that ran parallel to the water and connected their little town with the next one down the shore. He saw a figure walking slowly along there. A man it was, young, wearing something across part of his face and limping as if the bottoms of his feet were blistered. The man's shoulders and the way he swung his arms seemed familiar, and for a moment Paolo didn't understand why. He stood up, studying him intently now. The man stopped and put his hands to either side of his mouth, as if calling to someone. Paolo couldn't hear what he said, but he saw Enrico whirl around and then drop his fishing pole right into the water, and go sprinting back along the pier and then down the road.

Paolo waited a few more seconds to be sure; then he turned and hurried toward the flower garden to give his daughter the wonderful news.

ACKNOWLEDGMENTS

I have, as always, a number of people to thank: my wife, Amanda, and our daughters, Alexandra and Juliana, first of all, for their steady love, support, and wisdom. I'd like to express my gratitude to Peter Grudin and Robert Braile—two close friends who are also superb writers and editors. They took many hours out of their lives to go carefully through the manuscript of this novel and offer suggestions and corrections. I'm grateful to another friend, Peter Sarno, for his consistent support of my work through the newsletter and Plus Side essays and the publication of many of my earlier books. My heartfelt thanks, also, to two superb editors, Chris Werner and David Downing. Their careful readings and our detailed back-and-forth inspired good ideas, saved me from serious missteps, and undoubtedly made the book better. My appreciation, also, to Max de Zarobe, who, with his wife, Virginie, owns a magnificent vineyard, Avignonesi, in a part of Italy very close to the place where this story is set. I'd already chosen that location when I discovered Max, so the hand of fate may have been involved, but I'm grateful to him for a good deal of the factual information about winemaking at that time, and in that part of Italy, and for an incredible tour of the vineyard and a remarkable lunch there. In his case, and in the case of Simone Gugliotta, who helped me with the fine points of the Italian language, any errors that appear in these pages are entirely my own. I'm grateful, as always, to my superb agent, Margaret Sutherland Brown, at Folio Literary. Final thanks to the good people at Lake Union who worked on the production and copyediting of the manuscript, especially Nicole Burns-Ascue and Sarah Engel.

ABOUT THE AUTHOR

Photo © 2021 Amanda S. Merullo

Roland Merullo is the bestselling author of twenty-five works of fiction and nonfiction, including *From These Broken Streets*; *Once Night Falls*; *The Delight of Being Ordinary*; *The Talk-Funny Girl*, an Alex Award winner; *Vatican Waltz*, a *Publishers Weekly* Best Books of 2013 pick; *Breakfast with Buddha*, an international bestseller; *Lunch with Buddha*, selected as one of the Best Books of 2013 by *Kirkus Reviews*; *Revere Beach Boulevard*, a *Boston Globe* Top 100 Essential Books of New England pick; and *Revere Beach Elegy*, winner of the Massachusetts Book Award for Nonfiction. Born in Boston and raised in Revere, Massachusetts,

Roland earned bachelor's and master's degrees in Russian language and literature at Brown University. A former Peace Corps volunteer, he has also made his living as a carpenter, college professor, and cabdriver. Roland writes a weekly essay series called On the Plus Side and lives in the hills of western Massachusetts with his family. For more information, visit www.rolandmerullo.com.